Slaves of Circumstance

Baron Alexander

Wilderwick Press

Forest Row, UK

Baron Alexander/Wilderwick Press
Unit 4 Ashdown Court
Lewes Road, Forest Row, RH18 5EZ
www.baronalexanderbooks.com

Dedicated to Chrystal

CONTENTS

CHAPTER ONE

RUSSIA

The gentle rhythm of the tracks click clicking at times lulled Jack to sleep and at others kept him awake. The scenery changed outside the carriage window in the way stations changed on TV: click, click. The room was small but first-class: two beds instead of four bunks. Click, click. The little table even had a flower. And the second bed, a lover.

"You up?"

"Do I ever sleep?"

"Believe me, you sleep."

Valeria threw a pillow at him. "I don't snore."

"How do you know?"

"I would have heard."

"From your sister?" Jack had an innocently sly smile.

"You're an asshole sometimes, you know?" Valeria flushed.

"Val, I'm sorry. I think I'm getting stir crazy."

"Then stretch your legs at the next station and don't bug me." She turned her back to him.

Jack sat up. "The beds aren't bad at all. I was expecting greater privation."

Val turned to him and sat up. "Privation? Who talks like that?"

"I thought you said you spoke English," Jack said.

"I do. Pretty good, too. But sometimes you speak prat."

"Where'd you hear that word?"

"The ticket office. Lots of English and Aussies."

"I'm jealous of how quickly you pick up languages. Why didn't you become an English teacher?"

"You're envious, not jealous. And I didn't because there's no money in it and we already have too many teachers. Why didn't you become an investment banker? You, with your fancy MBA."

"Long story. Another time." He paused. "Vodka?"

"It's too early," Val said, her nostrils flaring slightly.

"I thought all Russians could drink vodka," Jack said.

"Yes, and they die before they turn fifty."

Jack poured himself a one-inch shot in his coffee mug. "I'll take my chances." He paused. "I've been looking at the map and the train schedules. I don't see anything that takes us up to where we need to go."

She was silent, head lowered just enough to shield her eyes.

"Val?"

"There's a slight problem," she said, slowly.

"Uh-huh?"

"There's no train or road to Uelen."

"What?"

"There's no . . ."

"I heard you. But you said you knew the way."

"Yes, but not by train." She was starting to make Jack's blood boil.

"Hang on a bit. We've been travelling four bloody days on this, this *thing*, and there's no connection to Uelen?"

Val was silent, biting her bottom lip. Despite his growing frustration, Jack thought she looked particularly striking at that moment. "We need to fly to get where you want to go," she said finally.

"We could've flown from Moscow. Why endure this train?"

"Because you wouldn't have taken me."

The logic was sound in a way. He wasn't going to argue.

"OK. No harm. We've enjoyed ourselves." He smiled at the memory of the night before. "So, how do we get there?"

"There's a problem. The area is like the old USSR and heavy with military. The ground isn't even suitable for trucks. We have to fly in, and we need permission to do so."

"We? Fly? Permission? Too many red flags. I wanted to cross without the authorities, and I thought that's what you wanted."

"I know, and I do. But your plan was crazy. You can't cross the Bering Strait. And definitely not on foot. It's suicide." Her voice was strong, defiant. She looked at him straight in the eyes.

"You didn't think to tell me that earlier?"

"You wouldn't have taken me. I don't believe you would have taken this trip without knowing that first and I needed to take this trip with you."

"And I'm happy that you did, but I need to get back to the US and I can't go from Europe. I figured I'd go all the way east and figure it out from there." Jack realised how ridiculous that sounded. *I'm a cliché*, he thought.

Valeria was quiet, waiting to see what Jack would do. She reached for his mug and took a sip. Then another.

"I can get us to the US," she said.

"Then why did you need me?"

"I don't have the money and I thought maybe you'd share your plan with me during our trip. I assumed you had one."

Jack took a sip and handed the mug back to her. He smiled. "OK, so what's the plan?"

∞

"I wouldn't turn on a computer much less open the internet without operating through an encryption service." Jack Harding said it casually, but was dead serious. He hadn't stayed alive these last ten years as a wanted man by luck. "If spam can find you, anyone can find you."

"Aren't you being just a bit paranoid?" Valeria Polzin was rubbing a towel against her head, knowing it would take an hour for her hair to dry. The rest of her was wrapped in another towel. *Men are so easy to manipulate if you're prepared to have sex with them*, she thought.

"When you turn on your computer or phone, it searches out connections with the network. It's like starting a bonfire in the middle of a starless night. If there's anyone around, you'll be noticed."

"OK, Mr. Bond," she said, smiling. She could see that Jack had forgotten about any deceptions. "But I don't know how else to contact him. I don't have a phone number and it's been years since I've seen him."

"And I don't have a computer here."

"I have a phone. You can use that," she said.

"But there's no security on it."

"Get over it. This guy's our best chance."

Jack thought about it. He didn't like it. It was rushed and he was developing a sense of something inside him. A warning. Val wasn't telling him something, he knew. Maybe he should just disappear in China or

Mongolia for a while. Finally, he shook off his anxiety and took her phone.

"What's the address? OK. Name? OK. Message sent. Now we wait."

"Vodka?"

∞

Andre was escaping the madness of the house by retreating into the garage. He was to prepare the propane cylinders for the BBQ and fill the small stainless pots with a special lighting fluid for the warming trays and fondues. It wasn't hard work. The garage was detached from the house and only a couple of dozen paces from the front door. The propane was stored along the back of the garage, outside. Checking was just a matter of retrieving and putting the cylinder in the backyard where the BBQ was located. The tricky part was the fluid. It was a very fine, light fluid that was flammable but not in the way gasoline or propane would be. It burned slowly with a blue flame. He rubbed it between his fingers to get a feeling of it.

Sitting on an empty paint can near the wall of gardening tools, Andre began filling the little pots. Each had a lid that could be adjusted, allowing more or less fluid access to the oxygen it needed to burn. He carefully poured the fluid in, put on the lid, and set it aside on the concrete floor. It was important that he didn't spill any.

After he had done his fifth pot, the house party burst into his garage sanctuary. Doron, Nicki, and Vlad each had a girl on their arms that Andre didn't recognise. They stumbled a bit on the door's threshold as they walked in. A handful of children followed them.

"Is the chocolate hidden in here, Uncle Nicki?" a little voice said. It belonged to the grandchild of the owner of the house, who was currently in prison. Only a short stay, but he was missed.

"Only the best goodies are kept here. Let me see what the secret fridge is hiding." Nicki opened the old fridge and pulled out a beer. There were no sweets there.

"Nice set-up. No wonder you come out here to spend time by yourself. Peaceful." He was rummaging around the tools and making Andre uneasy.

"Stop messing around, Nicki. Let's get back to the party," Doron said. The girl on his arm was getting cold and whispering in his ear.

The children were holding little candles that looked like miniature lanterns. They weren't much larger than what you would put on a cupcake. *Probably some party favour handed out to the children to keep them occupied,* Andre thought.

Vlad was a bit further into the party spirit than the others. He found another empty can and sat next to Andre, his friend on his knee.

"Andre, my brother. What's taking you so long? You left ages ago. People are asking where you went. Mom is asking where you disappeared to."

"Just getting the fuel ready for the BBQ and fondues," replied Andre.

"Let me see that," Vlad reached for one of the little pots. He moved the lid and laughed to himself. "Do you like that Anna? Do you think it'll work?" She nodded obediently and got up to get another drink from the garage fridge. He reached for her bum but just managed a little pat.

"Thomas, what do you think about this little bomb?" Doron was getting into it.

"It's not a bomb, Thomas. It's a little pot of fuel that will keep the food warm. It's dangerous. Be careful." He was busy filling the last of the containers. The sooner he finished and returned, the sooner he could be rid of these guys.

Thomas put down his little lantern and examined the pot Vlad was holding and Doron was pointing to. He picked it up and moved the lid back and forth. "What else does it do?" he asked.

No one answered because at that point, the lantern must have lit the spilled fuel and a blue flame started glowing faintly from the concrete floor. It was a small disaster, easily fixed with a foot or a bit of sand. Instead, the girls let out a shriek. Andre couldn't remember if it was in fear or excitement. Vlad leapt to his feet and located the fire extinguisher. He pulled the pin and began spraying everything and everyone with the white powder. It was an industrial-grade fire extinguisher liberated from one of the government offices Vlad protected during his day job. The room was covered before the little blue flame was remembered and extinguished.

"What the hell, Vlad!?" Andre didn't want to breathe or talk with all of the fire retardant in the air. Worst of all, he didn't like sudden movements.

In return, the others were laughing and cackling like the drunks they were. The girls began to twirl to maximise their exposure. Vlad turned the nozzle on himself to ensure coverage. The little boys laughed and screeched after they realised it was safe and when they saw the adults enjoying themselves. Only Andre fumed.

"Let's get a picture," one of the girls said. It was Anna. She was laughing and stomping her feet, bent over with the scene. She pulled out her phone and directed all of the parties to stand together so she could take a picture. "This'll be our Christmas card this year!" she howled.

Andre looked at the mess. The white covered the fridge, the gardening tools, the workbench, the vice— everything. "You know this'll take me forever to clean up," he said to no one in particular.

"I'll help you, Andre," Vlad said, sincerely. "But not today. Today, we party."

"Don't you think we should stay sober long enough to see him arrive?" Andre asked.

"Dad would take it as an insult," Doron said. He was already outside and wanted to be part of every conversation.

"Dad'll just be happy to be home," Nicki said. "And I don't think his mind will be on that anyway." He pulled his girlfriend closer, a little rough, and gave her a long kiss. She obediently kissed back and moved her hands onto his, which had grabbed her front.

The children had run back into the house as soon as the picture was taken. They wanted to show everyone inside how much fun they were having with their cool uncles.

"I'll be happy to see him back in one piece," replied Andre. "I won't believe it until I see it."

"Enough of all this misery," Vlad said. "Let's get back into the house and enjoy ourselves. Do you need any help?"

"I'll take the fondue pots, you and Nicki can take the propane to the BBQ. Thanks."

"With pleasure, Andre. With pleasure," said Vlad. They all made fun of Andre but he was the youngest and they still protected him, too.

Amidst the jostling of bodies, Andre felt his phone vibrate. He put down the fondue pots and looked at his phone. It was a message from Valeria. She needed to see their father

THE FAMILY

When the train came to a halt, Jack gathered his few belongings. He had learned to live with very little. He didn't carry a phone or a watch. Just a good pair of shoes, which he wore, three pairs of underwear, socks, and T-shirts, a spare pair of jeans, a fleece with a zipper and pockets, and an outer leather jacket. He stored these in his knapsack along with a Swiss Army knife, water bottle, passport, and money. Today, he carried his money in a pocket sewn into the inside of his jeans, inaccessible unless they were off. He put the passport in his outside pocket.

Valeria had a knapsack three times the size of his as well as a handbag, some plastic shopping bags, and her phone, watch, and jewellery. Jack put his bag on his back and helped carry hers onto the platform.

"What do you have in this thing?" he said, beginning to breathe heavily.

"Just the bare necessities," said Val.

Jack shook his head. "Any sign of your friends?"

"They'll be just outside the station waiting for us. Look for a yellow van with a green stripe."

"Sounds interesting." Jack picked up Val's knapsack and heaved his way through the crowds. Most of the people were just stretching their legs and he found the station relatively empty.

"Mr. Jack," a thick accent said. Jack turned to see an outstretched hand.

"Hi, you must be Valeria's friend," Jack said.

The man paused slightly and nodded to Val. She smiled at him. "Yes, my name is Vladimir. But please, call me Vlad."

"Thanks for picking us up, Vlad. I don't know what I'd have done without Val."

Vlad picked up Val's bags and carried them to the van. Inside were two more guys. They moved over to allow Jack and Val to sit down. Vlad went around to the driver's seat and got in.

"We've been having some trouble with the police lately. They've been checking passports at checkpoints on the highway. Do you mind giving me your passports just in case?" Vlad put his hand out in anticipation, driving with his left.

Val put her passport in Vlad's hand. Jack hesitated until Val put her hand on his thigh, reassuring him that everything was OK. *I don't like this*, he thought, but then handed over his, as well.

The checkpoints never happened and they arrived at a farm after almost an hour's drive. Jack lost track of where he was. He had tried to remember road signs along the way, but he couldn't see much out of the van and his Russian was patchy at best.

The van stopped and the doors opened. Jack was escorted into a building just off to the side of the house. The two extra men walked behind him and Val as Vlad led the way.

"Vlad, how do you know Val?" Jack asked. They were holding the door open for him as he walked in. He saw a white powdering covering everything. Inside, there were four large men, all in leather. He stopped cold. Then he backed out of the door but came up against the two men who were walking behind him and Val.

"Val? Vlad?" Jack tried to see them but couldn't. "Val? What the hell did you do to her?"

"Don't worry about her. Worry about yourself." The speaker pushed him inside and the four men grabbed him. The man behind Jack pulled out what looked like a video recorder. When it was on, he nodded to the others.

Jack resisted and tried to determine what was happening. It was happening so fast. Memories of Joe and that night with his parents flooded back. He started to shake and his body became cold.

Three of the men held him firm. They were each built like a brick house. Jack squirmed, lunged, and pushed. At 6'2" and 230 pounds, he was no weakling, but these men were hard. And they didn't say a thing.

The fourth man approached Jack with a knife. He lifted it above his head and slowly brought it down, allowing him to see the futility of resistance. A hand pulled at his shirt and the knife went behind. It was sharp and the fabric fell away, pressure ever downward, exposing his flesh. There was a faded scar along his abdomen where Clog had him stabbed ten years earlier. There were other cuts and scratches from Valeria but those were mainly on his back, out of sight for now. Jack felt a totally different level of terror as the knife reached his waist.

The man with the knife unbuckled the belt, undid the button, and unzipped Jack's jeans. *What the hell?* His mind screamed in terror as he saw himself from outside his body. He saw the man with the video recorder, the three men holding him like statues, and this thing with a knife about to open him up like a rabbit for stew.

The fourth man barked instructions to the others. Jack was thrown to the ground and his jeans were removed. One man held his shoulders and head while the other two grabbed his legs. The fourth man approached with the blade. Jack lay on his back, on his jacket, front exposed. The two men held his legs up so he was spread in the most vulnerable manner. The knife and the sheer terror of what it was going to do to him froze Jack to his core.

He felt the punch and the taste of blood without seeing who did it. They hit him again. The fourth man, satisfied at the terror induced, kneeled and pushed himself into Jack. At this point, Jack wanted to die—of terror, of pain, and of shame. The fifth man continued to record, but Jack had lost notice of him long ago.

The second man was rougher. He wanted Jack to cry out. He wanted to hear the pain as well as see it. Jack was punched, slapped, and eventually whipped before the second man raped him mercilessly. There was no laughter, no music, and no joviality. Jack grit his teeth and his eyes rolled into the back of his head. Soon, his body could feel no more. He had reached sensory overload. He had become a piece of meat to be consumed.

The third man was not as rough but made up for this with depravity. He made Jack move into different positions, pushing his head into the powder on the concrete floor. The room smelled of lighter fluid and something burned. For Jack, it was hell. His mind and body cried out for it to stop.

It was a full hour and twelve minutes, according to the video taken, before the fourth man finished. Jack was bleeding internally and had sustained burns, whips, and fists to his body. *At least they didn't kick me when they finished*, he thought.

The men left and Vlad returned.

"Do we understand each other or do I need to provide another lesson?" he said in his thick English accent.

Jack couldn't speak. His face was swelling up and he curled into a fetal position and shook violently. Vlad brought a blanket for him.

"It's time to take you to your quarters," Vlad said. He helped Jack up. All of the clothes were left on the floor and he was moved to a building beside the garage. Between the buildings, Jack struggled to breathe in the fresh air and feel the warmth of the sun on his face. He feared he would never feel it again.

When Vlad opened the door, Jack could see a row of bunk beds and mattresses on the floor. More than thirty bodies lay in various forms of sleeping and cowardice as they saw Vlad. He was walked over to a lower bunk bed and pushed onto it.

"This'll be your place. It is a lot better than being on the floor. These are your roommates. Don't get any ideas. You've had your first day. This can go easy or hard. If you resist, I'll bring your friends back tomorrow and the next day and the next day until your body is ground into dust. You're a little older than we like but it provides variety. Don't make me regret helping you." He left and the door locked from the outside.

Inside, there were no windows. There was a dull yellow light in the corner next to what looked like a toilet. Jack could see girls and boys, but mainly girls, ranging in age from eleven to seventeen.

Do any of you speak English? he said to himself. He couldn't make a sound. The pain and the swelling made that impossible. Instead, he turned his back to the silent eyes looking at him and tried to make himself fall asleep. His last thoughts were about Val. *If this happened to me, what did they do to her?*

∞

He learned nothing of Val. His days consisted of cleaning himself and being raped by men. *Why is it always men?* he thought. *Why can't I have a woman rape me? What's wrong with us men?* After a month, he stopped thinking anything whatsoever. He knew he had it better than the young girls and boys. They were forced to have sex twenty or thirty times a day with men older, fatter, and more perverted than he had thought possible. He saw their bleeding bodies and the shame, the vacant look in their eyes, and the absolute lack of laughter. *If I don't get out of here soon, I'll become just like them.*

"What do we have here?" The voice belonged to a distinguished gentleman with a wedding ring and polished shoes. He wore a tie and had a cross pinned on his lapel.

"Who would you like tonight?" Vlad asked, adopting his best manners.

"I'll have the old boy and those two girls."

"Excellent. I'll send them right in."

The man disappeared and Vlad grabbed an eleven- and a sixteen-year-old. They looked like sisters, both blonde and slim with a similar nose. He jerked his head to Jack to follow. They were directed to the main house and up the stairs. *The master bedroom.* VIP, thought Jack.

As he walked between their quarters and the main house, he realised it was dusk already. Early and getting cold; October in the middle of Russia. He stole a glance and looked again across the empty fields surrounding the compound. It was miles from anywhere and each time he saw it, he tried to figure out how he was going to run away. Five men escorted the boys, girls, and himself to the rooms next to their quarters. This was not the first time he had been to the main house or seen the hopeless expanse of land around him. But it was the first time when, after seeing again what he was up against, something inside him broke into an even smaller piece. *I'm never getting out of here.*

∞

He guessed it was almost three months later when he was summoned by Vlad and told he was going on a trip. Andre was going to take him to his new master, who would decide what he wanted from Jack. Doron went along to help.

"Did you father get back safely?" Jack tried to get Andre to talk.

"Yeah, almost four months ago."

"No, I mean I heard he went to America."

"Oh that, how did you hear that?" Andre became suspicious.

"Shut up or I'll make you shut up," Doron said. He motioned to slap Jack but didn't.

"I'm sorry. I just wanted to say that I can pay more for my freedom than whoever is paying your father for me." Jack had played his only card.

"You don't have a say in this," Doron said.

"I agree. That's why I was asking about your father. Maybe you should run it past him?"

Doron looked unsure and Andre just blinked.

"How much?" Andre asked.

"How much did you pay for me? How much are you getting for me? How much can you earn from me? If you let me know that, I'll better all of it." Jack saw hope. He knew he couldn't run. Either they or the winter would kill him. Greed was the answer.

"You want to know the economics behind our business?" Andre asked.

"I guess so," said Jack.

"We got you for free. We get everyone for free," Doron said. "But we get a lot renting your ass out. We must be selling you because you're not bringing in enough."

My sale could be my death sentence, thought Jack. "But the others. They must bring you in quite a lot."

"Of course. We're not Communists. We're not a charity." Doron laughed.

"Do you ever ship people to America?" Jack asked. He held his breath. *Was it too soon to ask?*

Both Doron and Andre paused. Jack could feel the foot come off the accelerator. They were thinking of how to answer that.

"Yes, but only for virgins, young children, or special orders. You would never be shipped. Besides, the market isn't worth it. American has its own supply." It seemed like Andre forgot himself for a while and spoke to Jack like a real person. "Say a child goes missing," he explained. "Within forty-eight hours, a quarter of them are snapped up by the pimps and operators. That kid'll be earning money for his master within the day and should last a few years if they are handled properly. Costs nothing. So why should they pay for foreign imports?"

"OK," Jack said, trying to focus on getting to the States. "What if I wanted to pay for my voyage to America, alongside these special delicacies, what would that cost?"

"I would need to ask my father. And he'll be mad. He already sold you," Andre said.

"You can tell the buyer I escaped and you had to shoot me. The new guy will understand. Besides, the next piece of meat is as good as or better than me, presumably." Jack was sweating. He didn't like the way the conversation was turning.

Silence. Then a phone came out and Andre talked to his father.

"A hundred thousand US dollars will get you to America on the next shipment. Can you do that?" Andre was genuinely interested, as was Doron.

"Yes," Jack said without hesitation. His gut told him that it was ten times the going rate, but it didn't matter what they asked for. It was his neck and he needed to live to fight another day.

"How are you going to pay? I can't say yes to my father without payment."

"I need to be in America before I pay in full. If you get me onto a computer here, I can wire half now and the rest when I am standing on American soil."

Andre looked at Jack. He had to pull the truck over. Doron was silent. This time they both talked to their father but Jack didn't catch much of it. When they finished, Andre turned the truck around.

"Father said if your payment doesn't arrive you will be dead by morning."

Chapter Three

STAYING ALIVE

Despite the horrors of the last few months, Jack's most terrifying memories were from ten years ago when his oldest and most trusted friend shot and killed his parents in front of him. The man turned out to be his biological father. Moments after he killed himself, Jack discovered a trove of information and money that allowed him to stay alive, despite being on the CIA's kill list.

Jack hated Joe for years until he realised he had been given the means to plot his own revenge. Joe may have been his biological father, but he had also spent a lifetime as a deep-cover CIA operative in the world's most inhospitable regions, pitting wits against the world's most intractable tyrants. The CIA money he now had access to was hidden and virtually untraceable, unknown to the mandarins of Washington or

Langley. Only a handful of people knew about the accounts and all of them, as far as Jack knew, were dead. Except for him.

Dirty money. Blood money. Money for killing and making war. Jack had used some to help facilitate Tim Bull's audacious plan, but there was plenty left. He had never determined how much because he never took more than he needed. It was just sitting earning interest in anonymous Swiss and Singaporean and Caribbean accounts. *Maybe my life these last few months is a punishment for what I've done,* he thought. His sense of shame and disgust at his present plight was not enough to wash clean the evil he had been part of last year. *Revenge may be best served cold, but it's still choking me.*

"I'll need a computer and some time."

"You'll get what we give you," Vlad said.

Jack was calm. "I need time to download the encryption software and then log on—however long that takes. After that, the transfer should be in your account within the next two hours."

He was in a room with the father and sons. The father was silent, brooding, and watching him as if he had three heads. Jack couldn't determine whether he was plotting to kill him or just wondering what was unfolding before his eyes. He nodded to Vlad and Jack was given a laptop.

"Thanks," Jack said as he started typing furiously. This was his chance.

Vlad, Doron, and Andre stood behind Jack, watching everything. No one spoke.

"OK, I'm in. What are the details?"

When they gave him the account number, he just stared at the paper. Valeria Polzin, Bank of Moscow. He looked at them.

"Surprised?" Vlad enjoyed this. "She's our fucking sister, you moron. Now close your mouth and transfer the money."

He did but was careful to not disclose how much the account held. It was a smaller account he used for living. He had never accessed the motherlode; he knew of those accounts but didn't mess with them for fear of triggering an alarm at the CIA. As he printed confirmation of the payment instructions, he could see the father smile. Nikki had dialled Valeria's number and handed the phone to their father. During the lull, Jack had an idea.

Every computer and location has a unique address. If he could send himself a message, he would be able to track these animals down later. For the first time in months, he was beginning to believe there would be a later. He did a quick ping to the laptop, copied the address, and began typing out a quick email to himself.

Before he finished, he felt a god almighty punch to his head. It felt like metal but was probably someone's fist. He heard the laptop shut and his body being dragged out of the room.

When he awoke, the four men in leather were there. Another man held a video recorder. Beside him was an eleven-year-old girl. What followed was something Jack spent the rest of his life trying to forget. He watched as she was submitted to the same horrors he received from these men—screams, blood, and eventually the sound of bones breaking. Her body crumbled and they threw her aside. He had thought there was nothing that could make him feel more fear than his first night, but he realised there was no bottom in the depths of man's depravity. He didn't fight and took the beating. He felt the tearing of his asshole as they did things to him no animal would bear. His eyes swelled up and his ears rang with a high pitch he would carry with him whenever he shut his eyes. This time they were laughing. This time, he prayed.

It lasted almost an hour after the little girl's death. Jack had become unconscious and couldn't be sure. When he came to, Vlad was standing above him.

"Congratulations, Jack," Vlad said. "You're a free man. I hope you enjoyed my father's parting gift. It's a reminder to send the other half when you reach your destination. We will have someone watching you in case you decide to renege. My father is not the most trusting of people. He wanted you to learn this lesson on your skin so you wouldn't forget."

Jack looked where Vlad was looking. There was a red blister on Jack's buttocks, but even this was hard to see with all the blood and shit that covered his body.

They actually branded me, he thought. Vlad started laughing when he saw Jack's eyes. *And they shit on me when they finished.*

"You'll be leaving in a couple of days. You'll have special transport." Vlad left Jack to find his own way to the dirty hose that served as the shower.

∞

He was pushed into a container stuffed with adults all looking to go to America. Each had paid an enormous sum to their traffickers. Jack felt lucky. Being a sex slave had only one outcome: death. Whether it came from the beatings or suicide, it would come. He had seen it in the eyes of the children who were sitting next to him after a particularly heavy beating. These were girls who had to service 300-pound men, married men, politicians, pastors, and everyone in between. Girls who would never know innocence, having been fucked or beaten a thousand times before they were old enough to vote.

But that needs to wait, thought Jack. *I just need to get back to* US *soil.*

The trip wasn't pleasant but at least he wasn't being raped daily. He was sore beyond belief and he feared infection. The container he shared with sixty others was forty feet long by almost eight feet wide. They had enough room to sit down and there was an area for a toilet in the corner. It consisted of some containers to urinate or defecate into. This was shared by both men and women. There were containers of water for drinking and it was rationed carefully. Food consisted of some dried meat and dog food. There were breathing holes in the container but the air was heavy with body odour and the putrid smell of human waste. As the summer sun beat down, the stench became a whole new form of torture.

This trip lasted thirty-nine days. *Almost as long as Noah's adventure,* thought Jack with little humour. The pain was like a knife on his nerves. Sitting hurt. Shitting hurt. Everything hurt. He could feel his muscles wasting and body becoming thin as all his reserves were consumed just to stay alive. When he felt the container being moved by the dock equipment, he knew they were on the final stretch. Seventeen people died during the trip and they were placed in the corner where the water once was. What little of it remained was moved next to the doors and people almost stopped using the toilet.

∞

"Welcome to Mexico, my friends," a voice said. None of the other inhabitants of the container could understand the man with the cowboy hat. Even Jack had to cock his head to understand what he saw. "Help these people now," the voice said to six young men. They came running and assisted in moving the people into two busses.

"You hungry?" the same voice said with humour to the starving group in his bus. "We'll be at your destination shortly. There'll be lots of food and you'll need to rest. You still have a long journey ahead of you." He didn't care that no one could understand him. He spoke in Spanish.

"Excuse me?" Jack didn't know much Spanish and the man could recognise a gringo when he saw one. "Do you speak English?"

"You American?" He started laughing so hard, he began coughing. The driver also began laughing. He picked up the CB and spoke something to the other bus driver. Jack could only imagine what the joke was.

"Yeah," Jack said. He was in so much pain and the sun was so bright he could barely hold a thought.

"Then you must be in some serious shit to be with this crowd." He tried to calm himself. "My name's Daniel."

"Jack. Nice to meet you." He didn't care if Daniel was his name. At least he was talking and not punching.

"I'd say likewise but we're not in polite society. What brings you into this situation?"

"Long story," Jack said. "Look, do you have an aspirin or any medicine? I would love to see a doctor before we do what I think you're suggesting."

"It will be a long hard walk to get across, but we have more to talk about before that. I'll see if I can get a doctor to look at you. We're not animals like some in our industry. We're just facilitators, trying to put food on our table and raise our families. No different than any businessmen."

Jack had initially liked this guy but was getting more wary. "That would be great. Thanks."

Nearly an hour later, they pulled into a dusty compound with numerous villas. Three stray dogs roamed, ribs showing. The family dog sat fat and content on the porch next to its master.

"Welcome back, Daniel. Any trouble?" the master asked.

"None, Señor Lalo."

"Good. Get them cleaned up and fed and we'll talk to them later. Make sure the translators are ready."

Washed, fed, and rested, the group reassembled, eager to go to America.

"My friends, you have been on a long journey. I can only imagine the hardships you had to endure. But it isn't over yet. We still need to get you over the border. To do that, you'll need to pay us money." Lalo waited for the translators to finish.

"It will cost you $2,000 per person, which we will collect from your wages on the other side. We have arranged work and accommodation and you will soon be living the American dream."

There were murmurs of appreciation and even a giggle. Despite the horrors they had endured, their spirits were unbroken. They were free.

"I want you to rest for the next three days. Eat and get strong again. We've grilled some meat for you. On the evening of the walk, we will provide you with a guide and there will be no stopping. If you are too weak, you will be left behind. Get strong and get ready. Next week you'll be in America, land of the free!"

The group applauded weakly and then dispersed, grabbing some food and juice. No alcohol was offered and none was desired. They were drunk on the expectation of their dreams coming true. *These guys aren't being trafficked for sex*, thought Jack. *Everyone is being too kind.*

As Jack walked away, Daniel pulled him aside.

"Gringo, I need a word with you."

"Go ahead," Jack said.

"Señor Lalo has planned an extra charge for you. He is of the mind that you might be dangerous to us."

"Dangerous? How?"

"Because you're an American, being smuggled in from Russia or some such place and then being smuggled into your own country. You can walk straight in and be welcomed with open arms. If you aren't, then you must be afraid of the law."

Jack didn't say anything. He thought he was OK, but he just couldn't take the chance. He needed to get back into the States to make everything OK.

"Or you *are* the law," said Daniel, staring at Jack.

"I'm not the police."

"Then you won't mind carrying a package across for us. You'll still have to pay the normal transit charges. The package is our insurance."

Jack could only guess what that package contained, but he had no choice. "OK, that's fine with me. As long as it's not too heavy."

Daniel laughed. "You won't barely feel it."

Jack was left by himself, the dust and movement of all the others fading into the distance. *Believe me, I'll feel it*, he thought. *Every single ounce.*

∞

On the appointed day, the busses parked a few miles from the international border around 4 pm. They waited in a single-file line behind their guide. When Daniel gave the nod, the guide began to walk. He didn't look at them. They would either keep up or be left behind. Jack tried to stay close to him, the three kilograms of cocaine sitting in his knapsack next to his water bottle and some dried meat.

"How long before we get there?" Jack asked.

"We just started. Don't think about it," the guide said.

"I just need to pace myself."

"Just be glad it's not summer. The temperature is perfect now. We'll walk until the moon can no longer guide us, probably just past midnight. We'll rest and then continue from 4 am until we reach our destination. Tomorrow will be hard. Conserve your water."

"How long is the walk tomorrow?"

"Until we get there. Usually in the evening, 8 or 9 pm." The guide picked up his pace so he didn't need to keep talking to Jack. He was there to guide, not talk.

No wonder they call them coyotes, Jack thought. He didn't waste any more energy on talk. He had received some antibiotics from Lalo's doctor and some aspirin for the trip. He put a lot of talcum powder on the body parts that might chafe. *And*, he thought, *I can always use the cocaine if I need more energy—or if I want a sure-fire death sentence.*

The first hour was the easiest, but he was worried about how to pace himself. He had no choice but to keep up with the coyote. It wasn't until the fourth hour when he started realising how long this journey was going to be. When they reached the eight-hour mark and midnight had passed, he collapsed along with the rest of the walkers.

"What are those?" he asked, pointing to plastic jugs of water.

"Some good Samaritans. They leave us water. It can mean the difference between life and death during the summer. Now, the weather isn't too bad. My suggestion is to fill up your water bottles. We wake in four hours." With that, he found a spot on the scorched little stones and went to sleep.

"Amazing," Jack mumbled. "I wish I could do that." He noticed the others doing the same. He tried and soon fell into a deep sleep.

The next morning, most people were already walking before he received a gentle nudge from someone's boot. "Thanks," Jack said and got himself up and walking immediately. *No breakfast, I guess.*

The actual cross was anticlimactic. "That's it?" Jack said. There was a hole in the fence and the guide stood back to ensure everyone who was still with him went through.

"There was a time when we could cross through a hole in the border like this, have our people pick us up, and take us closer to the checkpoint," the coyote said. "We would get out and walk only a half dozen miles in the desert before our guys would pick us up. But things have changed. Now we stay away from the checkpoint and rely on our people more than ever. The US can't monitor 2,000 miles of its border with Mexico. Our job is to get you to the pickup point, then it's up to you." He was walking again now that his group was through.

"Twelve more hours?" Jack asked. No one replied. It was walking time. Talk was over.

He soon understood why the second day was harder. The water ran out. Dehydration started to kick in and his muscles began to ache. No one showed weakness but he knew if he was hurting, so were they. Only the coyote seemed unaffected. When they stopped, Jack ate the last of his salty dried beef. *I hope it's beef,* he thought as he tore a piece off and started chewing.

"Maybe we should take a break?" He was starting to hear little groans and people were slowing. He was in agony.

"If we stop, you won't be able to start again. We continue. Only one more hour." The coyote looked back and saw the line lengthening. "If you have water, drink it while walking. Fill yourself up."

But his body rejected the water. It was under too great a punishment. Those who let themselves go too long without drinking threw the water back up. The coyote was becoming restless. "Stop messing around. We are close. Pull it together. It's not that hard. Much harder in summer."

They all persevered.

When the vans came into view, they tried to pick up the pace, but their legs could only put one foot in front of the other. There was nothing left in the tank. There were eight vans and one 4x4 pickup, the type a boss would drive. Its door opened as the exhausted men and women approached. All the vans opened.

"Eight per van, let's go! We don't have all day." The voice was different—a new master.

The men and women crammed themselves into the eight vans and the doors closed. Each one left as soon as the doors closed. Jack never saw or knew what happened to them. He had tried to join one of the vans but was held back by a large white guy, a good six inches taller than him.

"You have something of mine," the new master said.

"Ah, of course." Jack retrieved the cocaine and handed it to him.

"Thank you, and welcome back to America." The big white guy planted a fist into the side of Jack's face, which caused stars to swim in front of his eyes. They left two jugs of water and a salami sausage, which fell into the sand next to Jack's face. He could smell it before his eyes could focus.

Chapter Four

MODELS WANTED

"Oh no, we're almost out of gas. I'll have to stop," Tammy said to her daughter.

"We're going to be late," Chrystal said.

"It'll just be a second. We won't be late."

Tammy pulled into the station and stopped next to the pump. She chose the cheapest gasoline and put it into the tank. She flipped the lever on the handle to fill it up; it would stop magically, she thought, when full. "Have you ever . . ." she started to ask Chrystal a question through the open window and then stopped, her hand in her pocket. She pulled out a bill. Twenty dollars. She clicked the lever off and took hold of the handle, watching the total on the pump eating up all the money she had to survive on until the end of the week. She stopped at $19 and then inched it up towards $20. She missed and the total showed $20.12 due.

"Do you have twelve cents?" she called through the window.

"Uh, yeah. Here." Chrystal pulled out a quarter.

"Thanks." Tammy went to the cashier inside and paid.

Tammy had been a college graduate and received her bookkeeping qualifications before marrying Corey Alberts, a solicitor. They had Chrystal and she decided to be a stay-at-home mother. She wanted the best for her daughter and her husband agreed. Chrystal was smart, funny, and talented. Growing up, she tried out and got most of the lead roles in plays and musicals in her school. They were the perfect family.

When Corey served the divorce papers on her, she was devastated. She had no idea and had made no contingency plans. They sold their marital home and rented an apartment in a good area of town. They had enough money, Tammy thought, but it went so fast. She got a job and was just about able to make ends meet. Six months ago, she got laid off. The recession, she was told.

Chrystal was relatively unaffected by the whole divorce and did well in school but didn't pursue a university degree. She eventually became the manager at a local branch of a national clothes brand. She made decent money but wanted something more from her life.

"When I'm rich and famous, Mom, we won't have to worry about silly stuff like filling the tank. We'll have a chauffeur to drive us around. We won't even need to open doors. We'll have staff for that." She smiled. They were close, and she felt the frustration and shame of her mother as though it was her own.

"You're a good girl, Chrystal. Don't worry about all that stuff. Just keep working and don't give up."

"Don't let the bastards get you down, huh?" Her smile was infectious. "Anyway, fingers crossed. It might be our lucky day. Wait, it's just here. To the left. Great."

Tammy pulled up and put the car in park. When she started to turn off the ignition, she saw the sidelong look from Chrystal and thought against it. "I'll wait here until you're done. It'll give me a chance to catch up on some reading."

"*National Enquirer*?"

"No," Tammy smiled. "Just a book."

"How to dissect a frog?"

"Dickens. *Great Expectations*," Tammy said.

"How appropriate. Wish me luck!"

"Love you, sweetheart. Break a leg!"

The door slammed and Chrystal disappeared behind the agency's door. Girls and some guys were coming and going out the same door, all young, fresh, and full of hope.

It was almost two hours before she returned. Tammy had dozed off and woke to the door opening on the passenger side.

"I got an offer!" Chrystal was flush with excitement and was leaning toward her mother.

"Wonderful! I knew you'd do it." Tammy was genuinely excited for her.

"But it's big. They went on and on about how I have this look they've been searching for and how they know all the big agencies and how I'll be a big star. They told me they have a shoot coming up soon and asked when I could be available." The words flowed and tumbled out in her excitement.

Tammy was a bit more cautious. "What about your current job? It's steady pay. You wouldn't want to lose that. Jobs aren't easy lately."

"I know. But they're saying I can make between $5,000 and $15,000 per month doing modelling."

Tammy blinked. "That's a lot of money. Are they for real?"

"Absolutely. And I want you to meet them. They know all about you and they said they'd like to meet you."

"I was just about to say that I wanted to meet them before you make such a big decision."

"They're based in Los Angeles so I'll need to move." Chrystal said this and regretted it as the words left her mouth. She knew her paycheque covered the rent. Her mother's alimony cheque barely covered food and utilities.

Tammy paused. "When can I meet them?"

"Let me talk to my boss and see what notice I need to give. Maybe they'll allow me to take some holiday time, just in case it doesn't work out. When we know, I'll call the agency back and we can both go in."

She's smarter than me, Tammy thought. "Sounds like a plan."

∞

Chrystal's boss wasn't pleased with her job offer. He told her she could have two weeks' vacation time immediately but if she wasn't back by then she would lose her job. Chrystal agreed and phoned the agency. They were able to meet her and her mother straight away.

"Good afternoon, Mrs. Alberts. Your daughter has made quite the impression on everyone here. Have a seat while I buzz Lyle." The receptionist was pleasant and professional and smiled a lot when she talked. The entrance was clean and had four-foot pictures of celebrities on all the walls, many with signatures and messages of gratitude.

"Thanks for coming, Mom. Can you believe it?"

"It looks impressive. I checked them out online and they seem legit. I just want to see the whites of their eyes. I don't want you getting involved with drugs or messing around with the cameraman."

"Mom! Don't talk so loud. They're professional," Chrystal said. "And besides, I'm a grown woman."

"That's what I'm afraid of."

They were soon led into another room with four men, all seated comfortably on leather sofas and armchairs. They got up when Tammy and Chrystal entered.

"Lovely to meet you, Mrs. Alberts," Lyle said, shaking her hand.

"Please, call me Tammy."

"I can see where Chrystal gets her looks from," he said. "I can't believe you're old enough to be her mother."

Tammy knew it was empty flattery but found herself blushing nonetheless. "Flattery will get you everywhere," she said with a smile.

"Have you thought about modelling yourself?" The question was out of left field and sent a jolt though Tammy. Chrystal, who was chatting with the other men turned around and raised her eyebrows, smiling.

"No, I've never done anything like it."

"Would you like to try? I think it would be a great mix to have a mother and daughter available for photo shoots."

Tammy was beyond flattered. She melted. "Me? Photo shoots?"

"Why not? Listen, we've got a slot open now with our professional team. Let's take some shots of you and Chrystal and see how they turn out. If you like it and if I'm right, we may be able to extend a similar deal for you."

They took some test shots that afternoon, and Tammy was surprised at how much she liked it. It made her feel young and sexy again. She was offered a similar deal to Chrystal on the spot. As they left the agency, they turned to each other and squealed with delight.

"I can't believe it," Tammy said.

"I can't believe how hot you are!" Chrystal said. "They really made you look great in those shots."

Tammy feigned hurt feelings and then giggled. "I feel like I'm eighteen again."

"What should we do about the apartment?"

"I'm happy to give notice and go. The agency wants us there next week. You have two weeks to decide about your job. If we have to come back, we'll get another apartment." Tammy had a spring in her step and glint in her eye. "As the generals would say, sometimes you need to burn your bridges so you can't come back. We're going to make this work, sweetheart." She gave her daughter a hug. Life was turning around. Good times were ahead.

∞

They gave most of their possessions away and took a bag of small keepsakes. They were starting anew. When they flew to LAX, a driver was waiting for them with a limo to take them to the studio on the other side of Los Angeles. He never left their side and took their bags and attended to everything, including checking them into a luxury five-star hotel.

"Champagne on ice!" Tammy was more excited than Chrystal.

"Careful, Mom. We haven't signed anything yet."

"Don't be such a party pooper. One drink won't hurt us." She popped the bottle and poured two glasses. "To the future," she said.

"The future," Chrystal said.

They settled in the room and heard a knock on the door. "Five minutes," came a voice.

"We'll be there," Tammy replied. She turned to her daughter with a smile. "I still can't believe this is happening. Look at this place. I feel like a millionaire already."

"I know. I keep pinching myself," Chrystal said. "I can't wait to start."

On their first day, they took only their purse with their ID and some credit cards. When they reached the studio, they realised that it was a mistake to have brought it along. Their minder took care of it for them. Besides, they were changing clothes nonstop and it was hard to keep track of silly things like ID and some maxed-out credit cards.

"You look beautiful, Chrystal. Now, I would like to get you more comfortable in front of the camera. No, you are doing fine. But we have found being photographed naked releases the inhibitions of the model and makes it much easier for anything else."

"Excuse me?" Tammy was feeling a little self-conscious. "I'm not sure if I'm comfortable with that."

"I am," Chrystal said. "I've heard this before. All the models do it."

"Don't worry, Mrs. Alberts. No one's forcing you to do anything. Let Chrystal do her thing and you can do yours." The man behind the camera smiled.

"All right," Tammy said slowly. She watched her daughter get ready.

"Beautiful. You're a natural." Chrystal posed and became more confident. They seemed to know what they were talking about. Tammy went to get a coffee.

Before they knew it, three days had passed and each one was full on. *This modelling is hard work*, she thought. As she sat in a plush armchair, she noticed that pornography was being played on the television sets. Why hadn't she noticed this before?

"Is this normal?" she asked the receptionist.

"Yeah. Another division of the agency deals with adult films. They have their fingers in everything."

"Funny. I never noticed it before today." Tammy said it more to herself, but the receptionist shrugged and turned back to her work.

After an exhausting two weeks of frenetic work, Chrystal was flush with excitement. "I'm telling my boss that I'm staying. We're making a fortune and, frankly, I don't want to go back to our old life."

"I know. It's harder work than I thought but it's honest, and the pay is unbelievable. If you're up for it, I'm ready to stay, too." Tammy was proud of her daughter and happy to be part of her dream.

"Do you think we can take this weekend and do something nice?"

"What are you thinking?" Tammy said.

"Just spend some time together."

"But we are spending every waking moment together," Tammy said. "Don't you get bored with me?"

"Never. But I've been asked by Scott to go with him to a party on Saturday night and thought we could spend the day together."

"Scott the guy with the tattoo?"

"Mom, they all have tattoos. He's nice and sweet. And I could use a good night out."

"Sounds like you've got it all figured out. My girl's all grown up." Tammy was hesitant, but couldn't be prouder.

Life continued like this for the remainder of their first month in LA. They had taken a serviced apartment near the studio to reduce travel expenses. The studio had arranged it. When their paycheques finally arrived, neither of them could contain their excitement. They wanted to see how rich they were.

"And this is only the beginning," Tammy said, the envelope unopened in her hand.

"Let's do this together. One . . . two . . . three." They both tore open their envelopes.

They both stared at the contents. Then they pulled out the second paper and looked at it. They weren't laughing.

"What does yours say?" Tammy said.

"Nothing."

"What do you mean nothing? Doesn't it show you how much you made?"

"Yeah, but that's the thing. It's nothing. Our income is $5,000 but they deducted all of the expenses they had incurred on our behalf. The air tickets, luxury hotels, limo driver, clothes, food. Everything. It says that I owe them $1,230." Chrystal was speechless.

"Same here. But I owe them over $3,000. I don't know how this is possible."

"There must be a mistake. Let's talk to Lyle and get to the bottom of this. They're really nice guys. I'm sure we can sort it out." Chrystal was already putting the envelope into her pocket and walking toward the door. Stunned, Tammy followed.

When they returned to the studio, Lyle was meeting with Scott and the other crew. He looked up when the Alberts women walked in.

"Hello, ladies," he said. "What can I do for you?"

"Sorry to bother you, Lyle," Chrystal said, "but I think there's been a mistake with our paycheques."

"Oh? What's wrong?"

"It says we owe you money. How can that be?"

"Don't worry about it. It is normal in the modelling business. Because of tax and regulations, each of the models is an independent contractor and we need to charge every service we provide. It's just the first month. You'll make it back in no time."

"But it's a lot of money," Tammy said. "I owe you over $3,000. How will I ever pay you back?"

"Don't worry," Lyle said. "We can discuss it later. There are lots of opportunities in our agency. Some pay more than others. We can discuss it later."

"I would like to discuss it now, if possible," she said. "I'm very nervous. I've never been in this situation before. I think I would be better off not working if I end up owing you so much money each month."

Lyle's smile disappeared. "You will find that everything is clearly set out in your contract. We have been totally transparent with you. Besides, you signed a two-year deal. If you want to leave, you would need to pay us $50,000."

Tammy suppressed a gasp. *This was the big leagues*, she thought. "I'm sorry, Lyle, I didn't mean to offend. It's all so new to us."

"I understand. Look, it's simple. We have some shoots to do in the adult entertainment division that may be suitable for you. It pays twice as much and should get you out of debt in no time." He smiled at her and put his hand on her arm. It was friendly.

"I'll do it," Chrystal said. Tammy swivelled to look at her. "It's nothing, Mom. It's modelling. I can be like Mariah Carey. Look where she is now."

"Mariah Carey was a prostitute, not a porn star. And she was sixteen. And she sings."

"OK, but you know what I mean. It's all good. It's all modelling. And I'll be an actress. Maybe I'll be able to leverage this into a movie deal somehow." Chrystal was convincing herself more than anyone else. Lyle and the other men nodded their support. Tammy pursed her lips.

"I'm not sure, honey. Try it out if you want and if anything doesn't feel right, don't do it."

"You don't have to do anything you don't want," said Lyle. "Everyone's a professional here. It's not like we're strangers either." He was in a good mood again and had his hand on the back of Chrystal's neck.

"Tammy," he turned back to the mother. "Let's meet up later this afternoon to discuss how you can increase your income without doing something you're not comfortable with, OK?"

Tammy nodded. She watched her daughter go through the doors. She didn't want to think about the rest. *This modelling world is a tough business*, she thought. She found out that her daughter did the porn scenes while Lyle was talking to her later that afternoon. Tammy agreed to do some nude photos to increase her comfort level in front of the camera—and to increase her paycheque.

When they both were sitting in their apartment later that evening, it was as though a line had been crossed. Chrystal had enjoyed her shoot that afternoon and had booked more the next week. She was meeting Scott for a romantic weekend at some rich guy's home.

"Maybe we should call it quits?" Tammy said finally.

"Mom, I can't go back. Besides, look what we have achieved. How many people get to be part of these shoots?"

"Yes, but at what cost? You're doing porn, for Christ's sake."

"It's not that bad. They guys are gentle and I kind of like it." She was embarrassed to say it.

"I just hope you know what you're doing. I'm getting the feeling that if I don't join in, I'm going to be out on the street."

"Talk to Lyle, Mom. He'll get you some better shoots."

"I'm just not getting anything, sweetheart. If I don't get any shoots, we don't get money to pay for all this stuff, and I can't have you take care of me all the time."

"It's not a problem. And we'll get our big break at some point. You'll see."

But they didn't. Lyle weaned Tammy off any shoots until she agreed to try a sex movie. Tammy was embarrassed at her daughter's success and felt she wasn't pulling her weight. She agreed to try it.

When she arrived on set, there were two men in leather outfits. They tied her up, whipped her, beat her with their fists, and raped her repeatedly on camera. When it was done, Lyle explained that this is what the public wanted. Hard-core sex that shocked. Tammy understood it as punishment for her resistance.

Meanwhile, Chrystal learned that Scott wasn't interested in any romantic weekend at a rich man's house. He was merely escorting her to be the entertainment for a house full of old men. There were eight other girls there. They were all expected to show the men a good time. Scott made sure that everything went to plan. *I've become a whore*, Chrystal thought as the fourth man entered her that evening. He was pushing sixty, overweight, and sweaty. His wedding ring got caught in her hair when he pulled her violently during their time together.

When the cheques came at the end of the month, neither were surprised. They still had not earned enough to cover their debts. Tammy was doing four porn movies a week and was being rented out on the weekends at separate locations to her daughter. Lyle knew it would be weird for them both to be at the same party. At the end of each evening, they ensured no tips or gifts were given to the girls. If there had been, they were confiscated. "There's no need for you to have money, girls. We take care of everything for you. All you need to do is be beautiful and show up." Scott said this on more than one occasion. Tammy and Chrystal no longer argued about it.

"We can't afford to stay in our apartment," Tammy said after the second paycheque. Her voice was without emotion, stating the obvious. The events of the last couple of months had taken the spark out of her.

"I was thinking the same thing," Chrystal said. "The other girls share a large room, dormitory-style. Maybe we can try it there for a while until we make some real money."

"OK. When do you want to move?"

"Why not today? All they're doing is charging us for staying here."

Tammy was feeling weary. It was a big decision and the two of them were accepting it as inevitable. She was healthy and looked great for her age, but she felt every day of her thirty-eight years. She felt as though she had aged five years in the last two months. Her daughter still seemed fresh and upbeat, but she could see a sadness in her eyes. There was no more talk of Mariah Carey and big contracts or movies, or anything other than washing, changing, and getting ready for the next shoot or party.

When they moved to the dormitory, there were eight girls to a room. Each had a little table for their things. It was like living in a camp.

"Been here long?" Tammy asked a young girl, who couldn't have been more than sixteen.

"Just got here," she said.

"You look young. Shouldn't you be in school?"

"No. Dropped out. Left home. Dino found me and saved me from sleeping rough. I'm hoping to be discovered through the agency. They have hundreds of famous people as their clients. I may be the next big one." Her enthusiasm was genuine, her teeth white and eyes clear. It made Tammy turn away with guilt.

"Good luck, little girl," she said as she got her bunk organised. She took the bottom bed and Chrystal took the top.

"Everything OK, Mom?" Chrystal asked.

"Yeah. Everything's great," she said. It was becoming harder to lie.

∞

Soon Lyle decided that Tammy and Chrystal should do house parties together. Clients liked the idea of renting a mother-daughter team. Tammy started drinking and Chrystal began to take drugs to keep her perky and to dull the dark thoughts that had started chasing her. The little girl in their dorm was put straight into porn and then rented up to thirty times per day. It was no different than for any other of the new recruits, but for some reason she cracked. Tammy found her dead in the toilet. She had swallowed whatever drugs she could get her hands on, drunk half a bottle of vodka, and desperately slashed her wrists until she bled out.

"She could be you or me one of these days," Tammy said.

"I know, and it may still be. I've heard about some snuff movies where they take the girls and unleash their S&M men on her, only to finish her off by opening new holes in her. She dies screaming as her blood flows out of her while watching four men rape her simultaneously in holes created by knives. I'd kill myself if I thought I'd have to face that someday."

Tammy held Chrystal. They wanted to cry but there were no more tears. They had dried months back. "We need to find a way out of here before they separate us," she whispered.

Chrystal's eyes widened and she nodded. They would take their chance the next time it presented itself.

"OK, girls, show's over." Scott's voice filled their sleeping quarters like a band saw. "We'll get the bathroom cleaned up. In the meantime, back to work." He walked through the bunks and clothes, calming his girls as a shepherd does his flock. His presence was merely to protect his assets and maximise the investment of the agency.

He looked at the crumpled body of the little girl, head twisted from pushing herself behind the toilet. *Plenty more where you come from, little girl*, he said to himself. He pulled out a little cylinder and tapped the white powder on the fleshy bit of his left fist between the base of his thumb and his index finger. He raised it to his nose and inhaled. *Better than a cup of coffee*. He smiled and left the clean up to someone else. He stopped next to Tammy and Chrystal.

"We're leaving in an hour. That little bitch was supposed to join us. I'll grab two girls and you two and that should be OK."

"OK, Scott. Sounds good."

Scott put his hand gently on both Tammy's and Chrystal's faces, almost like a caress. "You two are something else. I wish everyone in here was like you. Want some?" He pulled out his little cylinder of powder. Tammy shook her head but Chrystal nodded. He tapped some out on a table nearby. When he watched Chrystal snort it, he put some more out and had another line himself. As he turned to leave, Tammy noticed a trace of blood coming from his nose.

When they were loaded into the car, three girls sat in the back and Tammy sat in the front with Scott. It was a luxurious black sedan with tinted windows. As they drove off, Tammy could smell alcohol on Scott.

"We're going to be a while. These fuckers are ways away. Almost two hours. But it'll be worth it. Heavy tippers." He popped some pills at a traffic light and added, "But don't get any ideas. All tips come back to me, right? It costs a lot to keep you beauties living the life." He smiled at them through the rearview mirror.

It was twilight now and the car reached the edge of the city. The highway stretched out in front of them like eternity. The four girls watched the road vacantly. Shutting down was the only way to survive.

As the car sped up, Scott's body tensed and curved, hands gripping the steering wheel. He let out a low animal growl as pain overtook him. The girls in the back were scared that he was angry but Tammy was afraid for a different reason. They weren't about to be beaten. Scott was having a seizure.

The car lurched to the left, then right, then felt like it would flip. His foot seized and pushed harder on the gas. Oncoming cars swerved out of the way. Tammy heard Chrystal scream and made an instance decision that she wasn't going to let them all die because of this asshole. Then she saw an opportunity.

She unbuckled her seat belt, knowing it meant certain death if they crashed. She grabbed the steering wheel and screamed for him to let go. His head was slumped and his hands slackened. She realised he wasn't having a seizure, but a heart attack. His body didn't resist but his foot was still pushing the accelerator. She had to stop the car but also couldn't take her eyes off the road or hands off the steering wheel.

"Mom!"

"It'll be OK, sweetheart, just stay calm." She said it but didn't remember anything later. Everything was in slow motion. The road was straight and there wasn't much traffic. That was a blessing, if there was such a thing. The other girls were too frightened to scream, barely teenagers and barely broken in by the agency. Just another couple of runaways picked up within a day of disappearing.

She moved the shifter into neutral and the engine roared as Scott's foot was still on the gas. His body was slumped forward and she needed to elbow his head away from the steering wheel. She wedged her body between his and the wheel and took control of the car.

The road's shoulders were wide and she took the car off the highway when it was below fifty miles per hour. She put on the hazards and the cars behind her raced past, hoping to avoid any accident. They hit the gravel shoulder and she made sure not to swerve.

"Everything's OK, girls. We're going to be OK."

She couldn't feel any breathing from the body behind her but his snot and drool ran down her bare back. She realised that her dress had torn and her top was hanging loosely around her waist, but she ignored it.

As they slowed, she began to believe they would live. Her body was coursing with adrenaline she didn't think she had. The girls were cheering. She didn't hear anything but the sound of the gravel, the roar of the engine, and her own breathing.

The car kept rolling as she elbowed Scott. He didn't move. She repositioned herself and moved his leg from the accelerator. The roaring ended and they finally stopped. Silence.

She was shaking. She put the gear in park, turned off the ignition, and returned to her seat. The cars on the highway sped past, oblivious to the five lives that had nearly ended. She readjusted her top and looked for a way to fix it. She opened the glove compartment and froze. There was a stack of money and a gun.

"You okay? Anyone hurt?" she turned to look at her daughter and the two young girls.

"No. That was amazing!" one girl bubbled. The other was nodding but saying nothing.

Tammy looked directly at Chrystal. "It's time. We're leaving."

"Where to?" the little girl asked.

Chrystal didn't need to say anything. She nodded.

"Listen, girls. If you stay here, you're going to die. Not tomorrow and maybe not next year, but it will not end well for you."

"But we'll get in trouble if we leave," said one. "They'll hurt us." She started to cry.

"I know. And they'll hurt you if you stay. Because that's what they do."

"I'll take my chances with the agency. I'm in enough trouble with my parents. I can't face them being mad for this, too. Lyle will find us and then it'll be worse."

Tammy was about to say something but changed her mind. "OK, it's your decision." She got out and walked to the driver's door. "Help me with this, Chrystal." She opened the door and undid Scott's seatbelt. He slumped forward.

"We need to get him to the side of the road. Let the two youngsters stay with him or come with us. We don't have any time to waste." Chrystal didn't say anything as she helped drag the body to the side of the road. He looked dead.

"OK, girls, decision time. I'm leaving in five seconds. You can come with us or stay with your slave owner."

"We're not slaves," the first girl said. "We're models."

"Yeah," said the other. She looked like she was going to something further but stayed quiet.

"All right. Well, you're two girls on the side of the road. Someone will pick you up. Whoever they are can't be worse than the garbage we've been with already. Even if they rape you, at least it's better than your usual day."

They waited for the girls to exit the car and wait by Scott's body. Tammy gave them some cash and told them to go to the police and go home, hoping they would change their minds once she left.

Then they pulled away, hoping to get as far as possible from their nightmare. Chrystal, in the passenger seat, counted the cash and eyed the gun. Neither of them had used one before. The cash would save their lives, but they hoped they wouldn't need the gun.

"We need to find different clothes and a new car, and somewhere to rest before we decide what we do next."

"We should go to the police," Chrystal said.

"I know, but I need some time to think, sweetheart. We're free for now. I don't want to go to the police only to be thrown in jail, or worse, returned to those animals." She looked at her daughter. It was over a year since she had driven a car, uttered the word 'free,' or even had a plan past surviving the day. It felt strange but good.

Chrystal's scream caused Tammy to turn her attention back to the road. She saw him just a second too late. She hit the brakes and he hit the car, broke the windshield, and rolled over the top. She wasn't paying attention and didn't have time to swerve.

"Fuck. Can't we get a break?" She pulled over, put the car in park, and went over to assess the damage—both to the car and the man she may have just killed.

Chapter Five

ALIVE

Jack was happy to be alive, but wishing he was dead. Guilt for his part in the June Terror ate at him constantly. His ordeal of the last six months felt like karma. He felt as though he deserved the unrelenting punishment for what he had done. At this moment, with his eye swelling shut, and his mouth full of fresh blood and dirt from the ground, he also began to feel a new emotion.

It was anger that got him to his feet. It was that unquenchable rage that was pitted deep within him that allowed him to survive Clog all those years ago. It allowed him to withstand the beatings and physical torment inflicted upon him by Vlad and his crew. He knew, even when he was beginning to give up hope, that if he survived, he would get revenge.

He allowed himself a small sip of water, enough to wash the sand out of his mouth. He allowed himself another as a reward for making it onto US soil. In normal circumstances, he would find his way to the police and hand himself in. They would question him but, as he was a victim, they would help him get back on his feet. But as far as the authorities knew, Jack Harding had never left the US. Harding was the name of his biological father, Joe. He had had fake passports and identification made and he could make them again, but they couldn't be made from the US Department of State passport office. Those would show him as Jack Woods, an out-of-work MBA student and former CIA asset (now dormant) who had disappeared roughly ten years earlier. Questions would be asked that he couldn't answer. Until he was able to reassume his false identity, he couldn't go to the police.

He needed money to get to where he had buried the necessary items to help him in this type of situation. *Well, not exactly a situation like this,* he thought. *But I'm glad I have it. Now all I need to do is get there. I just wish they had put me in Alaska instead of Arizona. Whatever happens, I still need to cross another border, and I need cash to get there.*

"This isn't that bad, Jack," he said out loud. There was no one for him to speak to but it felt good to talk. For six months, just opening his mouth meant a punch, or worse, something put inside it against his will. He started talking to himself in his head and was happy to talk to himself out loud. "Could be a lot worse." He laughed. He walked close to the highway but out of sight of any patrols, aiming for Interstate 10. He figured he could catch a lift there.

He brushed off the salami and bit into it. It was greasy and the outer rind was thick with pepper and a string that was woven like a poorly knitted sock. His fingers became full of the slippery fat as he gnawed at the meat inside the rind. In the end, he ate the rind.

"Not bad at all," he said. "Could be a lot worse, considering."

He made sure he didn't eat too much. He didn't want to be sick. He took another sip of water, put everything into his knapsack, and continued walking. "Kind of them to leave the knapsack," he said. "Real saints." He smiled. Talking to himself was like a comfortable madness.

His luck held and he reached the interstate close to a regional hospital. He walked through the empty streets of South Tucson's suburbs, wary of some neighbourhood watch member who might call the police at the sight of a man covered in rags and dirt. Perhaps it was because he was white that no call was made. He was convinced if he was Mexican or black, the police would have been on him in no time.

He saw the on-ramp to the interstate and positioned himself to go west. He would take the first ride he could get and play things by ear. It didn't take long before a Volvo station wagon stopped alongside him.

"Where you off to, friend?"

"West, sir," said Jack.

"Hop in. Is that all you have?"

"Yes, sir."

"Frank. Call me Frank. Tell me, I could use a cup of coffee. How about you?"

"Thank you, but I don't have any money."

"My treat. Please. It looks like you've been down on your luck and could use a helping hand."

Jack's head bowed and his eyes filled with tears. He couldn't speak. He hadn't known kindness in such a long time. "Tha . . . that would be fantastic. I would appreciate it. Thank you."

Instead of entering the on-ramp, he turned right and drove beneath the interstate to a nearby McDonald's. There was a Walmart there, as well. He went through the drive-through and ordered himself a coffee and an Egg McMuffin. Jack nodded his agreement when asked for one as well. They didn't stop. Frank put his coffee in the coffee holder and returned to the inter-state. When he had reached cruising speed, he opened his breakfast.

"How's yours?" he asked.

"This is the best thing I've tasted in over half a year," Jack said.

"Mine's pretty good, too," Frank smiled. After thinking for a moment, he said, "Is everything OK with you?"

"Yeah. Just going through a rough patch. You know how it is," Jack said. He didn't want to share anything. He just wanted to get to safety.

"OK. I'm not asking anything you don't want to tell me. I'm happy to listen if you want to talk."

"What do you do?" Jack asked. He could see this guy wanted to talk. He had finished his breakfast and was now sipping his coffee. He never remembered it tasting so good.

"I'm a pastor working with the hospital from time to time. I live outside of LA. That's where I'm going."

Jack didn't say anything.

"I don't believe anything happens by accident," Frank went on. "There's a reason you're in this car with me. God has a purpose for you, Jack."

He kept driving, drinking his coffee. Jack was quiet, unsure of what to say to that. *If he only knew*, he thought.

"Do you mind me asking you a personal question?" Frank asked.

"No."

"Have you accepted Christ as your personal saviour?"

Jack almost choked on the coffee. He knew about God as much as the next guy but he wasn't religious.

"Uh, no, sir."

"Would you like to?"

"Uh, Frank. I'm really glad you picked me up and I can't thank you enough for the food and coffee, but I'm not in the right frame of mind for this."

"I understand. It's my job," he smiled and shrugged. "I have to ask because I believe what I said. God has a plan for you."

"From your lips to God's ears," Jack said. Then: "Sorry, I didn't mean to be disrespectful."

"Not at all. I've said my peace and now I'll listen to you. Where are you off to?"

"Canada," Jack said. "Just above North Dakota."

Frank paused. "Then shouldn't you have been going the other way?"

"I just wanted out of where I was. This is fine. Besides, you've been really nice to me."

"You'll need to make your way back through Las Vegas and then up the interstates. It's a long way."

"I've got time."

"Why there?"

"I have some things I need to retrieve."

"Family?"

"Dead."

"Sorry," Frank said. "Brothers? Sisters?"

"Only child."

"Look Jack, you can stay by me if you need some time to get on your feet. My wife is wonderful and we have a large home. Our kids have grown. It wouldn't be any trouble."

Jack was touched. "Thanks, but you've been kind enough and I don't want to put you out any more."

"Not at all. I enjoy talking to you. It makes the drive go faster."

"I really appreciate it, but I need to keep moving. If you're going into LA, could you drop me off by a good spot to catch the traffic to Las Vegas?"

Frank wanted to say something. He had met a lot of young men who had hit rough patches only to see their lives spiral out of control. Jack looked like a decent guy and didn't deserve the meanness of living rough. "I'll do whatever you want, Jack, but I think it's a mistake. You have no idea of the evils out there. Unfortunately, I see many things that sometimes test my faith in humanity and even my faith in God. I wouldn't want to see you fall victim to this."

"Thanks. You really are the salt of the Earth. If it helps your conscience, you make me feel that there is hope for humanity. You remind me of a good friend I am looking forward to visiting in Canada. She works with the rejects of society, those who are discarded as sub-human. She works hard to educate them and keep them out of gangs. She welcomes them with open arms when the world turns its back on them because of the colour of their skin or lack of education. She takes in sixteen-year-olds who have witnessed their parents being butchered in front of them and who have never spent a day in school. The school system in Canada would say they were stupid; she would say they were unloved. She welcomes people like that into her school and, within two years, these damaged souls are reading at almost their age level. Like you, she sees that all things are possible in this world. Her cup is forever half full. Mine, these last ten years, has been anything but."

"Sounds like an amazing woman," Frank said.

"She is. I will never meet Mother Teresa, but if ever there was a saint walking this earth, it is Isabella of Winnipeg."

Frank was silent. He wanted to say more but something in him told him to be quiet. They drove on in silence until they reached the point where Jack had asked to be let out.

"Here's a good spot to catch a lift toward Vegas. Still time to change your mind though."

"Thanks, Frank. You've been the first nice person I've met in over six months. I'll remember this day as a good day."

Jack opened the door to leave, and Frank put his hand in his pocket and came out with some cash. "Here, take some money. It's not much, but at least you'll be able to get some food along the way and get washed up. Maybe get a clean set of clothes."

"I don't want to take your money, but I will simply because I need it. Do you have a business card or something with your church's details on it?"

"Of course. Call me at any time day or night." Frank wrote his cell number on the pamphlet.

"It was good to meet you, Frank." Jack meant it.

"Good to meet you, too, Jack. Take care of yourself and God bless you in your travels."

Frank drove off and Jack was alone again on the side of the road. *But free*, he thought.

He put his backpack on and started to walk toward the best position to catch the Vegas traffic. He bent down to tie his laces and walked across the road.

He heard the screeching of the brakes at the same time as he saw the lights. Before he could do anything, the grill was upon him and he hit the windshield. He jumped upward and that saved his legs from being pulverised, but he felt his body impact the glass windshield. He felt the car moving forward and him rolling over the top and onto the highway's shoulder. He was still alive. He could feel his feet and fingers.

Before he blacked out, he saw what looked like two angels running toward him. They weren't wearing much, but that could have been his imagination.

Chapter Six

THREE'S COMPANY

"Is he dead? Did I kill him?"

"No, Mom. I think he's still alive."

"We should leave him here. We have our own problems." Tammy started walking back to the car but stopped herself. She was no murderer.

"Help me pick him up," she said. "Let's get him in the backseat. We'll deal with him when he wakes up."

"He's too big to lift," Chrystal said.

"Then let's drag him. He's all skin and bones anyway."

"And he could use a bath," Chrystal said. "Do you think he's a hobo?"

Tammy looked at Jack. He had a few days' stubble and the teeth she could see from pulling back his lips looked healthy. "No. He's been beaten up a bit and we hit him pretty hard, but he's no bum. Let's put him inside and get out of here."

It took a lot more effort than they thought. Eventually, Tammy backed up the car immediately next to Jack and they pushed and dragged him into the backseat.

"If I knew we'd be doing all this work, I would have worn sensible shoes. This is going to ruin my heels."

Tammy paused and then laughed for the first time in forever. It felt good.

Chrystal joined in and they smiled at their new freedom. "So, where to?"

"Let's get as far from those monsters as possible. It's too easy to get lost out here in the dark, so we'll have to stick to the main roads. That means Vegas and then Denver, and on from there. We'll figure it out as we go."

∞

When Jack regained consciousness, he was lying on his side speeding along with two women in the front seat. It took a while to regain his bearings. The collision felt like nothing he had experienced to date, but he felt extraordinarily fortunate. By jumping, he'd managed to miss the metal of the grill and car hood completely, his entire mass being absorbed by the windshield. He allowed himself to move his torso a bit. He was sore but could move. He wiggled his fingers and rolled his shoulders. He bent his arms and began to feel for blood or scrapes with his hands. He could move his legs and ankles and swung his legs behind the front seats, using his arms to push himself up into a sitting position. He hoped he didn't have any internal bleeding.

"Hi," he said.

The car jerked violently and then regained its course. He could see they were driving the speed limit despite the shattered windshield. The driver was peering between the fragmented parts and the frame to see enough of the road.

"Welcome back. We thought we'd killed you," the driver said.

"How're you feeling?" the other one added.

"I feel like I've been hit by a car," Jack said. He managed a small laugh but it hurt. *Maybe my ribs are broken.*

That lightened the mood and the women laughed. "What were you doing on the highway, anyway?" the driver asked.

"Trying to get a lift. Looks like I succeeded."

"Tough way to go. I'm Tammy and this is my daughter, Chrystal. We're heading east."

"You'll need to get your windshield changed," he said.

"Yeah, that might be a problem." She was concentrating on the highway. "At least we're on a divided highway. No oncoming headlights."

None of them saw the flashing red and blue lights come up from behind them until it was too late. Jack put his head down and Tammy's composure evaporated. She took her foot off the gas, indicated right, and slowed down onto the shoulder.

"I can't be found," Jack said. He was fumbling with the backseat and found the button he was looking for. He folded the seat down and crawled into the space that led to the trunk.

Tammy looked behind her just as she saw the seat being pulled back into place. She looked at her daughter and didn't need to say the words. They would find out his story later.

"Can I help you, officer?" The words were almost comical with the smashed windshield, skimpy dresses, and stolen car. She wondered whether the police had discovered Scott's body and the two girls. Were they searching for them?

"Please turn off the engine." The officer looked in at them. "Licence and registration ma'am." His face flashed red and blue from the car parked behind them.

Tammy became flustered. "I don't have either, officer."

The trooper looked at Tammy and her daughter. He shone his flashlight into the car, sweeping the insides. "I'll need you to exit the vehicle, ma'am."

She undid her seatbelt and opened the door. Her dress felt obscene in the night air and she could feel his judgement of her as her heels met the gravel.

"Have you been drinking?"

"No, sir."

"Then why were you swerving earlier?"

"I was startled. We had an accident earlier." She pointed to the windshield. "My nerves are shot."

"Why didn't you call for help?"

"We don't have a phone."

The trooper paused. No one goes out without a phone, especially two women in party dresses.

"What happened to the windshield?"

"We hit something. Probably an animal. We stopped but couldn't find it. We didn't feel safe in the middle of nowhere waiting for someone to attack us so we decided to drive on to Vegas."

"Where you from?"

"LA."

"Where you going?"

"Denver."

The trooper looked at her with pursed lips. "Do you have any firearms or explosives in the car?"

Tammy's eyes widened. "No, sir."

"Have you recently been on a plane or near an airport?"

"No, sir."

"You know you're required to have your licence and registration with you at all times?"

"Yes, sir. We just forgot it, that's all."

"Ma'am," he addressed Chrystal. "Are you OK to stay here? I need to ask your friend some questions in the car."

Chrystal nodded, petrified. She remembered the gun and cash in the glove compartment. "She's my mother." She regretted saying it the moment it got out.

The trooper paused again. "Ma'am," he said to Tammy. "Come with me for a moment. I need to check on your car and ask you some questions."

Tammy felt the ground moving toward her. The weight of everything that had happened crashed down upon her shoulders in one great wallop that buckled her knees and caused her to vomit. The sudden movement caused the trooper to back up, unbutton his pistol, and rest his hand on its grip.

"Is everything OK, ma'am?" He sounded concerned and wary in equal measure.

"No." She started to cry. "Everything is not all right."

"Stay in the car, ma'am," he said immediately as he saw Chrystal opening her door. He reached for his radio and asked for backup. He asked Tammy for her name and if she was able to walk.

"Yes. I'm sorry. My name's Tammy."

"Tammy, what's going on?"

She looked at him for a long time before she was able to talk. The longer she stared, the hollower her eyes became. She felt her freedom slipping away. It was brief and glorious, but it was over. Thoughts of suicide and throwing herself in front of the next oncoming vehicle entered her head. *I can't go back*, she thought.

"This isn't our car. It's our pimp's."

"Excuse me?"

"We're whores. Prostitutes. Call girls. Sluts. Shit under your boot." Tammy was crying as the words came out. *You've probably seen us doing porn. Hard core. Forced blow jobs until we vomit, S&M beatings, everything*, she said to him in her mind. She regretted saying what she said to him out loud but needed to say it to herself.

The trooper was looking at her cautiously but with sympathy. "How did you come by this car?"

"Our pimp had a heart attack. He's dead. We decided to take it and run."

The trooper was silent. He wasn't used to roadside confessions. He was wondering whether to arrest them or help them.

"We're not bad people, officer. My daughter and I were given a modelling opportunity. It went sideways and one thing led to another. Before you knew it, we had lost our way. We couldn't leave. They took our ID, money, everything."

A backup cruiser arrived and parked in front of them.

"Are you going to arrest us?" Tammy was terrified of going back to Lyle. It made her feel sick.

"Not yet," the trooper started. His voice was compassionate. "I would like to check on your story and run the plates of your car. I think you've been through enough."

Tammy felt a twinge of hope.

"My colleague will take you and your daughter to our station in Vegas. You'll need to make a statement. If everything checks out, you'll be free to go." The trooper had children of his own and he saw his daughter when he looked at Chrystal. *There, but for the grace of God, go I*, he thought. "We'll have a doctor look you over as well. And Tammy?" He paused to clear his throat. "It will get better."

Tammy saw his mouth moving and heard the words. It was all so numbing. She half expected to "pay" for her release in services. *Maybe there are good people in the world*, she thought.

The other trooper was helping Chrystal into his car. Tammy joined them. "We'll get a tow truck for your car," the trooper said as he started driving.

The original trooper called for the tow truck, only to find it would be almost two hours before it would arrive. He pulled out a triangular warning sign from the trunk of his car and put it on the shoulder fifty yards behind the parked car. He affixed a flashing yellow light to it to give drivers as much warning as possible. He took a roll of crime scene tape from his car and wrapped the parked car. It was evidence, and he didn't want it tampered with.

His radio squawked and he returned to his patrol car. A seven-car pile-up needed his urgent attention. He would return to the abandoned car later. He hit the sirens and sped off into the darkness.

Jack listened while trying to not make a sound. The pain of his ribs and bruised muscles kept him on the edge of tears. The fear of arrest and the police without his manufactured ID kept him quiet. When he was certain they had all left, he flicked the lever on the backseat and entered the car. All he could see was the faint flashing of the yellow light on the warning sign. He pulled through his knapsack and stepped outside.

He felt for the front door and found it open. He looked for food or something he could take with him. He knew he didn't have much time before someone returned. He opened the glove compartment and froze.

A gun. Money.

He left the gun and took the cash. Things were looking up.

∞

Jack started walking in the direction of Vegas. He didn't know how far it was. He walked on the shoulder of the highway, knowing that if a trooper came by he would stop. He didn't know what he would say but figured he'd play things by ear. He was in the Mojave Desert and he had no intention of straying from the highway.

As his options tumbled within his head, he saw the glow of a settlement in the distance. It took another thirty minutes before he realised it was a small town he had never heard of called Baker. On the outskirts of town, he found a motel willing to let him stay without ID.

"Kinda late, isn't it?"

"Ah, yeah. I'm just exhausted. I can't go any further tonight," Jack said.

"Better safe than sorry, I always say. Besides, our rates are a lot better than Vegas!" He was smiling. He wasn't the sharpest knife in the drawer but the night shift didn't require him to do much other than sit and watch things. Jack was the first client he had checked in in over a year.

"I just need a room for tonight. How much?"

"Sixty dollars."

"Perfect." Jack handed over a $100 bill.

"There's free parking around the corner," the attendant said.

"Thanks. Already parked," Jack lied.

"Check out is at eleven unless you want to stay longer."

"Thanks. I'll see how I feel tomorrow. By the way, is there a clothing shop in town?"

"Yep, just a block away you'll find everything the town has to offer."

Jack took his key and went to his room. It was retro in a way that was genuine—it simply hadn't had a change of décor since 1980. But it was clean and he was bone tired. He didn't have time to digest the events of the last few hours. He put his head on the pillow and didn't move until the sun was in his eyes the next morning.

He didn't want to move or wake. His body was sorer than ever. He rolled himself out of bed and made his way to reception. He paid for two more nights, just in case, and then walked the couple of blocks to a pharmacy to get some pain killers. He also picked up a toothbrush, toothpaste, and dental floss. He felt embarrassed to talk until he cleaned his mouth. His next stop was to find some clean underwear and socks, T-shirts, and jeans. He found a nice flannel jacket and some good walking boots to match. He felt like a new man.

He just needed to find a vehicle. There were no car shops, just a mechanic. He tried that and found an old, fixed-up pickup that they were prepared to sell for cash, no ID required. He wasn't sure if it would withstand much scrutiny but at least he had a bill of sale from a reputable establishment. Hopefully it wouldn't get him arrested if stopped.

His body was aching despite the medicine. He grabbed a trucker's breakfast at the local greasy spoon and headed back to his room for some sleep. He locked the door, closed the drapes, and hit the pillow. He couldn't remember feeling that good for a long time.

∞

Three nights extended to seven before he was ready to move on. His body needed rest. It was worn down, stressed, and desperately in need of nourishment without the anxiety of being beaten or sodomised. Even those memories became distant—until he closed his eyes at night. He was determined to overcome his trauma, however long it took. First, he needed to get his identity back, and that was in Canada.

He felt guilty about taking the money from those women. They had been through exactly what he had. They knew his pain. And they probably didn't have a CIA stash of black money waiting for them.

Only the country music station in the truck kept him company as he made his way to Vegas. He started to think that, given enough time, those women would be back in prostitution. He had taken their money and he doubted they had any cash stashed in those skimpy dresses. He felt responsible. He had screwed up their getaway by being in the wrong place at the wrong time.

"But they almost killed you," he said aloud.

Yeah, but they could have left you on the side of the road. They didn't, despite what they had gone through, his thoughts responded. *I can't live with another death on my conscience. I'm going to find them.*

"Fat chance of that. Two hookers in Vegas?"

Two victims in Vegas, he corrected himself. *Who went to the police station.*

"Whoa, wait a minute. They'll think you're connected. What happened to keeping a low profile away from the authorities?"

I'll just wait around the station. They'll show up. They'll need to be coming and going to give statements and whatnot. You just slept a week before you were ready to get going.

"Yeah, but I got hit by a car." But his better nature was winning out. He resolved to find the station and stake it out until they arrived. If they didn't show after a couple of days, he could go to Canada with a clear conscience.

∞

His truck didn't stand out in the countryside. It was an old Ford F150 pickup with a cab large enough for a backseat. In 2006 it would have been fantastic. It had a massive 5.4 litre V8 engine and consumed fuel like a desert consumed water. Perhaps that's why he was able to buy it cheap. Whatever the case, it ran, but it looked all of its twenty years, and on Vegas's shiny streets, it looked conspicuous. He parked around the corner from the main entrance to the police station so he could see anyone coming and going. If the two women arrived, he would see them.

On the third day of his stakeout, he resolved to leave at sundown. The backseat was littered with McDonald's food wrappings and empty coffee cups. He allowed himself to smoke on occasion but didn't want to make a habit of it. The tank was full and he had bought a lot of canned drinks and water in anticipation for the drive. Chocolate bars and coffee he'd find on the way.

"Sorry, ladies, but I've got to go," he said. Then, "I have to stop talking to myself."

As the engine roared to life, Jack saw what he was now hoping he wouldn't. Tammy and Chrystal were leaving the station. *How did they get in without me seeing them? Doesn't matter, I should go and talk to them.* He put the truck into gear and drove toward them.

"Hi," he said, driving alongside them. They ignored him, thinking him a creep. Realising this, Jack tried a different approach. "Remember me? I'm the guy you drove over and left in the trunk of your stolen car." He delivered it with a little grin. It worked. They stopped and turned toward the open window.

"Look, mister. We're really sorry about that but we've got problems of our own," said Tammy.

"I think you may have forgotten something in your glove compartment," he said.

"I know. The cops found it and we've had a lot of questions to answer. The gun was linked to a killing in LA. We've been held until now while they checked it out. Apparently, our prints aren't on it and they're giving us the benefit of doubt."

"That's not what I'm talking about," he said.

"What else could there be?" As she said it, Chrystal pushed herself next to the window.

"I thought those bastards just took it," she said. "Do you have it?"

"I do. I didn't want to leave town without giving it to you. I couldn't help but overhear your explanation to the trooper and I didn't want you to be left with nothing. Especially since you need to start from scratch again."

Jack's words sunk in slowly. They had just been staying in the remand centre, a limbo of criminals and those charged with crimes, awaiting their fate over the gun in the glove compartment. They saw the hungry stares of the prison guards as well as those awaiting direction within the penal system. They were given some sweatpants and shirts from a sympathetic officer but nothing else was pleasant about their stay.

"Do you have it with you?" Tammy's voice was desperate.

"Sure. Here." Jack handed over the cash, made neat within an envelope.

Tammy opened it and counted it, her eyes widening slightly. "Thanks. . . ."

"Jack, the name's Jack."

"Thanks, Jack." The two women huddled over the money, looking even more vulnerable as they protected the one thing that would keep them from the street.

Jack put the truck in gear but then paused. "Before I go, I thought it only decent to ask if you wanted a lift somewhere. I'm heading north to Canada. You're welcome to catch a lift. It'll get you far from whatever's going on with you here."

"We're done with the police, I think. I've got their card and I can call in if need be." Tammy was talking to Jack but equally to herself and Chrystal. Her daughter nodded in anticipation of what Tammy was thinking. *This is an opportunity*, they both thought, *and we should grab it*. "If you're offering, we'd be very thankful and happy to accept." She opened the door and paused. "But don't expect anything. We're just hitching a lift."

Jack's hands raised off the wheel. "I'm just offering. Believe me, it's the last thing on my mind."

Tammy looked at him oddly. *Maybe he's gay*, she thought.

Almost reading her mind, Jack spluttered, "Not like that. I mean, I'm just trying to do the right thing."

Chrystal got in the back, used her foot to clear the junk food, and closed the door.

"Sorry about the mess. I've been enjoying my freedom."

"I think we've got some time to hear each other's stories," Tammy said. She closed the door and Jack drove on. "But let's get out of here first."

"Buckle up. We're only stopping for fuel and toilets. I'd like to drive through the night and get some distance between us and the past."

No one disagreed.

Chapter Seven

ROAD TRIP

Jack drove for hours and his two passengers sat in relative silence. It had been near the end of the day when they left Vegas. The power of the engine was reassuring as it pulled them further away from their respective nightmares. As the black ribbon of highway stretched before them on that spring evening, they each allowed their minds to be convinced that they were OK. Jack had bought some pillows and blankets and Tammy and Chrystal propped them against the windows and fell asleep.

Alone with his thoughts, an endless highway before him, and at least twenty-four hours straight driving before they hit the border, Jack began to plan how to deal with his predicament. He could chance going to the passport office now and resume his old identity. That would be his fall-back position, but it would open him to being re-contacted by the CIA and put him firmly back on their radar. He couldn't cross the Canadian border officially without a passport, so that meant walking across some godforsaken field and hoping he didn't trigger the motion sensors. He would buy his hiking gear in Fargo, North Dakota. The crossing at Pembina was a major trucking route. Further west was Neche, which looked good but was still too close to Pembina. He would find a spot west of Walhalla where there was some tree cover and walk across. He might get caught, he might not. Whatever happened, it wouldn't be worse than what he had been through.

He would give the truck to Tammy and her daughter to do with as they wanted. He was done with it. He would suggest that they get some identification as soon as possible. It would be easiest if they claimed to have had everything stolen, and just start over. They had enough money to stay in a hotel during the process. *They'll be fine*, he thought.

Jack adjusted himself on his seat. It was a big truck with a big windshield and lots of room inside. He had been driving for four hours and needed a break. He pulled off the interstate into a truck stop. The lights were bright and led him directly to the pumps. He filled the tank, got a free coffee with the fuel, and decided to get some chocolate bars to keep him awake. As he got into the car, his eyes had a slight stickiness as he blinked. He looked over and saw his two passengers fast asleep. *I think I'll close my eyes for ten minutes before I continue*, he said to himself. When he opened them next, the sun was up and his mouth felt like it was full of glue. Some drool had escaped his lips and his coffee was cold.

"Anyone need to use the facilities before we continue?" He saw the stirrings of Tammy and Chrystal and knew his own needs.

"Ah, yeah," Tammy inhaled deeply and exhaled. She rolled her head and shoulders as she worked out the kinks of her sleep.

"Sleep well?" Jack asked.

"Better than I thought possible," she said. She was blinking funnily as if her eyelids were stuck when they closed. "Honey, let's grab a bite before we go." She gave her daughter a little shake.

"Uh, OK." The familiar exhale and breathing of one just waking came from the back. Chrystal had cleared the entire backseat and was lying down as though it was a bed. She slowly sat up. "Where are we?"

"Just about halfway between Vegas and Denver," Jack said.

"That's it?"

"I closed my eyes and fell asleep. Sorry."

"Better alive than dead," Tammy said. "Let's take advantage of it and get a good breakfast. I think it'll be easier to drive in the daytime anyway."

They got out, stretched and groaned, and stumbled the first steps as their muscles and bodies woke up. By the time they got to the flat-roofed restaurant, they were walking normally and feeling hungry. No one took a second glance at them and they ate without in-cident.

"Feels odd, doesn't it?" Jack said.

"What does?" Tammy replied.

"This. The normality of it all. I don't know what you've been through—I can only guess—but I've been through a really rough six months and this is the weird-est normal thing I've done yet." He took another sip of his coffee and then a bite of his hash browns.

Tammy nodded but didn't say anything. She was monitoring every person who walked in and ate with tension. It wasn't normal for her yet.

They finished, used the toilets, and returned to the truck. "Next stop, Denver."

"That's what you said last time," Tammy smiled.

"Just keeping everyone on their toes," Jack said. He liked that they were starting to relax. He had a coffee to go, despite the four he had had for breakfast, and re-joined the interstate.

∞

Denver came and went, as did fuel and toilet stops. They only grabbed sandwiches and snacks along the way. When they reached Omaha, it was dark again and Jack's eyes were like rocks. Tammy had taken the wheel for a four-hour shift during the day but he couldn't sleep. He just stared into the distance, watch-ing the landscape change and stay the same. By the time it was different, he had forgotten what the other looked like. The process repeated itself in his zombie-like state.

"Drive through the night or rest at the next truck stop?" Jack would need Chrystal to drive if they were to go through the night. He needed at least a couple hours' sleep and the backseat was calling his name.

"Let's drive through," Chrystal said. She was fresh and ready to take the wheel. After Omaha, it was straight ahead until they hit Canada. "I hope you don't mind the radio while I'm driving."

"I'll take a shift, too," said Tammy. "You can sleep in the back, Jack, and take over after we're tired."

"Sounds like music to my ears," he said. "Let's put some fuel in the tank and my belly and then I'll see you when you need me to take my shift."

They hadn't talked much up until then. Just the normal conversation about the traffic as they passed through cities, the poor quality of most of the coffee they were drinking, and the concrete-like food they were eating at the truck stops. No mention was made of any of their experiences. Nothing was asked or offered.

The big sky, country music, and general sense of being in redneck country made Tammy and Chrystal feel far from the horrors of LA. In a strange way, it reminded Jack of his months with Vlad. Same open countryside, grain crops, and big men in trucks. It caused him to twitch and at times he found himself crying for no reason, especially during some of the country music ballads on the radio. He was glad the other two were distracted by their own thoughts.

Something caused Tammy to start talking after she got behind the wheel. Perhaps it was being in control, or maybe it was Jack's non-threatening nature. Perhaps it was the fact they had gone almost thirty-six hours and not one question was asked of her about her past, the police, or the accident that nearly killed Jack.

"I can't believe you survived that collision," she said.

Jack was curled up in the back and wasn't ready to talk. He was enjoying his full stomach, warm blanket, and soft pillow. "Huh?"

"What are the odds that the three of us would be in a truck driving to Canada?"

Jack sat up. "Infinity to one."

"Crazy. If you had any idea of what we've been through, it would seem like the worst luck to have hit you. But it turned out to be the best thing that happened to us."

"Maybe, but I'm still sore as hell. I look like an aubergine under these clothes."

That got a chuckle.

"Seriously, Jack, we both want you to know that you showing up with the money was something no one we know would have ever done."

"I heard what you said to the trooper. I couldn't live with myself if I didn't at least try."

"Do you want to know what happened to us? We're really as ordinary as people come. I was a stay-at-home housewife and mother, recently divorced. My daughter was a manager of a clothing store. Neither of us had ever even jay-walked or had a speeding ticket before this. Then we got sucked into a world of glamour and promises."

"You don't need to tell me," Jack said.

"But I want to. I want you to know that we're not crazy."

"I never thought that."

The truck drifted a bit and the tires touched the shoulder, causing Tammy to bring it back in lane with a jerk. "That's how we were stopped last time," she laughed ruefully.

"Excuse me?"

"You got up in the other car and startled me. The car swerved and a cop just happened to see it. That's why we were pulled over. Nothing to do with a dead pimp, broken windshield, or possible fugitive in the backseat."

Jack's ears pricked at the word 'fugitive'. "Is that what you think I am?"

Tammy shrugged. Chrystal had turned in her seat so that she could see both her mother and Jack. She also shrugged. "You mentioned something about not being picked up by the police."

Jack laughed. It seemed so long ago. "That's a long story. I'm not that kind of fugitive. I was heading back from Europe and wanted to go by train overland because of all the troubles with the airlines. I had hoped to cross the Bering Strait by foot."

"That's impossible. It looks close on a map but there have only been two confirmed cases of people walking across. One was in the late 1990s, a father and son, from Russia to Alaska. I don't know how they did it but they were stranded on some ice floes, actually had to swim in the ice water and virtually died before being discovered in Alaska. I saw a documentary on it." Chrystal said this in response to the strange looks she was getting from both Tammy and Jack. "Besides, the Russian military would never let you near it to begin with."

"Yeah, I found that out the hard way. I trusted someone, only to be sold to traffickers. I endured things I would be ashamed to confess to my god, if I were so inclined."

"Me, too," Tammy said quietly. "I sensed that about you."

Chrystal was about to say something funny but decided against it. They rode in silence for a while.

"Wouldn't you want to do something about it?" Jack finally asked.

"You can't. It's all over the world, all over the US. No one cares or else it wouldn't be happening," Chrystal said. Tammy nodded, keeping her eyes on the road.

"But what if you could?"

"I'd kill every motherfucking one of those evil bastards with my own hands," Tammy said. It was feral. It made Chrystal shudder because she knew she meant it.

"I think there'd be a line a mile long of like-minded people," Jack said. "A while ago I began thinking about what it would take to make an impact. I would need help from people I could trust."

"You're sounding all serious," Tammy said. She liked Jack. So did her daughter.

"I am serious—but I'm also seriously tired right now. I don't have a plan yet, but I'm working on one. Think about what you'd do and let's talk in the morning. I can barely carry a thought I'm so tired." Jack allowed his body to collapse on the backseat and, within a few minutes, he was in a deep sleep.

When he opened his eyes, it was daylight and Chrystal was driving. He woke at the sound of the engine slowing and the truck turning into an empty mall parking lot. He sat up in time to see the familiar sight of a McDonald's.

"Welcome to Fargo, folks. I couldn't stand another trucker's breakfast," she said. "There's a gas station just over there and we can stretch our legs and use the toilets here as well as any place."

"Thanks for letting me sleep. I guess I needed it," Jack said.

"I'm not just a pretty face," she said. "I actually enjoyed the drive. I've never driven a pickup truck before. I can see why people love them so much. Makes ya wanna grab your fella and hit the backroads."

Jack's radar was pinging. Was this flirting? He really never understood it and was convinced he was incapable of it. He put it out of his mind—it was the worst possible thing he could broach at this stage.

Their journey felt like one meal after another, with a lot of nothing in between. It felt good to do lots of nothing. It was over their morning bacon and sausage muffins that Jack progressed his plan.

"We're going to need to split up shortly. You need to get your passports and, ideally, driving licences, or you'll find yourself in a whole lot of unnecessary trouble." Jack couldn't avoid it. They wouldn't be of any assistance if they couldn't cross a border or even survive a speeding ticket.

"That makes sense," Tammy said. "But that could take weeks. Are you leaving us?"

"I need to get to Canada and there's only one way that I know how."

"You're going in illegally?" Chrystal was almost laughing. "Who does that?"

"I know. But I have some stuff stored there and only I can get it. It'll help me with what I'm planning to do."

"So you have a plan?"

"Not 100%, but one is forming. Whatever happens, I need to be able to interact with police forces and border controls without being concerned."

"I'm in," Chrystal said. Tammy looked at her, surprised at her energy. Then she also nodded.

"Great, but I'm not sure what we can do just yet. Besides, you need to get your passports."

"And driving licences," Chrystal said. The food was gone and she was drinking her coffee while looking at Jack. He tried not to notice.

"OK, there's a sporting store over there and I need to get a few things. There should be a phone store somewhere in the mall. We'll get two pay-as-you-go cell phones. I won't be calling you but you'll be able to contact me on this for at least a month or so. If you change your minds, I'll understand."

"We won't," Chrystal said quickly.

"I'm heading to Winnipeg. When you get your stuff sorted out, drive up there and call me. We'll figure out what to do then."

Jack bought some quality hiking boots, a waterproof jacket and poncho, a hat, a knife, and a better knapsack. He packed some dried meat and fruit. He wasn't planning on walking for long. The whole hike should be fewer than thirty miles. After that, he would hitchhike to Winnipeg.

Tammy and Chrystal agreed to drive him just past the small town of Walhalla and then return to Grand Forks while their passports and driver's licences were processed.

"All you need to do is say you've lost your passports, you don't know where or how, and just realised it today. You'll need to do the same for your driver's licences. All the information is already in the government computers. You're doing nothing wrong."

"Do we need to tell them anything?" Chrystal's bravado was fading as the reality of dealing with federal and state governments and the possibility of being arrested for what happened started weighing on her.

"We don't need to tell them anything, sweetheart," Tammy said, putting an arm around her. She wanted to protect her little girl and felt her anger in her throat at the animals who put them through their hell.

"You're just tourists heading up to Canada," Jack said. "Keep it simple. You don't have any major plans, just to drive and enjoy the spring and summer in the north. Maybe you'll go to the lakes in Ontario, or who knows. They won't care because you already had passports and driver's licences and just need new copies."

"And we can get them expedited," Tammy added.

"Yeah, it'll still take about a month," Chrystal said. "What'll we do for a month in Grand Forks?"

Jack laughed. "It's not that bad. Could be a lot worse. If you prefer, you can drive to Minneapolis and wait there. They may even surprise you and get your documents to you in a week or so."

"We'll be fine," Tammy said. "When do you want to go, Jack?"

"I'm finding myself reluctant to leave you but I need to press on. The sooner the better."

Nothing was said as they piled themselves into the truck. Jack drove. It was almost three hours before they reached Walhalla. It was a little town known only for the modest skiing facilities nearby. Jack hoped that ridge would help shelter him where he planned to cross the border.

He turned west at Walhalla and made his way down the dirt roads, but not as far as the Pembina River or Frost Fire ski resort. He then turned north and followed the roads until he could go no further. They were less than five miles from the border.

"I would have thought they'd have drones and towers," said Tammy, looking skyward.

"Or at least a chain-link fence," said Chrystal. She had her hand over her eyes as she looked into the unending distance.

"Well, this is as far as you are going. I'll wait for an hour before I make my way across so you're a good distance away in case anything goes wrong." Jack found himself tearing up. He wasn't an emotional person but the connection he had with these women cut to his core.

"We'll be OK," Tammy said. She gave him a peck on each cheek and a strong hug.

"You take care of yourself, Jack," Chrystal said. "I plan to see you in Winnipeg." She kissed him on the lips, soft at first and then harder than either he or she expected. "I'm sorry," she said, slightly embarrassed at her actions. She pulled away and gave him a little nod, then turned away.

Jack looked at both of them, speechless. He managed a little wave and a smile. All he could think about was that kiss. Other than his crying, which came from nowhere, he forgot that he even had emotions until that moment. So much had been torn from him, he expected to feel numb forever. *I guess forever just ended,* he said to himself.

"I'll be fine," he managed to say. "Take care of yourselves and don't take any chances. If you make it to Winnipeg, I'll be there. Check into a hotel near the train station and call me. I'll be with you within hours. If I don't see you again, it has been an honour to have met you both. You give me hope."

Tammy was in the driver's seat trying to turn the truck around on the narrow road. Soon the only thing Jack could see was the dust trail, fading brake lights, and a distant silhouette. Then he was alone with just the border and the might of the entire United States of America if he got this wrong.

Chapter Eight

WALK IN THE PARK

After the initial adrenaline of unpacking the hiking gear and seeing Chrystal and Tammy look at him with both concern and something approaching affection, Jack settled into the task ahead. The pickup truck had disappeared over ten minutes before and in front of him was a short hike into Canada. The road was gravel and he could see the long grass, scrub, and the soft wood trees that filled in the areas between the farms. He checked his boots and ensured they were double knotted. He had a buck knife on his belt and a compass in his pocket. He had a mid-sized backpack, which he secured with straps around his waist. He pulled down on the straps that went over his shoulders and pulled the whole pack snugly against his back. He didn't want any movement when he walked.

His body was sore and tender. The more he rested, the softer he became. He felt the grass against his leg and saw his jeans become wet from the ground. "Bloody swamp shit," he said to himself.

It wasn't a swamp, just the prairies recovering after a winter. It was only five minutes into his hike before he felt his boot slip into a boggy section. The water and earth surrounded his boot and calf and sucked it in. There was no resisting. If his boot wasn't so securely on his foot, he would have lost it. It took a gentle, constant pressure, but he got his foot above ground and made sure his next steps didn't see a repeat performance.

"Five miles," he muttered. "Piece of cake."

The trees were barren, the grass yellow, and the sky maddeningly blue. Not a cloud to be seen. In other circumstances, it would be considered a good day to go for a walk or hang out with friends with a beer and BBQ. Today, Jack was walking to freedom.

In the end, he had decided to go as far west as the Frost Fire ski resort. It was only an extra couple of miles on a straight road. It was little more than a beginner's slope but it was the best resort for hundreds of miles. For Jack, it had the added advantage of being close to the Pembina River, which meandered its way to Canada. His plan was to stay covered by the trees by the river and enjoy the view. It would likely be closer to fifteen miles because of the meandering, and it didn't even go due north, but it was infinitely better than walking on the highways or through a farmer's field.

Worst-case scenario, I'll be in Canada by the end of today, Jack thought. *Another day to hitch to Winnipeg and then I can . . .* He was mid-thought when a blinding pain took hold of him. He heard his voice inhale a scream three octaves higher than normal. He felt a piece of metal clamp hard through the flesh on his calf. It hurt but he knew it would be worse later. He realised that the metal had probably stopped at the bone. The nerves of his skin and flesh were severed.

His body dropped as though he was shot, landing hard but cushioned by the backpack. He was pinned to the earth by a trap set for an otter or possibly larger animal. The pain was unbelievable; different than the mental and sexual torture in Russia, more intense than the gruelling walk of Mexico or being hit by a car in California. It was primal. Primitive. He was little more than an animal trapped and waiting to die. It took a full minute before he could catch his breath. There were tears on his cheeks from the shock. His body's adrenaline and survival instincts kicked in. There was no time for crying, only to stay alive. Still, the tears ran freely down his cheeks.

He removed himself from his backpack and tried to see what type of mess his leg was in. He cursed himself for being so stupid. When he looked down, he became fearful. The trap wasn't set for small animals. It was metal with jagged edges, like teeth, closed tightly against his leg. There was blood beginning to soak through his jeans and pool beneath his leg. He reached for his backpack, found some rope and tied it above the trap. He didn't care if it was the right thing to do. He needed a tourniquet before he bled out. He tied it tight and then tied a second knot to prevent any movement. Then he passed out.

When he awoke, it was dark. He was cold but not dangerously so. He couldn't feel his leg. It felt like wood. There were no bolts or screws or anything he could undo to release himself. He tried to open the jaws but they must have had a locking feature because he couldn't budge it. It just created more pain. It wasn't long before the agony overcame him and he passed out again.

This time, it was daylight and the birds were singing. He had become part of the landscape and he noticed that the small animals and birds had come in close to him. He saw the beavers in the river and a fox finishing off a meal not far away. The only animal he needed to fear were the bears the trap was set for.

"Where the hell did all this come from?" he said to himself. The gorge itself must have been cut by glacial melt. He looked around and began nodding his head in agreement with his suspicions that it must be part of some national park, not private land. "Then why is there a bear trap where hikers could come across and why the hell am I in it?" Jack found some water in his pack and drank deeply. He was wet and mildly cold but that was nothing against the pain. He fished out his dried meat and ate half of it. He didn't think he even needed that much when he started out. "This whole hike is a farce. I should be in Winnipeg by now," he growled.

He watched a pair of elk emerge from the treeline to nibble at the grass. The iron-grey stone of the river bed was covered with the spring water. Jack shook his head, which caused even more pain to shoot from his leg. He found himself whimpering. "I'll be dead by this time tomorrow. Even if the blood loss has been stemmed, I probably have tetanus. To top it all, I have no bloody cell coverage. Why even have a damn phone?"

He tried to bend his knee and bring the trap closer to him. He refused to die from something as stupid as this. His pack had become a prop for his head and he had already found his rain poncho to lie on. It didn't make him any dryer but it helped. His leg was stiffening up and the pain was blinding. He reached for the rusty metal trap amidst the starbursts of light behind his eyes as the pain pushed him closer to his limit. He felt the irregular surface of the metal against the tips of his fingers. It was cold and unyielding. The whole experience was dreamlike—except for the pain. That was all too real.

Jack felt the muscles in his chest and back tense as he put his hands on the trap. He put every fibre of his remaining strength into the action. Instead of freedom, all he heard was a click as his squirming caused the trap to tighten further. His body spread eagle, back arched, as fresh screams burst from his open mouth. The new pain caused his body to spasm as if jolted with electricity.

The elk ran away and there was a flutter of wings as birds took flight. While most of the animals ran away, there were some who crept closer. The mountain lions and lynxes weren't interested in the strange prey, nor was the bobcat that hunted silently before the latest outburst of primitive screaming. Jack didn't allow himself to pass out. Suddenly, he saw the outline of a creature coming toward him. The smell of blood must have lured it. All Jack could see was the mass of fur emerge from the woods, walking slowly with the confidence that it was no one's prey. Its head was down and the lumbering movement was both cautious and determined. It was alone. It didn't need help to finish Jack off. When the bear raised its head and looked directly at him, it was just over a hundred yards away on the other side of the river.

He watched the bear amble slowly, occasionally taking a look at Jack but equally sniffing the ground and surrounding areas for food. It came to the edge of the river and looked down for fish. The river continued to flow gently around the paw that was planted in the water. Then another step. And another. Soon the whole bear was in the water, belly deep. It kept walking as if the river was an annoyance and not ice-cold winter runoff. Briefly, it was forced to swim as the water became too deep. Jack caught himself swallowing hard when he realised that the bear was no longer swimming and was walking again. Despite the insane pain, the fear of imminent death was greater. He reached down and seized the trap.

"There must be a release lever," he muttered to himself. The salty sweat of pain was dripping into his eyes, burning them. His hands started to search the sides and bottom of the trap instead of trying to open it. Opening it seemed to tighten it. His body was bent over as he searched.

He looked up as the bear took its first step out of the river. He stopped fiddling with the trap, leaned back against his pack and stared at the bear. Its rear quarters hulked up and his head was splayed into the fur. The nose was massive and twitching as it got closer. The mouth seemed to be moving. Was it licking its lips? It was only twenty-five yards away. Jack was dead and he, like all prey in nature, knew it. He stopped fighting and waited for death to take him. Even the pain of the trap ceased to bother him. It was as though a natural anaesthetic protected him from the pain of the end. He closed his eyes as he waited.

The bear smelled the blood. Food. He continued forward, the stones of the ancient riverbed scratching against his claws. It ignored the familiar smell of rotten vegetation next to the river. The creature before it had a new smell and it was overpowering. The bear was next to him, and it sniffed the whole leg and body. The great snout and nose nuzzled the now-dry pool of blood. It licked at it. As Jack's body was on top of that blood, the bear used its snout to push him aside. He was tossed like a rag doll. The pain returned and he screamed.

The scream frightened the bear and its head jerked violently. Jack was no longer sitting still. He moved away from the bear but was still tethered to the trap. He crawled in an arc but could get no further from the bear.

The beast stood on its hind legs and let out a roar that proved to Jack that there were even scarier things than what he had gone through. Fear compounded and his bowels released. He felt the shit and urine fill his pants and begin the embarrassing journey down his leg. He was no longer prepared to die. His body was scared but fighting to live. Above him, the head of the bear rolled as the roar continued for what seemed like an eternity. He could see the spit and slime of bear snot and drool coming from the mouth. Then suddenly, the roar stopped and its body came crashing down next to him. Then everything went black.

Chapter Nine

PATRIOT

"And then what'd you do, Jet?" The teenager in jeans and a lumberjack jacket had turned toward the driver of the F350 pickup truck. His eyes were wide and he was smiling in admiration.

"What do think I did? I got the hell out of there as fast as I could!" Jet smiled as Arthur hooted and howled. He had told Arthur this same story a dozen times with the same effect. Jethro Brown had been staying with a militia outfit in Idaho for a number of years. He believed in America and the ideals of the constitution. He didn't believe that their rights should be regulated out of existence. So he didn't pay his taxes, renew his driver's licence, or do anything else demanded of him by the federal government.

The story he told Arthur was about when the IRS, FBI, and BATF raided the militia camp. It wasn't that the members owed that much in tax. In fact, they made barely more than minimum wage and many didn't work. But Jet believed the federal government was afraid of the precedent being set. He believed that if others followed suit, the entire edifice of the federal government would come tumbling down and patriots such as himself would be able to rebuild the country as it should be.

Some of the militiamen had opened fire on the authorities and both sides sustained casualties. When the point came for the officers to storm the complex, Jet and others used an underground tunnel to pop out behind them and disperse into the other states. Jet ended up in North Dakota.

What Jet didn't say was that he had already decided to leave. While he loved the ideals, he found the racism and anti-Semitism of many of the militia both infantile and historically incorrect. Law and justice were colour-blind as far as he was concerned. And the idea of a handful of Jews controlling the world was simply farcical. He wasn't so stupid as to voice his concerns and just wanted to be left alone.

It was by chance that he met Linda Harrington almost three years ago. She was a nurse in Bismark and had a young teenage son in need of a strong male role model. After a year of dating, they got married and moved to Jet's place just outside of Walhalla. She continued to work as a nurse in nearby Cavelier's hospital. It was small by anyone's standards but she was paid well and enjoyed being with Jet. He was a gentle and natural father, and Arthur loved being with him.

Today, they were checking on their traps. He didn't care if it wasn't totally legal. He heard about a mean bear in the vicinity and thought he'd sort it out for the community. Because that's what people should do. They help each other. He brought Art down to hunt and fish and teach him how to live off the land.

When he had reached the area, he saw what looked like a man trapped and a bear coming toward him. It took a few moments to remove the .308 Winchester slung over his shoulder and assume a prone position on the ground. He ignored the wet stones and rested the rifle on his left hand, which formed a base through his elbow that rested on the ground. He removed the dust caps from the rifle sights and took a couple of deep breaths. He chambered a round and focussed. He needed to kill with one shot. He wasn't going to shoot at the bear's head as it was moving around roaring. He had the angle to take a chest shot, hoping to hit the heart. If he missed, he would enrage the bear and the person would be mauled to death seconds later.

Art was motionless and lying prone next to him. Jet inhaled and then let the air out slowly. At the bottom of the breath, there was a short interval before he would inhale again. That was when he pulled the trigger. The shot was absorbed by his body and the bear went down hard. Jet was up and running before the bear hit the ground. He chambered another round and felt for his

.45 pistol. If he saw so much as a twitch, he would fire another shot into the bear's head.

There was a spray coming off his boots as he ran along the shoreline. It was faster than running in the brush and long grass. The man's body was stationary and the bear hadn't moved.

He gave the rifle to Art with the instructions to aim at the bear's head and fire if he moved. Jet went to the trap and depressed the lever that allowed him to open the jaws. The body of the man was limp and he smelled of fear and shit. He felt terrible for his trap to have done this but would think about that later. Now, he needed to get the man to his truck.

With Jack pulled clear, he approached the bear with his .45 drawn and ready to fire. He picked up a stick and poked the eye of the bear. Nothing. He lifted the eyelid and then push downward on the exposed eye. Nothing. He turned to Art.

"Looks like we'll be eating bear for a year. Look at the size of him!"

"How's the guy?" Art had lowered the rifle and had removed the shell from the chamber. *Unless you are planning to shoot, keep the chamber clear.* He could hear Jet's voice in his head.

"He'll be fine. His leg looks a mess. I'll have Linda look at it when we get home."

"What do you want to do with the bear?"

"I'll try to get the truck here and then we'll take it with us. Alternatively, we'll need to at least gut it and take some meat out of respect."

Jet was able to get the truck down next to the river and they spent the next thirty minutes removing the intestines, bladder, and bits of the internals that would otherwise ruin the meat. When they opened it up, Jet was pleased to see the results of his shooting. The bullet hit the top half of the heart. Sometimes animals continue on for a few steps but, lucky for Jack, it stopped dead in its tracks. If it had fallen on him, he would have been crushed. As it was, Jet needed to use the winch to haul the carcass into the back of the pickup. The suspension lifted the front of the pickup as the thousand pounds eased into the back. Jack was put into the backseat of the double cab and their guns were laid on the floor next to him.

He drove straight to the hospital where Linda worked.

"You what?" She was trying to understand how Jet even could put out a trap like that. "It's inhumane. Isn't it illegal?"

"Let's just see how bad this is before we get too carried away," Jet said. "And can we keep this quiet? I wouldn't want this to show up official if possible. Just in case there are questions."

"Sometimes I don't know what I'll do about you, Jethro." She always used his full name when she was angry. She turned her attention to the leg. "Are you conscious, hon?" Jack had begun to moan.

"Uh, yeah. Where am I?"

"You're safe. You're in a hospital. You had an accident and everything will be OK. I've given you some relief for the pain—it must hurt like anything—and I've given you a first shot of tetanus immune globulin and some general antibiotics. I've cleaned the wounds and disinfected everything. I also took the precaution of treating for any possible spores or other nasties that may have gotten in there. You are a very lucky man."

"Thank you," Jack said, waiting for the fearsome pain to kick in at any time. It didn't.

"Thank this man here," she said, tugging at Jet. "He is the one who shot that bear." She ignored the minor fact that he was also the one who laid the trap.

"Thank you, sir," Jack said. "I thought I had died twice out there."

"You're welcome. My name's Jet."

"Jack."

"Nice to meet you, Jack."

"And you, Jet." Jack raised his arm to shake Jet's hand. It worked and he was amazed at how much better he was feeling. "These drugs must be something else, because I'm feeling no pain here."

Linda smiled. "I just hope I didn't overdo it. I imagined you have had enough pain for quite some time."

Jack laughed. "You can say that again." He was settling into his pillow when he remembered. "My pack. Did you manage to bring my backpack?"

"Yep. Art's got it at home for when you're recovering."

"Thanks," Jack said. His body relaxed and he felt himself drifting into a sleep.

"I'd like him to stay by us for the next week or so, if that's OK with you, Linda." Jet felt responsible for Jack, despite saving his life. He knew it was his fault.

"I was about to suggest the same thing," Linda said. She kissed Jet and let Jack fall back to sleep. Jet sat for a few minutes before he also left to deal with the bear. It needed hanging in a cool place and he didn't have a fridge large enough.

The damage looked worse than it was. Lucky for Jack, there was no trauma to any major arteries or nerves. Jet and Linda had decided there was no reason for him to see a doctor. She disinfected and inoculated the torn flesh before sewing it back into place. Jack would have a limp for a few months and he would have scars to rival Rambo on his calf but otherwise he was fine.

Jack woke in a room covered by yellowing wallpaper in a futon bed. Jack felt like he had been hit by a freight train. He was able to sit up but when he tried to swing his legs out of bed, he felt the sensation of disconnection. His legs were there and he could see them and feel them, but they weren't responding as they should. It was as though his legs had fallen asleep and just needed some blood to circulate and sort things out. He used his fists to massage his legs. He pulled them out with his hands and sat on the edge of the bed.

"Hello!" He sounded ridiculous and he knew it.

No response. There was a different smell to the place. The carpets harboured cigarette and possibly pipe or cigar smoke. A greasy air hinted at burned steaks overcooked in the kitchen the night before. The sun was just rising and flimsy translucent flower-patterned curtains did nothing to stop its effect on the room. A dog came in and stopped at the door. Even it was cautious of Jack. He whimpered and turned away. Five minutes later, a woman appeared.

"Hello there. I'm Linda, but you might not remember me from the hospital. You were pretty doped up. I hope you slept OK. Are you in pain?"

Jack tried to assess his environment. It was a time warp, thirty years out of fashion but clean and respectable. The woman was attractive and had a friendly smile. In different circumstances, he would describe her as sexy. She was in a robe but he could see a figure that was all woman. She moved and talked like a professional. Teacher? Lawyer? Nurse? He decided on the last one as she produced a thermometer and asked him to take his temperature. At least it was in his mouth. He really didn't want anything approaching his ass ever again. She was respectful and spoke soothingly to him. It added to his sense of disconnection from reality.

"Can I get you anything? Are you hungry?"

"I can't feel my legs," Jack said.

"Oh." She moved a little closer. "Do you mind?" She looked him in the eye before she bent down and began examining him, poking and prodding. Eventually, she left and returned with a rubber hammer. "Cross your legs." As Jack couldn't, she did it for him. "Now relax."

She tapped and Jack saw his leg move. She did the same on the other with the same result.

"Good news, no nerve damage. The legs are just in shock and should be functioning sooner than later. How's the pain?" She looked genuinely pleased about the result and concerned about Jack's welfare. He remained wary.

"I don't feel anything," he said.

"Hmmm . . . I think I should reduce the dosage. How much do you weigh?"

Jack thought a bit. He used to be 230 pounds but these last six months had taken a lot out of him. "I think 180 or something around there."

Linda paused. "We need to start getting some meat into you. I don't know if you remember what's happened, but I think you would enjoy some bear stew once it's ready."

Jack managed a smile. "That would be lovely." He wanted to say more but was embarrassed.

Sensing this, Linda asked, "Is there anything else?"

Jack hesitated but then realised there was no reason to be ashamed. "I need to go to the bathroom."

"Oh. I see." Linda smiled understandingly. "I'll get Jet."

She left the room and a large man returned. He was a giant. Well over six-feet tall and built like a mountain.

"Hi, Jet," Jack said. "I remember you from the hospital."

"How you doing?" he replied. "I think you wandered into my trap. Sorry about that."

He didn't know how to respond to that. He thought the mountain in front of him saved his life, but he was in fact the cause of his disastrous accident. He began to wonder whether Jet was mentally all there; why would he admit to something like that in the first sentence? Jack wanted to kill him but that was patently impossible. Instead, he said, "Not a problem. I should've been more careful."

"I understand you need some help." Jet stood awkwardly.

"Uh, yeah. I can't feel my legs and I need to go to the toilet. If you could help me onto it, I think I can do the rest."

Jet shuffled his feet and then moved toward him looking uncomfortable. He picked up Jack with surprising ease and carried him to the toilet. He put him on the seat and then left the room, closing the door behind him. "Call if you need any help or when you are done," he said.

Jack wasn't sure what rabbit hole he had fallen into. Sexy nurse and giant who traps bears? As he didn't have time to ruminate or pursue other options, he accepted his situation and tried to figure out what to do next. When that was done and he was back in bed, he tried to get a better sense of things.

"So you trap and hunt in that area? What about the authorities? Does the ski resort know you're doing this? It looked like a national park to me."

"I don't accept their authority," Jet said.

"You what?"

"They don't have authority to stop me so I do what I need to do. I don't hurt anybody and I keep in contact with the wardens. They know I'm there and don't have a problem with it."

"But I just about died," Jack said before he could stop himself.

"And I'm eternally sorry," Jet said. "I really didn't want to harm anyone. That's why we took you in. I want to see that you are treated and back on your feet as quickly as possible."

There was an awkward silence as the two men looked at each other, each determining what level of bullshit would be dished out in the course of their conversation. Linda sensed the unease and decided to make some breakfast. "Coffee, anyone?"

"Yes, please," Jack said. His body yearned for the simple pleasures of coffee, greasy bacon, and some fried eggs on toast.

"Jet?"

"Yes, honey, that'd be great. Thanks."

The conversation had paused for the moment and Jack was left alone to rest before breakfast. He was determined to understand who these people were and when he could get back on track to Winnipeg.

When he was lifted by Jet to the breakfast table, Jack found himself in a further surreal existence. He watched Linda cooking while Jet talked about his past. Linda seemed to be a normal midwestern beauty who followed society's rules about being a wife and mother. Her son, Arthur, sat silently at the table, watching Jet and his mother do their morning routine.

Jack found himself wanting to ask questions but silenced himself as the breakfast was served. Neither of the men got off their chairs. Linda glided around the kitchen, never saying a word. The men sat back in their chairs drinking their first coffee before breakfast and discussing the bear and how to deal with the meat. Linda's life as a nurse was never brought up. For Jet and Art, Linda's work was a distraction from her being a mother and wife. She brought in a steady income to the household and never complained, but there was something about her movements that hinted at a resignation to her lot in life. It took a few days before Jack realised that Art was Linda's son and Jet's stepson. He learned that Jet was ex-militia on the run, trying to stay below the radar and keep his nose clean. Linda was the lynchpin that provided the respectability, but she seemed oblivious to her role. Jack couldn't determine whether she was being extremely pragmatic or simply dimwitted.

After five days of a startlingly similar routine, Jack was ready to go. His flesh was tied up and would heal in due course. He developed a sense of anxiety about his situation. The house was isolated and the routine was unrelenting. Linda would go to work and return and then cook dinner. Before she left, she ensured that all of the men had eaten and that sandwiches, soup, or a casserole was set out for lunch. Jet seemed to roam the grounds like an animal. He didn't work or bring in any money. He hunted, read, and spent a lot of time at the local greasy spoon. Linda didn't mind. In fact, she was sympathetic to his plight. Art was in school most of the time when he wasn't glued to Jet's side. Jack didn't understand his role in the whole madness and was keen to be on his way.

"So what is it that you do?" Jack said after a lunch of leftover spaghetti and meatballs. Art was at school and he was alone with Jet.

"I defend the constitution of the United States."

Jack took another mouthful of pasta because he was speechless. He let the silence linger for a while. "And what does that entail?" he said eventually.

"I stay alive by trading with people locally. I don't believe in banks or money or any of that kind of stuff. I want to live the life of a free man." He looked at Jack and took a bite of his meatball. He chewed for a moment and then continued. "It's harder than you might think."

Jack started to have flashbacks of Russia and tried to stay calm. *He's a sociopath*, he thought. Aloud he said, "I think it would be nearly impossible to act independently of the government with all the regulations."

"That's it in a nutshell," Jet said. He had opened a beer earlier and was on his second. "But we need to think beyond the obvious with the government. They just want to turn us into a bunch of robots, paying taxes and birthing babies to replace ourselves."

Jack was silent. Despite the obvious madness and the scary, horror-movie design of the house, he agreed. He no longer believed in the American dream. The people who made it were the exceptions. The US was less socially mobile than England, the land of Jane Austen characters and Downton Abbey. If someone didn't do something, the US would drift from a democracy to a caste society—albeit in the guise of a transparent, participating, and inclusive democracy. The idea appealed to Jack but the reality of Jet's life grated against his understanding of the world. Jack wanted to cheer Jet's independence but feared it in equal measure as one step from sedition and the destruction of the status quo.

"You're a brave man," Jack said. "And I can see you are taking this seriously. How sustainable is your way of life?"

"So far, it isn't." Jet was surprisingly without guile. He seemed incapable of lying or hiding his own failings. "Linda supports us all and I try to be a good husband and father. She's the best thing that ever happened to me."

Jack was speechless. Jet could have told him he was the messiah with less effect. He expected crazy and wasn't prepared for honesty. He also couldn't square Jet's statements with his behaviour. On the one hand, he spoke like an enlightened man. On the other, he treated his wife like it was the 1950s. *No burned bras here*, he thought.

Jet continued. "All I want is to make a difference. I know I'm not a genius, but I'm no idiot, either. There is something wrong with how our society is functioning. At least I can live like I want for now. But that will eventually change and I don't want to face it."

"I think most people think as you do but they accept their life and circumstances. It is part of growing up and conforming." Jack was surprised at his own honesty. Jet's frankness inspired him to do the same. "I respect your decision to remain honest to your beliefs, Jet. I just hope you'll find something to give you satisfaction at the same time."

"Thanks, Jack. Not everyone gets me." He took a final slug of beer before crushing the can. "And sorry again for the trap. I can see it was a bit of a bone-headed thing for me to do."

"Honestly, I can't believe that I'm still talking to you. I didn't want to say anything earlier because you saved my life but it was only pure luck that I'm sitting here and not inside that bear's belly."

"I know. I really am deeply sorry. If there is anything I can do to help, you only need to call on me." His head was bowed in shame.

"Don't beat yourself up," Jack said. "It's done and over. And I'm really pleased to have met you."

Jet's head rose and his face was smiling again. "Thanks. It means a lot to me. By the way, you are welcome to stay here as long as you want."

"I wanted to talk about that as well," Jack said. "I need to get going. My leg is healing nicely. If you could get Linda to give me some spare bandages and some medicine, I'll be on my way."

Jet's face dropped and became serious. "Can I give you a lift?"

"Not really. I'm heading to Canada and I wanted to avoid the border crossings."

Jet raised an eyebrow. "Are you a criminal?"

"No," Jack said.

"Then why avoid the border?"

"I have my reasons," Jack said.

Jet was silent for a moment. "OK. Not my business. But I will get you across the border. I'll take you to within one mile. After that, you'll have to walk. When you are in Manitoba, you just keep walking north until you reach a paved road. Hopefully someone'll pick you up and then you can catch a bus from there."

"I appreciate that." Jack had finished his lunch and was already visualising the walk. "And thank you."

"Don't thank me until you reach your destination. That leg'll hurt you a lot on your walk. You'd be smarter to wait here until you are stronger and fully healed."

"Thanks, but I need to go. There's something in Winnipeg I need before I can continue."

"Your choice, but I'm here if you need me."

Jack reached out and they shook hands. *Life is stranger than fiction*, he thought. *And this guy is right out of the comic books.*

Chapter Ten

GREAT WHITE NORTH

Brad Schritt stopped for Jack on the gravel road just one mile north of the border. When the Silverado pickup stopped, no one was more surprised than Jack.

"Where you heading?" Brad tried to sound like this was something he did every day. In fact, it was the first stranger he had ever picked up hitchhiking. It was dangerous and exactly the thing his parents would not want him to do. He had just turned eighteen and graduation was around the corner.

"Winnipeg," Jack said. He threw his backpack in the back of the pickup as he put himself in the passenger seat. It was a new truck, or at least a recent model. It looked to be fitted out with all the extras. Brad saw the admiration and smiled to himself. He enjoyed being a bad boy with kick-ass toys.

"I'm heading to Winkler. Is that good enough?"

"Sounds good to me," Jack said. He was happy to rest his joints. His body sank into the seat, feeling only the seatbelt and hearing the heavy metal that pounded into his chest. Brad turned down the volume at first but then "Paranoid" started and he cranked it until the windows vibrated.

"Black Sabbath," Brad said. He could see the confused look on his passenger's face. It didn't make him turn it down and they drove without speaking as the music pulsated.

Jack smiled and lifted his eyebrows. He was happy to be in a vehicle and on the move. The walk was uneventful. Jet had dropped him within a mile of the border and he had walked across flat farmers' fields. He didn't understand why there was a border crossing at all if criminals could cross as freely as he did. *Maybe they did and the public just didn't realise it,* he thought. The whole process of illegally crossing the border without consequences made him uneasy. It was as though he realised that the emperor didn't have any clothes.

"What are you laughing about?" Brad said as he noticed Jack smirking. Thankfully, he turned down the music to talk.

"I was just thinking about life and how we enslave ourselves with imaginary chains. We are told something by those in power and we believe it, making it real. Yet it is no more real than our belief." Jack was watching a falcon land on a telephone pole as he spoke.

"Wow, heavy stuff," Brad said. "That's the kind of shit Ozzy would sing." He had a new respect for the hitchhiker. "What made you think of that out of the blue?"

"Not sure," lied Jack. "Maybe it's your music. Or maybe just being near such a long imaginary line separating Canada from the States caused me to think about how ridiculous and how important such lines are."

"What do you mean?" He was driving in autopilot mode. The roads were straight enough to land an airplane on. He turned to look at Jack more than he should have, keeping half an eye on the road. *Besides*, thought Brad, *these trucks virtually drive themselves.*

"Shakespeare said in *Hamlet* that 'nothing is good or bad, but thinking makes it so.' Milton's Satan said that 'the mind is its own place and can make a heaven of hell, a hell of heaven.' More or less. I may have missed a word or two but you get my thinking."

"Are you a professor or something?" Brad said, a bit less interested.

"No, just thinking to myself about how life is about perception. I then began to think about how our anxieties and frustrations and fears were probably about perception as well. We entrap ourselves with obligations and rules. These are mental constructs."

"Yeah, sure," Brad interrupted. "But you'll get a ticket if your perceptions aren't in line with everyone else's. You can't just walk around in a daze doing whatever you want. Take me, for example. I need to drive the speed limit. I can't drink while I'm driving. And if I do drugs, I'll go to jail. Everything I hear nowadays is about going to university or getting a good job. Or that I can't get a good job unless I go to university. Or if I want to keep farming pigs and potatoes, I need to go to university. I hear what you're saying. Sorry, what's your name?"

"Jack."

"Nice to meet you. I'm Brad. I hear what you're saying, Jack, but it doesn't apply to me. I'm not allowed to be free to think or do what I want."

Jack tried to refrain from smiling. He wasn't going to push the point. "You're probably right. I was just thinking and you asked. Perhaps it applies more to me right now." Jack wasn't looking to debate with a kid. *Brad would discover his chains in due course*, Jack thought.

The rest of the trip went well and the music wasn't returned to the ear-bleeding levels of before. They reached Winkler and Brad turned to Jack again.

"Where should I drop you?"

"Can you drop me next to a bank? And do you know where I can get the bus to Winnipeg?"

"Sure. I think the Greyhound picks up people by the gas station. Let me just check." He pulled over and consulted his phone. "Yep, it's right by this gas station coming up. Try to remember it. You need to buy your tickets online; the bus driver doesn't sell anything."

"OK, thanks. Are you able to see when the next bus is leaving?"

"There's a bus tonight at six."

"If I pay you cash, can you book me a ticket?" Jack fished for some bills from his pocket. It was US cash but he figured it would be acceptable. His portion of cash from the pimp's car was running out but all he needed was to get to Winnipeg. Everything would be fine after that.

"Sure. Just did it. Cost $22.50"

"Here's $30 US and keep the change. I owe you for the trip into town, as well." Jack was pleased.

"Thanks, Jack! I'm taking you to the mall. There's a bank in there and you can grab McDonald's or something. It's not too much of a walk back to the bus stop. Just remember where I said."

"Done and thanks. I really appreciate this."

"No problem."

Brad pulled into the mall parking lot and stopped next to McDonald's. Jack grabbed his pack from the back and slung it over his left shoulder. He walked over to the driver's door and Brad had the window down.

"It was good to meet you, Brad." They shook hands.

"Likewise," Brad said. "And I've been thinking about what you said. Maybe it might have some relevance to me, too." He had a slightly distant look in his eye.

Smart kid, thought Jack. "You'll be fine. And if you can, go to university and feed your mind. Then it'll take care of you the rest of your life."

"See you later, professor!" With that, the big engine roared as Brad accelerated. Jack hadn't even heard the engine when he was inside.

Jack looked at McDonald's and shook his head. *What is it about this place? Is Karma punishing or rewarding me? Every time I get a lift, I end up here.* Rather than fight fate, he went to change his cash to Canadian currency and returned to have a Bic Mac and some fries.

∞

The two-and-a-half-hour bus ride was luxurious. The climate inside was perfect and the seats comfortable. There were only three other people on the bus, so Jack spread out over two seats. He sat above the rear axle and leaned his head against the glass. He watched the blur of telephone poles and endless fields pass him by. It didn't take long before the reassuring motion put him to sleep.

"We've arrived, sir." The bus driver had walked down the aisle to prepare for the next batch of passengers. It wasn't uncommon for him to find people sleeping at the terminus. He shook Jack's shoulder gently.

"Hmmph?" Jack instinctively sat up and tried to open his eyes. They felt glued shut. He could feel the drool in the corner of his mouth. He removed the rest from his cheek with his hand. "Sorry." His body was stiff and he needed some pain relief for his leg.

"No problem. I just need to get the bus ready and locked so I can go grab something to eat. Unfortunately, that means you need to be on your way."

"Of course. My neck may disagree but that was a really good deep sleep. Thanks." Jack grabbed his pack and walked out the bus. He rolled his shoulders and head as he tried to get his body going again. The limp was still there but that was more about time than tiredness.

He heard a plane take off. Winnipeg's bus terminal was at the airport instead of downtown. He would need to take another bus to get there, but the exhaustion was overwhelming. He changed his mind and booked into the Sheraton hotel. All he could think about was sleeping and, having paid, went to bed without eating.

When he woke, he found his strength again. He had a massive breakfast of hash browns, soft basted eggs, bacon, and toast, all washed down with four cups of strong black coffee. It was just after 9 am when he emerged and found the bus stop to take him downtown. That dropped him at the junction of Portage and Main. It was only a short walk from there to the destination he had been aiming for since he made that deal with Vlad's father in Russia.

"Hello, Jack. It has been quite some time." A middle-aged woman with long red hair greeted him. Her face was freckled from the sun and crinkled from smiling.

"Hi, Isabella. I'm glad to see you are the same as ever." Jack gave a quick peck on each cheek and walked inside her home. "I assume you're still busy doing the same thing as the last time I saw you?"

"Busier than ever," she replied. "I'm opening a new school solely for new immigrants that aren't wanted anywhere else."

"You still running the school out of your house?"

"No, I found a spot with more room so I can take donations and food. Things were growing too fast and I needed help. We're a lot bigger now, and I even have paid staff."

"You mean you never paid anyone in your previous school?" Jack was amazed.

"Only a fraction of what they would make as teachers in a more conventional school. These are true believers who volunteer their time and love to educate these kids. If they didn't, the kids would end up on the streets—and that means gangs, prostitution, and crime." Isabella had been leading Jack to the kitchen as they talked. "Have a seat. I'll make some coffee. Want some leftover carrot cake?"

Jack was full from breakfast and didn't need the coffee. "Sure, just a small slice. I'll have my coffee black if you're having some."

When they settled over the cake and coffee, she eyed him carefully. She had noticed the limp and he was looking skinny and beaten up. "Is everything OK?"

"Sure, why?"

"For starters, I'm sitting with you in my kitchen having cake and coffee after not having heard anything from you for over a year. And, secondly, you look like you are either on drugs or lost a fight with a train."

Jack just about coughed up his last piece of cake. "Don't worry, I'm not on drugs. Just a really bad nine months. I'll tell you another time."

"Hmm. . . ."

Jack disregarded the disbelieving look. "I have something more serious to talk about. It relates to your work."

"Really? You becoming a bleeding heart all of a sudden?" She flashed a mock smile. Her multi-coloured shirt and jeans reminded Jack of a kindly teacher—which she was—and not the fount of information that he came for.

"I'm looking to redress the imbalance of justice in the world of trafficking and I need information, contacts, and the safety deposit box key." Jack trusted her completely. She was the closest person he had encountered who didn't have an ulterior motive. She was also the closest person he knew to a living saint. The Mother Teresa of Winnipeg he had told Frank about.

"When did you become interested in trafficking? And what do you mean by balancing the scales of justice?"

"That's part of my story I'll have to tell you another day. I don't know exactly what to do, but I need to do something. You've worked with almost every police agency in North America and have contacts in the anti-trafficking agencies that matter. I need to learn what is inside your head. I want to start by learning who the pimps are, who the johns are, and how the problem is currently tackled."

"And the key?"

"That's from Joe. I was to use it if things became desperate, and they are. It holds all of the access codes to the secrets he left me. It's time for me to unlock some of them. I am hoping it'll help me with my new mission."

"Mission? Jack, you are talking a bit like a crazy person. I'll give you all the help that I can but I want you to stay here and calm down a bit first. Relax, and we'll work on this together. Sounds fair?"

Jack smiled at the soft, patronising voice. It must come from working with children all the time. "Sure. Sounds great. When do we start?"

"No time like the present. I'll get you the information and you can go through it on my spare laptop. Once you have had a chance to digest things, we'll brainstorm the next step. I'll get the key now for you."

"Thanks, Izzie."

She lived in a large apartment in the middle of the core area of Winnipeg and sat above a retail space. Twenty-five years ago, she and her husband had decided to sell their house and buy a property that they could live in and use as a school. They found a large abandoned retail space large enough to school up to thirty children. The apartment above was modest but met their needs.

Teaming up with a public school, she was able to have her operation recognised by the education board. She used her own salary as vice-principal to hire additional staff. Volunteers came out of the woodwork to donate their time and educational materials. Rachel Decker, a Hutterite woman visiting the area, noticed her nascent school. When she talked to Isabella, she began to cry and vowed to assist in every way possible. Isabella was a Mennonite, a committed pacifist, and a Christian. Her work included all religions and ethnic groups. Rachel's colony decided to supply its excess food to her school. Soon, van loads of milk, honey, meat, and vegetables began showing up. She was able to feed her pupils breakfast and lunch—which aided in their education.

"They have nothing," her eyes would tear up when talking to Jack. "They are unwanted by everyone. I just wanted to provide a safe place for them to heal. You have no idea of the trauma they have faced. Some have seen their parents butchered in front of them. Many have been raped and beaten. I receive girls of fourteen with a reading age of four. But then," her tears gone and face beaming again, "after only two years, they are reading and writing at an age of twelve or more. One girl came in at thirteen with a reading age of five. Within two years, she was reading at her age level and, a year after that, was able to receive a scholarship to go to a private school."

"Amazing," Jack said. He knew this meant a lot to Isabella but it was beyond his ability to provide this type of help. His mission was more primal. He didn't know how to nurture. He also knew that getting help from a pacifist such as Isabella would necessitate her not knowing his full plans. He would assist her organisation if he was able to, but it all depended on what the box revealed.

"We outgrew our space after only three years and were able to rent extra space from the Full Gospel Mission Church nearby. Everyone wants to help but they don't know how." She wiped some residual tears from her face. "Enough about my dramas. Go see what's in the box and let's talk when you have reviewed the data on that computer."

Sensing the morning pep was talk over, Jack got up and began to leave.

"Oh, here's a key to the apartment," she said. "Don't make me regret this."

"You won't. And thanks again."

∞

Winnipeg was once a trading fort set in the middle of nowhere with grand historic ambitions. The confluence of two rivers around which the modern city's downtown site was the place where fur traders met and did business. It had become increasingly irrelevant shortly after World War II as major industries and headquarters moved east to Ontario and west to Alberta. Ironically, it wasn't until the trains began to roll again near the end of the 1990s that the stars aligned and all things Canadian were positive. Global commodity demand helped all Canadians and a housing boom began that was unaffected by the US-European bust of 2008. To top it all off, oil was found in the southwest of the province. It had always been the main hub for east-west and north-south traffic—especially for grain and materials bound for the port of Churchill. Set just west of the geographical centre of Canada, it should have become the Chicago of the north. Instead, it had become the destination of immigrants who weren't able to settle in Vancouver, Calgary, or Toronto. Because of Manitoba's high population of First Nations people, its downtown was referred to as "the reservation" by the less charitable or racist element within the populace. Whatever its past, trains now rumbled constantly through its centre and the city felt alive again.

With fewer than 700,000 people, Winnipeg was easy to navigate and people within their sectors of expertise tended to know each other. The world of welfare and poverty was no different. The authorities knew who the do-gooders were and vice versa. All parties knew who the bad guys were—drug dealers, pimps, petty criminals, and the rest of the spectrum of folks who make up a city. Jack knew that he would get a clear picture of the criminal inhabitants from Isabella's data. What he needed now was a plan.

"Can I help you, sir?" A smiling fresh face looked enquiringly at Jack. He was in the basement of the Scotiabank where the safety deposit boxes were.

"Uh, yes. I have come to take something out of my box."

"What number?"

Jack looked carefully but couldn't see a number. He showed his key to the young woman, careful to not let go of it.

"Ah, yes. This is a VIP box. It doesn't have a number." Her voice became even perkier. "I'll take you there myself. Please follow me." She turned and started walking, ensuring that Jack was following. She had to slow a few times as they navigated the lengthy corridors.

"Sorry about my mobility. Bum leg," Jack said sheepishly.

"Not a problem, sir."

They arrived in an area within a larger vault. The huge door was open.

"A bit outdated, but too difficult to remove," she said.

"Really lovely. Like looking inside a watch," Jack said.

They located the box and she inserted her key on one side. Jack did the same on the other.

"On three, two, one, turn." The keys turned and she excused herself. "Please press the button when you want me to return. When you are done, you can put the box back or wait for me. The front plate locks automatically."

"Thank you. I may be a while." Jack sat on the chair. He used the table in the middle of the vault. They had secluded booths if need be but he decided against it, as he was the only one there.

When the woman was gone, he lifted the lid.

REUNION

"Can you pass me the towel, Mom? It's over there, next to you." Chrystal had just come out of the pool, her hair slicked back from the water. She wore a one-piece instead of her usual bikini but she could feel the hungry eyes of every man and even some women on her as she walked the fifteen feet from the pool's edge to where her mother was sitting. The hotel was the best Grand Forks had on offer and consisted of 120 rooms wrapped around a central mini water park. It was designed for children and parents to enjoy themselves. A water slide snaked down within the large four-storey glass atrium. Rooms enjoyed views of the swimmers, as did the restaurants—one for breakfast and the other for conferences and formal occasions.

"How's the water?" Tammy handed the oversized towel to Chrystal. She was in a robe reading a celebrity magazine.

"Water's great. I can't get enough of it."

"I can't believe how much I am enjoying doing nothing," Tammy said. "And who would ever think of looking for us in North Dakota?" She was smiling.

"I don't think anyone is looking for us," Chrystal said, more hoping than believing.

"Anyway, we don't need to think about that nonsense. What do you want to do today? We could catch a movie or go for a walk, maybe?"

"Walking isn't the most entertaining thing to do in Grand Forks. Sorry, Mom."

"Look at the bright side: at least it's not winter."

"Why are you so positive this morning? We've been here almost a month and our only accomplishment is that we haven't become fat eating in restaurants all of the time."

"Don't be so down on things, Chrys. We are having a fantastic holiday, exercising in a great gym, swimming as much as we want, and eating gourmet food. You look fantastic by the way. Your body agrees with this break."

Chrystal blushed. "I don't feel great but thanks for that. I can't even wear my bikini yet. And I swim to get clean." She lowered her voice as she sat next to Tammy. "Every night when I close my eyes, they are there. I still feel what they did to me. I can't wash them out."

Tammy turned and sat on the edge of her reclining deck chair. She put her hand on Chrystal's shoulder and nodded. "I know. I try not to think about them, but they are always there for me, too." She grimaced. "I know they hurt you. But we survived. We're here, and we'll be fine." Silent tears began to run down both of their cheeks. She wiped them against the sleeve of her soft terrycloth robe.

"I love you, Mom," Chrystal said, hugging her.

"I love you too, sweetheart." Tammy shook her head as if it would erase the images that floated there. "Oh, I almost forgot why I was in such a good mood," she was smiling again. "I just got a message that our passports are ready for collection. We're good to go. That is, if you still want to."

"I was ready to go when we got our driver's licences," Chrystal said. She took off the towel and wrapped it around her waist.

"You like Jack, don't you?" Tammy was smiling. "He's a nice man."

"I do," Chrystal said. "I never thought I'd like any man after what we went through and definitely not so soon, but Jack is different. He has a sadness in his eyes and a determination in his voice."

"And he's not bad to look at," added her mother. They both laughed.

"How about a quick trip to the mall to pick up a few things before we head north?"

"I couldn't have suggested anything better myself," Tammy said. They got up with a new spring to their step and left the atrium for their room.

∞

"I can't believe that this time last year, I was the manager of a store just like that one."

"And now you are off to meet an international fugitive—or whatever he is—to do who knows what." Tammy took a sip of her coffee and changed lanes. She looked down briefly to see that she wasn't speeding. The road ahead and behind disappeared into an endless horizon.

"Shuddup. I want to do this. I want to hurt those people who did those things to us." Chrystal was serious. She didn't want to go from one disaster to another but Jack was not Lyle and he didn't promise anything. All he had was a plan and that was better than nothing.

"So do I, honey." Tammy became serious again. "But let's keep an open mind. We'll see what is going on and, if we like it, we'll stay. If not, we go home."

"Freedom, baby. Freedom." Chrystal was feeling good about herself. Her new jeans accentuated her figure and her top made her feel like a woman again and not just some meat with holes for men to lust after. "You like my new shoes?"

"I love them. You really look lovely." Tammy was proud of her. She had been through a lot and was bouncing back. She wished that her own spirit was so resilient.

"Seventy-six miles to Pembina," Chrystal said, reading the green sign at the side of the road.

"And not far from there to the border. I'm actually getting nervous," Tammy said, squirming slightly in her seat.

"The traffic is heavier than I would have expected. This is the middle of nowhere."

"Correction: we are just east of the middle of nowhere. The middle of North America is Rugby, North Dakota." Chrystal gave her mom a mock look of concern. "Hey, it's what you learn sitting around a pool for a month. Eventually, you start reading the fun facts of the state." They both laughed. "Besides, you can't blame people for not wanting to fly."

"Only because of cost, Chrys. If we had the money, believe me, I'd be flying instead of driving."

"I like the drive," Chrystal said. "It's therapeutic."

"Well, I've had enough therapy to last me for quite some time." She put on the radio. "Rock or country?"

"Rockin' country!"

"You really are embracing this, aren't you?" Tammy said with a smile. She scanned through the stations until she found one with good reception. "Looks like country it is. Yee haw."

Chrystal moved her shoulders and swayed to the music, dancing in her seatbelt. Tammy nodded in time with the beat and tapped her fingers on the steering wheel. They watched the massive tractors ploughing the fields making hypnotic straight furrows that blurred as they passed. It wasn't long before they were slowing to a standstill behind a line of cars waiting to enter Canada.

"There are six lanes. Why are they processing all of the cars in just one? It seems an unnecessary delay." Chrystal was watching the long-haul truckers form a line in lane six. She and Tammy were in lane one.

"Don't complain. I really don't want to have any trouble. They can probably sense our fear."

"Now you're making me afraid. We haven't done anything wrong."

"Be calm. Have some chocolate." She passed a package to Chrystal and had some herself. It was another fifteen minutes before they pulled up next to the black corrugated metal box with a large woman behind the window.

"Good morning, ma'am. Is this your vehicle?"

"Yes." Tammy burst into a sweat. This was the last question she expected. Did Jack steal the truck?

"What is the purpose of your visit to Canada today?" Her face gave away nothing.

"We've never been and wanted to take a look."

The woman's eyes looked down at something. A monitor? Notes? "Can I have your passports please? Pull your vehicle over in one of the inspection bays just up there." She pointed ahead and to the left. Tammy gave her their passports and did as she was told. Another officer was waiting for them.

"Please turn off your engine and step out of the vehicle. Both of you."

Chrystal's face was serious, as was Tammy's. They put on light jackets to stop the wind and stepped out of the truck. The tarmac with a simple metallic structure felt alien and their adrenaline made everything seem different. The inspection bay was spotless and the man facing them was professional and friendly, but his authority was absolute. They stood ten feet away as he began to look at the vehicle.

First, the door handles and steering wheel were rubbed with a little white piece of fabric at the end of a plastic handle. They used a mirror to look under the vehicle. Then they opened all of the doors. An empty coffee cup tumbled out the rear passenger door. With black latex gloves on, the officer lifted the mats on the floor, looked under the seats, in the glove compartment, and felt in the crevices of the seats. He worked systematically from the floor to the doors to the ceiling and everything in between. When he was satisfied there was nothing of interest, he looked carefully at the box and wheel wells.

Another officer came from inside the building with their passports and handed it to him. They spoke between themselves and the other officer returned to the main building. The searching officer turned to Tammy and Chrystal.

"Everything looks fine. I apologise for the search. You must have flagged something in the system. Have a good day." He handed the passports back to Tammy.

"Thank you, officer." She was shaking and the two returned to the cab without saying a word. They reversed out and accelerated up Highway 75 toward Winnipeg. It was quite some time before they spoke.

"What the hell was that all about?" Chrystal had lost much of her earlier confidence.

"Just security. One hell of a coincidence, but just run-of-the-mill security. Otherwise, we'd still be there."

"I couldn't breathe when they took our passports. I could feel their hands on me and the lies crashed on me like a massive wave."

"For me, it was the first question. I never recovered. I feel like a fraud."

"You've done nothing wrong. Neither of us have. We'll get through this. We need to understand that we'll have these moments and we just need to persevere."

"How'd you get to be so smart?" Tammy said. "I'm so proud of you, Chrys. You really are my whole life."

"Don't start talking like that, Mom. You'll make me cry." It was too late, and the tears were already flowing.

"And you're making me cry. I need to pull over." Tammy did and they enjoyed a good cry and then hugged each other.

∞

"Jack? We're here."

"Yeah. Not a problem. A little hairy at the border but no problems."

"No, everything's fine. Chrystal is looking rested and we're both keen to see you."

"Great. OK. Three o'clock at the Old Spaghetti Factory. See you then."

Tammy looked at Chrystal and smiled. "Looks like your boyfriend'll be here soon."

"Stop it, you're embarrassing me!"

"Anyway, we've got a few hours to kill so we may as well wander around here."

"What'd he say?"

"Nothing much. He was happy, I think surprised, to hear from us. Let's see how things go."

The two women looked like sisters as they walked through The Forks. They were both wearing designer jeans, ironed to show a crease, with black, high-heeled pumps. Chrystal wore a soft brown leather jacket that hugged her body and stopped short at the waist. Tammy wore the same one in black. They had treated themselves to the hairdresser before they left Grand Forks and they looked and felt like a million bucks. They walked like they were in a movie and most heads turned to watch them pass. They were no longer porn stars or sex symbols. They were striking and beautiful and proud.

"This place is exceptional," Chrystal said. "So far, I like Winnipeg better than Grand Forks."

The paths were all either cobbled or made of paving stones. There was granite everywhere along with statues and monuments to famous traders and founding fathers of Manitoba.

"There's lots of First Nations stuff, as well," Chrystal said. "I hate to keep saying it, but I can't believe where we are today compared to where we were only a month-and-a-half ago."

"What, you prefer walking in fresh air and chatting to being raped dozens of times a week?"

"Mom, quiet. What's got into you?"

"I don't know," Tammy said. "I am mad. I can't stop being angry. I know it's a downer when I talk like this and it'll pass. But when I see how beautiful and peaceful and clean all of this is, I can't help but be furious at the shit we went through. How we were degraded and made to feel smaller than a flea's shit."

Chrystal laughed. "I've never heard that before." Then, more seriously, "I know how you feel. You know I do. Let's enjoy the day and grab an ice cream after our walk."

Tammy linked her arm in her daughter's and they walked leaning in on each other. There were quite a few people there and they enjoyed the screeching of children with painted faces and heard some bands preparing for an evening performance. They watched the buskers and wandered the market.

Tammy's phone rang. "Hello? You are? Great. We'll be there in five minutes."

"What's up?"

"Jack got there early. He's waiting for us."

They got up and walked toward the entrance to the market where they'd noticed the restaurant named the Old Spaghetti Factory. When they got there, Jack was leaning against the wall, scanning the crowd. When he caught their eye, they could see the jolt that ran across his features.

"Wow, you two look amazing," Jack said. "You look like movie stars!" He kissed them both on the cheeks as they came close.

"Thanks Jack. You don't look too bad yourself." Tammy was all smiles and saying the things Chrystal wanted to say. She needn't have bothered, as Chrystal's eyes said it all.

"Jack, it's so good to see you. I can't believe it. This place is amazing." As she talked, she got closer and put her arm in Jack's. She stood close to him, almost like a cat as it purrs next to its master's leg. He didn't move away.

"I think it's warm enough to grab a table outside. Do you want to eat or just grab a drink and a snack?" Jack started to move away from the entrance door and felt Chrystal's body next to him. His body was becoming warm and his eyes felt more alive. Not long ago, he thought he would never think about sex again, but right now, his hormones were over-riding all logic or memory. He pushed that aside as they walked to the metal tables overlooking a pavilion under a permanent tent. People were dancing to an aboriginal drum performance.

"You're limping," Chrystal said, pulling away and looking him up and down. "What happened?"

"Let's just say crossing into Canada on foot illegally was more eventful than I had anticipated."

Tammy pursed her lips. "OK, but you'll be telling us the story before long."

"OK," Jack said, putting his hands up. He enjoyed having them in his life. They were fun and genuine. *And they saved my life*, he said to himself. *After almost killing me first,* the same voice continued. *I think I am going crazy. Why am I having these conversations with myself?*

The Old Spaghetti Factory lacked the view they wanted and they decided to take a table at the Beachcomber instead. It was right on the edge of the development before the grass and stone steps which acted as seats and overlooked the river.

"This is much nicer," Chrystal said.

"Agreed," Tammy said. "I want to sit so I can see the river."

"Me, too," Chrystal said.

"I'm happy wherever you put me," Jack said.

Chrystal closed her eyes as the thoughts of where she wanted to put Jack entered her mind. *Why am I so horny? This is insane.* She felt her buttocks tightening and her lower back arch slightly as her chest pushed out involuntarily.

Jack's mouth went dry as he thought he saw Chrystal have a mini sex fantasy. *Now I'm definitely crazy*, he said to himself. To the waiter, he said "I'll have a Molson Canadian and a look at your menu, please. Tammy? Chrystal?"

"Is that a beer? I'll have the same," Chrystal said.

"I'll make it easy. Me, too," Tammy said.

When the waiter left, the three put their elbows on the table conspiratorially. "So, Jack, what's the plan?" Tammy was looking straight at him and he could feel the same from Chrystal.

"We can't talk here," Jack said. "But I am pretty close to working out what I would like to do. I want to run it past you and see if you agree. It's pretty bold and it would mean the two of you taking prominent roles."

"In what way?" Chrystal said.

"Let's just say that we have a lot more cards than I thought. I think we can make a real impact to reduce this happening to anyone else—and do it in a sustainable fashion."

Their drinks arrived. "I'll drink to that," Tammy said, taking a sip before ordering salad nicoise from the waiter.

"I'll have the same," Chrystal said. She hadn't looked at the menu and wasn't that interested in eating anyway.

"I'll have the house burger, fries, and onion rings," Jack said. "And another beer all around, please." When the waiter left, he shrugged. "I'm hungry and need to put on some of the weight that I lost."

"We never said anything. And I like a man with a good appetite." Chrystal was moving past flirting and could have sat on Jack's lap with less subtlety.

"Have you booked a room anywhere?" Jack asked.

"No, we didn't want to do anything until we talked."

"Good. I don't have a place here and I'm staying at a friend's. I booked you a lovely room at a hotel just over there.

"Are you staying at your friend's or did you book a room there, too?" Chrystal asked.

Jack reddened, more than a little embarrassed. "Yes, I booked a room as well. I figured if we are working together, we should be close by."

"Working? Is that part of your plan?" Tammy asked.

"Yes. It is imperative that we create a sustainable source of income to accomplish our goal. But, like I said, we can't discuss that out here. Too many ears."

"Then let's forget about all of the cloak-and-dagger talk," Chrystal said. "I think this is the beginning of a party."

Tammy and Jack smiled. They clinked the necks of their beers together and took a deep drink. Just in time, their next round arrived. Jack ordered another round for all of them.

"I'd prefer a glass of wine over beer," Tammy said. "Perhaps a bottle of white wine for us, Chrys?"

"Yeah, that sounds perfect."

"Sure thing," the waiter said. "We've got a lovely pinot grigio from Italy on offer. It's a bit more than the house wine but it is spectacular. The house white is from British Columbia; it is a pinot gris and is quite decent. Which would you prefer?"

"I'm happy with the house white," Chrystal said. "Thanks."

"And I'll have a bottle of your house red, please," Jack said. "No sense in me drinking beer if everyone else has become civilised."

"Yes, sir. Your food will be out shortly."

The meal came and was devoured. More wine was ordered and drunk. The hours passed effortlessly and the sun eventually set.

"I think that's it for me," Jack said as the last of the twilight faded.

"I'd say let's go find a party, but I'm also feeling it right now," Tammy said.

"Me, too," Chrystal said, slightly slurred. "If I didn't know who you were, I couldn't tell you now. You have both become blurs."

"Then I'm glad it's not far to the hotel," Jack said.

"But all our stuff is in the truck. We never moved it over. Mom, I can't do it tonight. Can we deal with it tomorrow?"

"Absolutely. Right now, all I want to do is hit my pillow."

"Look, here are your room key cards. You're all checked in. Just go right up. Give me the truck's keys and I'll bring your stuff up now."

"Aww, you're such a sweetheart." Chrystal leaned over and kissed Jack on the cheek. "You really are a gentleman."

"I'm not sure about that," Jack said, looking away. "But go to bed and I'll take care of everything here."

"Thanks, Jack," Tammy said and kissed him lightly on the other cheek. "You're a good guy."

When they left, Jack found himself watching them go. So did a number of other guys on the patio. He paid the bill and headed to the truck.

Smells like a girl's truck, he thought. *Perfume and everything clean*. He grabbed two suitcases and what looked like a smaller bag of stuff they might want and walked to the hotel. He found their room and knocked.

"Hello there," Chrystal was in a robe, having just showered. Her hair was wet and he found himself drawn toward her. Tammy was asleep in the other room. He had booked a large suite for them.

"Uh, hi. Where to you want these?"

"Anywhere is fine."

"OK. I guess that's it for me. I'm off."

"Which room are you in?"

"I'm next door."

"OK, Jack. Good night." She leaned in and kissed him gently on his lips. Her wet hair was cold against his skin. "You really are a lovely man."

Jack didn't know what to do. He wasn't looking for anything like this, and yet his body wanted it more than his exhaustion wanted him to sleep. Despite himself, he found himself saying, "Good night, sweetheart. Try to get some sleep."

He heard the door click shut and he fished his key card from his pocket. His things were already in place and he simply kicked off his shoes, emptied the change and money from his pockets, and took off his clothes. He jumped into the shower, brushed his teeth, and put on the robe hanging on the back of the bathroom door. The night air and exercise of lugging their suitcases had woke him up. *I hope there's something on the idiot box.* He left a light on in the bathroom and closed the door to allow just a crack of light. Ever since Russia, he didn't like the dark.

He pulled back the covers and found the remote control. Just as he was about to turn it on, he heard a knock on his door.

Chapter Twelve

A Plan Forms

The blackout curtains were effective and the Manitoba summer dawn wasn't felt by Jack or Chrystal. He got up first, showered, and made himself ready. He tried to make as little noise as possible but he couldn't avoid the lampshade and just about knocked the TV off the desk when he reached for his wallet.

"What time is it?" Chrystal pulled the covers up tight around her chin and her hair looked a bit crazy. Washing so soon after going to the hairdressers sometimes defeated the purpose.

"Just after nine. Carry on sleeping. I'm just popping downstairs to have a coffee and perhaps read the paper. I'll wait for you there."

"Uh hmm." Jack could hear her opening and closing her mouth. She was willing herself awake. "I'll be down as soon as I can."

Jack sat on the bed next to her. "Last night was perfect." He kissed her and then got up toward the door.

"Yeah. Beautiful." Jack heard it just before the door clicked shut.

The hallways were deserted and he could see room-service trays outside the doors. Some had the paper delivered but uncollected, hanging on the door handle in a plastic bag. The art on the wall was a mixture of aboriginal images, landscapes, and autumnal colours. He found the elevators and headed to the restaurant.

He found Tammy sitting quietly with a carafe of coffee reading the front page of *The Globe and Mail*. Jack joined her and ordered a breakfast of poached eggs on toast with a double espresso and an orange juice. There was already a pitcher of water on the table.

"Slept OK?" Tammy couldn't withhold her smile.

"Like a baby," Jack said. "So did Chrystal. She'll be down shortly."

"She likes you."

"I know. I like her, too. I'm sorry if I've done anything inappropriate."

"Not at all. We're all adults."

"Sometimes, I don't feel like one."

"Just do me one favour." Tammy put down her paper and looked directly at Jack.

"Of course."

"Don't break her heart. She's had a rough year and doesn't need false hope. If you are both having fun, great. But don't let her believe it is something it isn't."

Jack was taken aback. "I'm as surprised as you are at this development. I wasn't looking for anyone. But Chrystal and I have found a bond and it feels great right now. If that changes, we'll jump off that bridge when we get there."

"Sounds fair. And I don't want to overstep the mark, but she's all I have. I will do anything for her. And nothing she does with a good heart will ever be wrong in my books."

Jack nodded slightly. "I will be honest and frank with you and your daughter the best I can. I just hope that's good enough."

Tammy returned to her paper and Jack waited for Chrystal to arrive. It was almost an hour before she emerged. Her hair was wet again and she had changed into a warm sweater.

"Morning, Mom. Morning, Jack." She smiled coquettishly and sat down. When the waiter came by, she ordered some toast and a carafe of coffee with a large water.

Jack tried to act naturally and began giving a history lesson. He wanted to impress them and had read up on the Forks before they arrived. "The Forks are significant because of the meeting of two rivers—the Assiniboine and the Red River. We sat last night overlooking the point where the two meet. The Assiniboine runs east-west and allowed the trappers to travel significant distances by water. There weren't roads or any other way to travel easily. And the Red runs north-south. In fact, halfway between Grand Forks and Minneapolis lies the source of both the Red and Mississippi rivers. The Mississippi travels all the way down south and drains into the Gulf of Mexico. In contrast, the Red travels all the way north and drains into Hudson Bay."

"Thank you, professor," Chrystal said and then leaned over to kiss him. She smelled wonderful with a hint of a perfume that lingered on him.

"If you don't care, I don't mind, but I find it interesting at how trade created cities and cultures. The Forks was the point where traders met. At the time, they traded furs but this grew and diversified as more settlers moved in. Trends changed but Winnipeg became the logical location for a lot of the shipping companies moving grain or commodities across the country."

"Fascinating," Chrystal said. She was still glowing. He could have been giving an account of the horrors of the holocaust and she would be flying high as a kite.

"That is interesting," Tammy said. "So what happened to Winnipeg? Until now, I had never heard of it. The way you talk, it should be much larger than it seems now."

"Good question. Economics, politics, and luck. None of this is important for our purposes, but it did give me some inspiration for my plan."

Chrystal leaned in. It allowed her to touch Jack and run her hand along his leg or arm as he talked. She couldn't help herself and Jack liked it. She could tell from his glances and the way the edges of his mouth turned up into a little smile.

"We are going to start trading something?" Tammy asked.

"Actually, yes. And I wanted to see if you two would be interested in running it."

"What is it?" Tammy asked. She was just a bookkeeper and this sounded too much for her.

"We can do it," Chrystal said before Jack said anything. Both Tammy and Jack smiled at that.

"It is both simple and complex. Simple in that we don't try and reinvent the wheel. We enter into the industry that I think is right for us. It's complex because we need to run a shadow operation within the company, effectively siphoning off one or two percent of its annual turnover to fund our revenge on those sons of bitches."

The two women were silent for a while. Tammy spoke first. "This all sounds very technical and beyond our abilities. What you are talking about sounds like a huge industrial concern. What do we know about trading?"

"Tammy, if there is one thing I have learned in life, it is that anyone can do anything if they have the will to do so. We have the will. And recently, I have also found the way."

"But don't we need a lot of money to do whatever this is?" Chrystal was trying to make sense of Jack's speech.

"That's the thing. I just found out that we have enough money to create a monster company. Our next problem is to find an industry to jump into that won't raise eyebrows. Something that needs a lot of capital and makes lots of money but is still opaque enough to siphon off a significant percentage of its cashflow without raising alarms."

"I guess property is out of the question?" Tammy said.

"It's good but not flexible enough for our purposes. We need to have reach and a reason to be crossing borders and dealing with ports and people of all persuasions. We need to be able to pay vendors and contractors all over the world in volumes that don't cause suspicion. We need to be trading something that gives us flexibility in pricing."

"I give up. What is it?" Chrystal said. Her hand was perched on Jack's arm and she was beginning to want him the more she touched him. She knew their discussion was important and life-changing but her body was elsewhere and it was affecting her ability to concentrate.

"I think we should begin trading something so boring that, even if people looked at our company, they would shrug and look elsewhere. Only people in the same industry will realise what we are doing and there is always room for another competitor in any industry."

"OK, Jack. Enough suspense. Tell us." Tammy was getting impatient.

"We start with gravel and sand. We expand into cement and then shipping. The world needs sand, and lots of it, for roads and other construction. Internationally, places like Dubai and China need a certain type of sand. They have a desert but can't use it for their buildings. We can purchase these aggregate companies on the stock market. We don't want to be the biggest, just within the top ten. Big enough to be important but not so big as to be a threat. The big guys will watch us and buy us up when it suits them. We will run the company in such a way as to not make us attractive. That is where the shadow division comes in. We'll also sell topsoil. We have endless amounts of the best topsoil in the world right here. We could transport it to the Arab nations and get top dollar for it. They would be able to create estates like they own in England or the US— green with grass and trees, rooted in the best topsoil, and so expensive, it would be available only to the wealthiest."

Tammy and Chrystal were silent again.

"But this is insanely expensive to do," Chrystal said. "I can't even imagine having this type of money to invest. And I definitely can't imagine running it."

"We have the money." Jack sat back on the chair and took her hand in his. "It's a long story and I can't believe it myself. I thought I had access to a fortune, but not of this magnitude."

"You're a millionaire?" Tammy said. "And you walked across the border illegally? I'm sorry to sound ungrateful and please don't take this the wrong way but you sound like a crazy person."

Jack laughed. "I feel a little crazy right now. But it's true and I'll show you so you don't have to trust me."

"Then why do you need us? Get proper professionals to do this," Chrystal said. She had become scared and intimidated by the scale of the plan. *He doesn't need me*, she thought, sadly.

Jack kissed her hand. "I need people I can trust and I trust you both with my life." It was as though he could read her thoughts at that moment.

"But you barely know us," Tammy said.

"I know you enough. You could have left me at the side of the road but you stopped, even though it was dangerous for you. You could have disappeared into the shadows but decided to come up here instead. I know it's tenuous but sometimes you need to trust your gut." He took a drink of water. "Besides, I'm not giving you the money; I'm just putting you in charge. I still need to figure out the logistics of how to transfer the funds and deal with ownership issues with all of the current regulation on money laundering and so on. It's not a walk in the park but we have the most important elements. We have the money and a good start on the plan. All we need are like-minded people to execute it."

"But this doesn't deal with what we were talking about. I want to feel safe and I won't until those animals are dealt with. For all we know, they have a bounty on Chrys and me and we'll wake up dead one day."

"We will deal with our situations as a test run of the plan. The business is only to create a sustainable source of money so we can pull it off. If we simply spend the money we have, it will eventually all be gone and that's it. I envision a plan that encompasses political lobbying as well as bounties on these bastards' heads. Having a fully operational industry gives us the tools to fund congressmen and women, senators in the States, and provincial and federal politicians in Canada. We need to change laws as well as kick those assholes back into the shadows."

"It sounds too good to be true. If life has taught me anything, it is to beware of things that are too good to be true. But we've come this far. Let's give it a try." Tammy's body language was one of disappointment rather than the excitement Jack had hoped for.

"I'm with you, Jack," Chrystal said. "Whatever you want to do, count me in."

"Thanks, but I need you to see it the way I do. If I can't, then there is no chance for this to succeed." He took another drink of water. "I'll show you the bank accounts and you can see it for yourselves. That is the major hurdle, I think. Once we can establish that the money is there, then it is down to how we invest it without going to jail or appearing on some authority's radar."

"OK, Jack," Tammy continued. "I believe you about the money. I still want to see it, but let's assume we have it. How do you invest it without setting off those bells?"

"This's the problem. But I think we can achieve it by creating a handful of hedge funds in international centres and tax havens. I don't want any single fund to have more than a billion dollars."

"There's more than a billion dollars?" Tammy was forgetting her doubt and was shaking her head.

"Yeah, that's why this is so fascinating. We have the power of funds that operate at the highest levels. Our problem is putting them into play. I believe we need to create a bank or buy one so that we can funnel the funds from where they are to our own control. From there, the funds are distributed among the investment fund companies we also create. Those companies then buy the shares of the companies we want to own. Ideally, we don't need to take companies private, but there may be times where we need to buy all of the shares. It would be better to only buy 51% with our fund companies, owning no more than three to five percent each. The lies will be on disclosure. We don't want anyone knowing that we own 51%, if possible. But even that is not the end of the world. What we mustn't do is have anyone find out that we—or I—own any of the company."

"Why?"

"Because that becomes our weakness. I'm still trying to find a way around this. Perhaps I won't own it and we simply create a foundation with a purpose that we determine. It then owns the company and can invest its dividends however it decides. We, naturally, then own and control the foundation. While it is called a foundation, there are jurisdictions in the world that allow you to own what otherwise would be a charity in the US or Canada. We need to be judicious with our disclosure."

"And where do we come in?"

"You will be appointed to head up the board. You'll be instructed and have lawyers and accountants to advise you. The less you say, the more others will think you know."

"Sounds scary but exciting," Chrystal was almost purring. "And all I wanted was to become a model."

They laughed and agreed to adjourn the discussions until after they had all digested the information. Tammy and Chrystal walked away feeling lightheaded, each for a slightly different reason. Jack returned to his room to find Chrystal waiting for him.

Chapter Thirteen

Sylvia

Jack was pleased to have a chance to revisit his safety deposit box. Chrystal and Tammy were on board and he was still trying to get his head around his budding romance with Chrystal. As he felt the smoothed grey edges of the metal box separate beneath his fingers, all of his concentration focused on it.

He opened a Moleskine notebook, which was set upon the top of the box's papers. In it was a set of instructions to Jack from Joe and the account numbers of the CIA slush fund. It also held important information that would form the seeds of his revenge. He leafed through it until he came to the place he was looking for.

"If you find yourself in need of someone artistic and capable of producing quality paperwork, I cannot recommend anyone higher than Sylvia Öst. She is an expert on passports and other dull things. But her counterfeiting skills are much more impressive. She

understands paper quality and can source anything you need. She is also fully comfortable with all polymer and hieroglyphics employed by government agencies to discourage counterfeits."

Jack didn't need money counterfeited, but he did require a birth certificate of sorts for the CIA funds—without it, the money was useless to him. He also didn't need a fake passport. He had left a Canadian and German passport with Isabella before he went to Europe the previous year. He had them made by Zed Mallic, another suggested contact from Joe. Zed had given Jack the key to the safety deposit box. Another contact, Brad Doerksen, had given Jack its location. None of them were as trusted by Joe as Isabella, which is why Jack trusted her the most. It was also why she was the person he needed advice from more than anyone.

∞

"I don't need to know the details," she said. "I trusted Joe and he trusted you. That's good enough for me." Isabella was tired after dealing with her school and the politics of poverty. Despite her brilliance, she couldn't understand why the government didn't do more to help the least fortunate in a more sustainable way. It caused her to short circuit and Jack was seeing the result.

"I'm not asking you to do anything by acting or not acting," Jack said. He was walking a fine line. Isabella was a committed pacifist but he knew she would sell her soul to make her kids safe. "I'm just asking for some advice."

She had poured herself a glass of red wine and her husband Cato was preparing dinner. He also worked to help make the school a success but was gifted in other ways—namely a mind like a computer and an oratory skill to rival his namesake. He worked for a massive financial company and ensured that Isabella could follow her dreams—he was able to subsidise their lives until her school was self-sustaining, which took longer than either of them anticipated.

"What can I say that you don't already know? From my experience, people ask for advice when what they really want is validation for what they have already decided." She tilted her head back to let the red liquid flow across her lips and into her mouth. "Hmmm. I needed that."

"I used the key," Jack began, "and it has presented me with an opportunity to help right some wrongs. I think it will help kids like the ones in your schools."

"Amen to that," she said. "So what's the problem?"

"I need to do something drastic, something big. Something so big it scares me."

"Fear can be good."

"To achieve this, the plan requires me to trust a person Joe named to help in circumstances like this."

"Who is he?"

"A she. Sylvia Öst."

Isabella's eyes narrowed. "I know of her. Are you planning to steal and replace the Mona Lisa? If so, I heard the one at the Louvre is already a fake."

"Nothing like that. I just need to have some papers found."

"Found? Are they lost or imaginary?"

"There's a lot of money involved. When Joe set this up, our current anti-money laundering legislation was only a glimmer in some bureaucrat's eye. Now, without proof of your source of funds, no bank or solicitor or respectable organisation will touch you. I need to deal only with top-drawer firms to achieve my objectives."

"So you need to 'find' the documents Joe misplaced?" She arched an eye and her head tilted slightly.

"Something like that. I just need to know if this Sylvia can be trusted."

"As far as I know, she's trustworthy. And Joe trusted her."

And Joe killed my parents, Jack said to himself. "Then I guess she's my best bet," he said aloud.

"That's it?" Isabella sounded disappointed. Joe was a shady character but they helped each other—usually opening doors at the CIA and Immigration Customs and Excise. That was always done to aid her kids. She knew that a brown- or black-faced immigrant born in Mexico or Eritrea didn't stand a chance in Canada or the United States unless people like her gave them a hand up in life.

"That's it," Jack said as though he was done. He paused. "If I wanted to compile a list of every pimp in North America, how would I go about it?"

"What?" She sat on the edge of her sofa. "What do you want with scum like that?"

"I'm trying to make the world a better place."

"Be careful, Jack. These guys don't play by the rules. The law doesn't seem to stick to them and there is always another person waiting in the wings to replace whoever is arrested."

"Possibly," Jack said, "but I need to try. The world's oldest profession is not prostitution, it's slavery. In both cases, there is the slave-driver."

"Nicely said, Jack, but to do this properly, you need to change the law. You need to go after the demand and the supply will dwindle. You need to attack those who take part in the services that the pimps are selling."

"Like France and other European countries," Jack said. "I agree. Fines of $5,000-10,000 instead of a slap on the wrist is a good thing. I would argue to make the fine as much as a month's income for the perpetrator."

"And the sex workers?" she asked. "What about them?"

"I view them as victims in this equation. I appreciate there are some who are there by choice. Not everyone in the sex trade is being abused or wants to get out, but those who are need help. Prostitution is not going away. I'm not living in a fantasy land. But we can make it difficult for others to take advantage of the sex workers by protecting them from pimps and attacking their clients."

Isabella was silent again. "Why the sudden interest? You've never talked about this before. Our last conversation was about a global conspiracy and international arms sales. You were going on and on about how countries should not be allowed to export guns or military materiel. Since you arrived, I haven't heard one word on this." A thought crossed her mind. "Wait, you weren't involved in any way with the events of last year?"

"Let's just say I've expanded my horizons," Jack said. "I'm not sure if either are solvable, but I can't just sit back and do nothing."

Isabella lifted her glass in salute. "That's exactly how I feel."

∞

Sylvia Öst lived in Montreal. She didn't speak a word of French but loved the city and the people. Originally of Swedish-Germanic descent, her family escaped the holocaust to settle in New York in 1937. She was born there and was classically trained in the humanities, and was fluent in Greek and Latin. Her parents spoke German at home and her nursemaid spoke Spanish. She was five when her parents noticed her proclivity for drawing and art. Tutors were brought in to educate her in the finer techniques of both eastern and western art, focussing on the method of mixing and applying paints on canvass. Sylvia found herself imitating anything that interested her, from paintings in museums to signatures on cheques. She grew up in a highly privileged environment but still enjoyed being able to see beyond the pieces of paper used as currency, whether as academic degrees or money.

"Why should it matter what university I go to?" Sylvia said. "It's just a piece of paper. I am the talent and it shouldn't matter what someone else says."

Her mother tried to calm herself and spread her hands on her knees. "You know perfectly well that a degree from Harvard is treated differently than a degree from a local state school. You are old enough to know the facts of life. You can be the smartest person in the room, but if you don't have the papers from a trusted organisation, you will never have any authority behind your statements."

Sylvia was good at her studies and did go to the suggested universities, but she developed an increasing cynicism toward authority. She was born during the hippie era, but neither of her parents were hippies. She grew up in the seventies to disco and long hair and Nixon's Watergate tapes. Vietnam was a bad dream and America was being held hostage by its addiction to oil, leading to huge inflation and social unrest. It wasn't until she was in her early twenties that she began to dabble in currency counterfeiting. It was more of a hobby and it was during this time that she met Joe. She was recruited as a CIA asset but her identity was protected by Joe. He, in turn, utilised her talents and she was able to do things she otherwise wouldn't have dreamed of. Corporate paperwork such as bonds and share certificates, signatures of generals and presidents on bank stationery and anything else that was required gave her an insight to the fragile nature of the global currencies and society's trust in its institutions.

Jack met her at the Ritz-Carlton and saw her before she saw him. She was sitting in a high-ceiling reception area on a sofa. The ceiling was painted with tropical palms and birds. "Chrystal, do you want to check us in and I'll meet you later? I want to meet Sylvia alone first."

"Sure," Chrystal said. Jack handed his passport to her and gave a nod to Tammy. The three of them decided to travel together, since they didn't know where events would lead them and didn't want to use the telephone or emails for communicating.

Jack had worn a sports jacket for the trip and found himself inhaling and buttoning it as he walked past the grand foyer into the palm room where Sylvia was seated. She was dressed all in white, with high heels and her hair tied up. Jack was expecting to see a ridiculous sixty-something sitting all in white—like a laboratory student in university. Instead, he saw a tall, striking woman with the confident lines of tailored clothing. She would have had blue-black hair when she was young. It still looked healthy but age was starting to show. It made her look distinguished instead of old and she didn't try to hide the inevitable aging process. *Wow*, Jack thought. *I didn't think they made people like her anymore.*

"Hello, Ms. Öst. I'm Jack." Jack extended his hand and they shook. She didn't get up. He sat down in the curved upholstered chair across from her.

"Hello, Jack. It's a pleasure to finally meet you."

That threw him. "You know me?"

"Know of you. Joe let me in on his little secret. He was so proud of you and he didn't have anyone he trusted to talk to. I'm sorry to hear about your parents."

Jack wasn't expecting this either. A rage exploded inside him and it took everything for him to calm himself. "You knew my parents?"

"No. I never had the pleasure of meeting them. Again, Joe only had good things to say about them."

"Then you know how they died?" Jack said.

It was Sylvia's time to be silent, her confidence slightly wilted. "Yes," she said slowly. "And I can't imagine how you must feel."

"Thank you for that," Jack said. "But the past is the past. I understood that Joe trusted you but I didn't have any idea he trusted you so intimately."

"Yes." Her smile and confidence returned. "Joe was a lovely man." She had a faraway look in her eye as she remembered some unshared memory.

"So I will trust you," Jack said. "I have a difficult problem to solve and I understand that you are the best person for the job."

"Let's wait before we talk details," Sylvia said. She looked to her left and right. "It is impossible to know who's watching."

Jack nodded. "What do you propose?"

"I have booked a room for tonight and will be taking a swim shortly. Meet me there in forty-five minutes." With that, she got up and walked away.

I guess I'll see you then, Jack said to himself, bemused. *Not sure if she's a prima donna or just paranoid.* He got up and headed to his room on the fifth floor.

∞

"Hello, Jack." Sylvia was already in the salt pool, located on the top floor of the hotel. She was wearing a white bikini and her arms were stretched outwards, reclining against the side of the pool. Her body was floating just below the surface. Her eyes were fixed on Jack and he refused to let his eyes leave hers. He took off his robe and left it on the curved spa chair and waded into the pool.

"This is a bit dramatic, isn't it?"

"I'm sure you have learned to be careful. Otherwise, you wouldn't be alive." She was looking at him curiously.

"I try to be careful. This is the most reckless thing I've done for quite some time."

"Come next to me. I don't want to shout."

Jack went over, taking in her body and the white fabric that covered her in the most minimal manner. "I'm here to talk seriously, Sylvia."

"Of course. What is it you need me to do for you?" As she spoke, she brought her arms from behind her and allowed her body to float downwards. She moved closer to Jack so that they were barely a foot apart. For his part, Jack began to feel uncomfortable with her lack of boundaries but held his ground. She said the words, but the double entendre was as subtle as a sledgehammer.

"I need you to give birth for me," Jack said. He used these words deliberately. *Two can play at this game*.

"Oh? I'll do my best for you, but I must warn you that my child-bearing days have long past." Her left hand was underwater and drifted into Jack. As he didn't move away, she allowed herself to accidently keep it on him. Her right arm rose to touch his face.

"Sylvia, I mean it. I'm here with my girlfriend. I need you to do some professional work for me." Jack was beginning to feel butterflies in his belly as he stood so close to her. Her left hand had begun to search and if he didn't stop this now, he would regret it.

"Oh," she said, pulling her right hand away. "Honest mistake. I was hoping to mix a little business with pleasure." She smiled as innocently and Jack could see that this act had worked for her numerous times in the past. Her left hand had stopped its searching but had not been withdrawn.

"I need some corporate paperwork done. It needs to be accurate to the highest degree. It needs to be in paper and electronic format, and it needs to check out."

"That's all?" Sylvia was still flirting, but it was dialled back a lot. She finally withdrew her left hand and returned to her reclined position along the pool's edge. The effect was to push out her chest and allow her whole body to float near the surface.

Jack didn't understand her behaviour but decided to press on with his conversation. *I hope Joe knew what he was doing recommending her to me*, he thought. He acted casually and adopted the same position against the wall, each of them floating just below the water's surface.

"I have a problem," Jack started.

Sylvia looked him up and down. "Not from where I'm looking." She gave him her innocent look again.

"Thanks, but I need to know if you can help me."

"Sweetheart, I have forgotten more than most people will learn in their lifetime."

Humble, too. "OK, but I need something and it's quite serious."

Sylvia brought in her arms and looked at Jack. "Every job is serious. Each one could be your last, or mine. Just tell me what you need and I'll tell you what you need to do."

Jack involuntarily scanned the spa area and, satisfied they were alone, began. "Joe has put me in a tough position. He has left me with access to a large amount of money."

"Congratulations."

"Yes, but I can't access it without setting off a lot of alarm bells."

"What do you want to do with it?"

"Create a structure that will be both flexible and transparent, operating in plain view while allowing me to carry out my objectives."

"Like bombing planes?"

Jack stopped cold.

"You see, Jack, there are no secrets. When I heard that Tim was involved, I knew something fishy was behind the June bombings. When you told me on the phone you had just returned from Europe last year and Joe had put you in touch with me from the grave, I put it together. I didn't know for sure until just now when I saw your face."

Jack remained silent.

"Not that I'm bothered. I find your actions both deplorable and exciting. At least you still have passion and believe you can change the world." She was touching his face again. "Frankly, I find it irresistible." Without warning, she grabbed the back of his head and put her lips on his, hard. Jack's lips responded but he was losing control.

"Sylvia," Jack pushed himself away from her. "Maybe in different circumstances, but I am really here to solve a problem—not create one."

"What's wrong, Jack? I can see your eyes feasting on me. I've already undressed you downstairs and here in my mind. We both want this. Why fight it?"

Jack untangled himself from her and went to the pool's ladder. He climbed out and put on his robe. As he looked back, he saw a different Sylvia. She was serious and her face was hard.

"Well done, Jack. You passed. I'll help you."

Jack's mouth dropped a bit. "Wha--?"

"I flirted, then threatened, then threw myself at you. Nothing dented your resolve. Oh, and sorry about the comment about Tim. I've worked with him and he was a great guy."

Jack felt like he was twenty-one again and had just learned that his parents were spies. The ground began to shift and his confidence turned inside out. This woman knew about him, his most terrible secrets and, most distressing, all about Joe. *Even I don't know everything about Joe.*

"Don't be surprised. It's a small world we operate in. Only a handful of people could have funded and orchestrated the June atrocities. Tim was one and his connection to Joe was too strong to ignore the coincidence of you now coming into my life."

"I'm sorry if I don't share your logic," Jack said. "I'm not admitting to anything other than needing your help."

Sylvia climbed out of the pool. Her long legs were athletic. She put on her robe.

"Look, we don't need to like each other, but I am the best there is, and I can keep my mouth shut." Her face was set and Jack got a glimpse into the beast that resided within her. "But I do like you, Jack, and I respect your actions—however mad they may at first seem. In fact, your logic isn't that different from the CIA's or FSB's counter-intelligence units."

Again, Jack was lost for words. "Thanks, uh, I guess."

"Now, tell me what you need and I'll get it done for you. By the time we're finished, you won't recognise your new self."

Chapter Fourteen

THE BEGINNING

"Thank you, Mr. Devellier. You have truly made this a painless process." Chrystal and Tammy rose and Luc Devellier followed.

"The pleasure has been all mine, Mesdames Alberts. We should have all of the accounts opened within two weeks."

"Why so long?" Tammy asked.

"Nothing to be concerned about, just the normal banking procedures. We need to comply with the anti-money-laundering legislation and do a criminal search on you but I don't see this being a problem. Unfortunately, accounts this size need board approval and they only sit once every two weeks."

"It's not a problem. We're more concerned that our capital investment is safe," Tammy said. "And we only want to work with the most reputable firms. Your firm came highly recommended."

"Thank you. You will find us easy to speak to and easier to work with. We may look small, being in Guernsey, but our parent bank is the third largest in the world. Your money is safe with us."

"I want to clarify one thing," Chrystal said. "You manage this money for us but we can still direct where you invest if we want to?"

"Certainly," Devellier said. "You can be as active or as passive as you want."

"And your fees?"

"Our fees are negotiable at this level. We generally take a percentage of monies under management but, as we discussed, we will simply charge a fixed fee of £1.35m per year."

"And confidentiality?"

"Subject to statutory filings, no one will know. You will, naturally, be responsible for your taxes if you decide to remit any profits into your country of residence. If, however, the profits are rolled back into the fund, we can minimise your taxes to nearly zero. We have a team dedicated to this. Your advisors can liaise with them at any time to ensure that we are complying with your tax planning."

"And everything we discussed is in your bank's proposal papers? I'd like to review this before we press the final button."

"Of course," Devellier said. "If at any time you need to review our relationship, we will fly to you and discuss it. Nothing is set in stone."

"You make it hard to say no." Tammy was smiling, hand extended.

"I look forward to seeing you both again soon," Devellier said. He opened the door to the boardroom and walked them to the elevator.

∞

"Like giving candy to a baby," Chrystal said as she popped another piece of steak in her mouth. "Went just as you said."

They were enjoying a meal with Jack before their flight off the small island in the Channel Islands. Guernsey was known internationally as a tax haven and its financial services sector was the largest employer on the island.

"This is just one private bank of a dozen in a dozen different jurisdictions we need to visit in person," Jack said.

"Yeah, a real hardship," Chrystal took a sip of her wine. "By the way, this is a great red."

"2001, Medoc near Bordeaux." Tammy was reading from the wine list. "Did you know that there were more vintage years declared between 2000 and 2010 than from any other decade in the last 150 years?"

"Are you reading that from the wine menu as well?" Chrystal asked.

"Yes, and there's a lot more here."

"Enough about the wine," Jack said. "It's great, and over twenty-five years old."

"Party-pooper," Chrystal said with a slight pout.

"We have a lot of work to do. Sylvia has come through trumps and, so far, we haven't had any queries about why you have access to so much money."

"Why should they?" Tammy asked.

"Why not? We need to be careful and assume someone is watching us at all times, even if only to make a pitch for some business idea." Jack lowered his voice. "A woman of great wealth can comment on how lovely the wine is, but try not to drool. You can afford the best and most expensive things the world can offer. You need to learn to be a bit more arrogant and circumspect."

Tammy and Chrystal nodded. "We know, but it's still very exciting."

"For me, too," Jack said. "But the stakes are high and we only have one chance at this. Our first objective is to get all of Joe's funds into play. Once we have control, we can begin to implement the next phase."

Chrystal raised her glass. "Next stop, Monaco."

"Then Andorra, Geneva, Liechtenstein, and Hong Kong," said Tammy.

"And then the rest," said Jack.

They drank, ate, and enjoyed their first victory. It was the first battle in what Jack felt would be a war before everything was over.

∞

Despite his initial doubts about Sylvia, she had been totally professional in her behaviour after that day in the pool. They pondered how they were going to make their plan work. "Victory may seem easy if you have money and all you want to do is open an account," She said. "But this is the single greatest hurdle most money launderers face. The second is actually transferring the funds into the account. When you transfer $10,000 or even $100,000, there are questions that need to be answered about your source of funds. But when you transfer $100 million or more, you need to ensure that your story is bulletproof."

This Sylvia provided and, while Jack held his breath at each step, the story was accepted and the documents were confirmed. He replayed their conversation and wondered at both the simplicity and complexity involved.

"We need to create a story that no one can check out," she said as she began searching through files on her computer. "It needs to be something that, when mentioned, piques their interest and then is satisfied almost immediately."

"How is that possible?" Jack said. They left Montreal the day after the pool incident and met in New York City, where Sylvia did her magic. Tammy and Chrystal decided to stay in Montreal for a few more days before re-joining Jack.

"When you meet someone new, you begin to talk and allocate him or her into their socio-economic pigeon-hole," Sylvia began. "It may not be politically correct to say this, but you first look at their clothes, hair, and personal hygiene. Then you notice the way their body moves—is it graceful, harsh, determined, or awkward? You decide whether the person is a player in their field or just a wallflower. You try to see whether they have power and whether they exercise it by the way other people defer to them or the way they speak on the phone. Their voice also betrays levels of confidence, fear, or indifference. One of the fastest routes to prejudice is asking what they do for a living or, if that is not appropriate, finding out how they made their money." Sylvia was talking while looking at her computer screens. She had five screens connected to her keyboard as she searched internet sites and her own records while making notes on how she was to create Jack's new identity.

"That seems backward," Jack said. "I would agree that we are all prejudiced to a certain degree. We can't help prejudging people by what they wear or how they act, but this is different. I need a story to overcome banking legislation. They don't care about how I look."

Sylvia stopped typing for a second and turned to him. After a second longer than was comfortable for him, she returned her attention to the screens. "If you hear that a person is a solicitor or doctor, you smile and say 'nice to meet you' or, if you're keen, you may ask what they specialise in. If you hear that the person is a successful entrepreneur who has recently sold his business for a billion dollars to Google or GE, you smile and try to sound congratulatory. But, deep down, the conversation about money is over. You have ticked the box in your head that says they have more money than they will need for the rest of their lives. Money ceases to be an issue in your mind. If you continue the conversation, it may be about art or politics."

Jack was listening politely. "This may be true. You're the expert, so I'll wait to hear what you think the solution to my problem is."

"Your problem is the quantity of money involved as well as the fact that you are receiving this windfall due to no effort on your part. Governments will be suspicious and bankers need to be reassured."

"Exactly."

"I think I have an idea," Sylvia said. She pushed back from her screens and swivelled to face him. "You were doing ancestral research to learn more about your family and where they came from. You know that your grandparents came from Germany to escape the holocaust. They arrived in New York penniless in 1937 and eked out a living doing menial work for the rest of their lives. Your parents moved west in the hope of finding something better. This is how you found yourself in the middle of nowhere, USA. As luck would have it, recent legislation governing banks require them to ascertain the ultimate beneficial owners of all of their formerly secret numbered accounts. Most banks have already been subject to this for ten years ,but the Swiss and Liechtenstein banks where your accounts are held have not been."

Jack looked admiringly at Sylvia. This stuff was pure nonsense and he loved it. He felt like he was in kindergarten sitting on a carpet being read a story by his teacher. "Is this true?"

"Everything I say is true because I can verify it," Sylvia said. "Because of the amounts involved, the banks hired a firm to find the descendants of the ultimate beneficial owner listed on their books. Again, as luck would have it, you are the sole beneficiary of these accounts."

"Sounds like a fairy tale," Jack said. "No one will believe it."

"Quiet. I'm not done yet," Sylvia said. "When they reach you, you discover that you are not Jewish and that your great-great grandfather was a successful German industrialist in the late 1880s who had the foresight to hide some of his assets from the authorities. He opened a number of accounts in Switzerland with numbers but no names. Despite their reassurances to the contrary, the Swiss maintained the name of the person who opened the account, which allowed them to trace it to you."

"Then why say I was Jewish at all?" Jack said.

"Because we need some way to kill off all your relatives and reduce your family tree to just one branch—

your grandparents with their one son who had one son: you."

"That's a bit unbelievable," Jack said.

"How? Your great-great grandfather, let's call him Meyer Hildebrandt, benefitted from Bismarck's bringing together of Germany. He was an arms manufacturer as well as a railway magnate, both creating the steel for the railway tracks as well as being the silent partner in many railway enterprises. This is why his name is not well known. In the early 1880s, he deposited fifty million Deutschmarks into accounts in Liechtenstein and Switzerland. This is the equivalent to two million British pounds sterling at the time, or ten million United States dollars."

"That sounds like an insane amount of money," Jack said. "How could he just make that much disappear?"

"This was before modern taxation and people's money was theirs to do with as they pleased. Meyer made this money in a dubious fashion and had much more on the books within his business. He wanted to ensure that the family was always wealthy. While his fears of social disintegration within Germany failed to materialise during his lifetime—he died in 1913 before World War One—the monies he set aside were to silently work, growing above inflation and not subject to the devaluation of the mark after WWI."

"Why? How would he have known to diversify out of the mark when he deposited it?" Jack said.

"Because everything was on the gold standard. There was no reason to invest in marks. The marks were converted to dollars or sterling or into gold itself by the Swiss and Liechtenstein banks. They are good at what they do and their primary concern was to retain the capital value of the money deposited. Most likely, some of the currency would have been converted to Swiss Francs. Some would have been used to purchase actual gold—let's say 100 kilograms, which was deposited one-third in Geneva, one-third in London, and one-third in New York. Most of the monies would have been invested in blue-chip companies via the stock markets in the US and England, as continental Europe had become unsafe for quite a few decades. The remaining monies would have been kept in currency accounts and kept liquid."

"Does it need to be so complicated?"

"Yes and no," Sylvia said. "You never talk about this, but I will prepare the paperwork to set out this story and ensure it is filed in all of the right places. This means that any pain-in-the-ass taxman can dig and chase and will find this story. Being Jewish, you lost all of your relatives in the furnaces of Dachau and Auschwitz."

"But you said I wasn't Jewish."

"Yes, and this ties into what Meyer was concerned about. He had enemies within Germany and the Nazis were persuaded to pressure his descendants. As they were no longer industrialists and were simply living off

Meyer's inherited wealth, the Nazis didn't find any use for them. Their assets were confiscated and they were labelled as Jews. It's much easier to kill enemies if they are labelled as such. It meant there was no legal process available and no one asked questions."

"Again, overly complicated."

"Again, yes and no. When those who dig into your past realise that your family was subjected to the horrors of the holocaust, they will stop digging. It is one of the no-go areas and you will gain moral high ground. You are a survivor and the monies you inherit will be treated as a sacred trust."

"And my need for secrecy will be understood," Jack added.

"Exactly. We need to provide a reason for the extreme secrecy. You don't want to meet bankers or investment fund managers, so you lend via your proxies—Tammy and Chrystal. We need to create a suitable pedigree for them, too. Good suits and manners will not be enough. They will have graduated from Harvard and done a stint at the London School of Economics before spending four years in Moscow dealing in commodity trading with a focus on Sino-Soviet relations."

"But they don't speak Russian or Chinese," Jack said.

"Don't worry about it. They speak English and are good-looking white women. In the sweepstakes of genetic lottery, they have hit the jackpot. You wouldn't be able to do this if they were Nigerian or Indian. This is another prejudice that will not be overcome soon."

Jack didn't say anything. She might be right.

"They just need to develop a little bit of arrogance and only speak English. They should learn some Russian and Chinese words like where the toilet is and how to toast a drink. Everyone drinks and some words need to be learned for that or they won't be believed."

"Sounds easy enough. What about me?"

"Your name is Meyer Hildebrandt, after your great-great grandfather. You never developed the affectation of calling yourself Meyer Hildebrandt the Fourth because you were, until now, relatively poor. You are a highly secretive and reclusive person who renounced your American citizenship when you were going through a phase in your early twenties. The Americans weren't prepared to do this unless you had another citizenship in place. You were able to get a German passport as a result of your heritage and you currently live in Monaco. This is important or else you would find yourself dealing with tax claims on your inherited windfall."

"Where do I live in Monaco? Surely, there will be press and other agencies wanting to check me out? Why would I be living in Monaco before I inherited? I thought you said I was poor."

Sylvia ignored him. "I have arranged for your address to be at an old CIA safe house. I can back date your existence there, including utility bills and bank statements. You won't actually live there, but neither will anyone else, and the CIA will be using it for their own purposes. They are not in the business of advertising their safe locations."

"And you can recreate all of this? All the documents, filings, and so on?"

Sylvia feigned hurt. "How can you ask that, Jack? Everything will be perfect. Even the imperfections will be perfect. One thing when doing this, we need to remember that people are human and they err. If everything is too neat, too perfect, it also becomes suspicious. We need to create a record that looks like it has just survived the ravages of time and war and distance. This is what I do." Sylvia brightened. "In fact, I am relishing the opportunity to do this. It is a masterpiece. It draws on a lifetime of talents I have nurtured and developed. Don't get me wrong, I'll be charging for this and I'll let you know where and how when I'm done, but you will become Meyer Hildebrandt."

"Sylvia, I don't know how to thank you."

"Just pay the bill promptly when the time comes." She smiled and returned her focus to her screens.

∞

"I want to raise a toast to the three of us," Jack said. "It has been six months since our first account opening and we have now dispersed the entire $7.2 billion into twelve different jurisdictions."

"Cheers," Tammy and Chrystal said in unison. They had rented a boat off the coast of Bahamas and were imperceptibly bobbing while enjoying champagne with their lunch. They had bought a selection of seafood from the restaurant next to the fishmonger. On a large platter sat a feast of oysters in the shell on ice, cooked prawns, langoustines, crab, and some pickled fish they couldn't identify.

Jack had gained back the lost weight and was looking muscular and comfortable. Tammy had met a number of suitors and was enjoying the life of the rich and famous, while staying conscious of keeping a relatively low profile. Money was rarely discussed and others judged her by her clothes and ability to be at the venues she attended—from political functions at $10,000 a plate to the private lounges at airports reserved for super VIP passengers. Chrystal was transformed into an international advisor to the super rich and managing director of a family office based in Montreux, Switzerland. She wore suits more often than bikinis these days, but still sported the ultra-high heels. And she still found Jack gorgeous.

"You seem to have come up with quite the structure, Mr. Hildebrandt," Chrystal said to Jack. She was snuggled next to him and her arm was linked with his. She was in a bikini and wrapped in a delicate sarong. Her skin had developed into a bronze that made her blue eyes stand out even more, but it was her smile that kept Jack hypnotised.

"I think we have all done well to make this happen," Jack said. "I think we should create a sub-fund by taking 10% from the account and let Isabella run it as a charitable investment house." He looked at both of them in anticipation.

"It's your call," Tammy said.

"I want to pay back something to that pastor who stopped for me when no one else would, and to Isabella, who has been an inspiration to me and so many others." Jack paused, as he was becoming emotional. "Otherwise, what are we doing?"

"Which comes to something I wanted to ask," Tammy said. "You have done so much to make this happen. Are you sure you want to go through with the rest of it? Chrys and I have been through a lot. So have you. But maybe we should just let sleeping dogs lie. We're comfortable and there's no reason to put ourselves at risk."

"I know what you're saying," Jack said, "but I need to do this. Besides, the fun is just beginning. We still need to buy ourselves the cash flow to make our plans happen."

"How do you want to do that?" Chrystal asked, becoming more serious. Her hand moved to Jack's leg, absent-mindedly fiddling with the seam of his shorts.

"We have a lot of cash available to us. I have been analysing a number of companies that would be suitable for us. Ones that are boring and invisible to most people and all connected to sand, cement, construction, and transport. We will need advisors, but we can buy control of these companies with the support of our investment funds. Due to Sylvia's work and the way we structured the investments, we don't need to report their connection to our main investment vehicle. We are looking at public companies, so all we need to do is buy up their stock. We can get about fifty percent of the purchase price from the banks. We can get an additional ten to thirty percent from the investment banks and pension funds. The most expensive money is the top ten to twenty percent of equity. This is where we invest our money. From the outside, it is a highly leveraged purchase. Internally, we just need to worry about controlling fifty-one percent of whatever we get."

"And you want me to operate the twelve funds through my family office?" Chrystal said.

"No. You will be heading up the bid through the family office. The funds will invest as though they are strangers and Tam will deal with that. You need to deal with the advisors and ensure that we don't get tangled in the legislation surrounding takeover bids."

"Unless we can do a friendly bid," Tammy said.

"Yes, that's the best," Jack said. "But we need to plan for the worst and hope for the best."

"Sounds like we've come a long way from fashion shoots and porn," Tammy said, shivering involuntarily as the images flooded back to her.

"But that's exactly where we are heading," Jack said. "You know my story and I know what you have told me of yours. Whenever you become too comfortable, remember the fear and hatred and desperation of those times. I want to prevent that happening to others. This money and these takeovers are just a means to an end. Our objective is to hammer those sonsofbitches so hard, they retreat back into the shadows. It is time the good people of the world start fighting back against the bullies who ruin our lives."

"Yeah," said Chrystal, "Fuck freedom of speech."

Jack paused long enough to receive a kiss from Chrystal. It turned into a long one and Tammy tried another oyster while waiting. "I think we should eat these before they get warm," she said to herself as much as the other two.

"Agreed," Chrystal said as her eyes ate up Jack before turning to the food.

"We can talk about this later. I'll give Chrys the details on the companies I have in mind. We can decide on whether this is sane or if you have an alternative suggestion. Just remember that we are looking for a strong cash flow from the business to have the freedom to take one or two percent of the gross to redirect to our purposes."

"This means actually running the companies," Tammy said. She used the back of her hand to catch some liquid that squirted from her mouth as she spoke.

"Yes. And I'm looking to you to do this, Tam."

"Why me?"

"Why not?"

"Why not you?"

"Because I need to implement the actual plan to deal with those sonsofbitches and it will take time and full concentration. Besides, these companies virtually run themselves. You aren't firing the brains. You are just representing the shareholders' interests as chair of the board. It will be up to you to find the right people to be CEO and CFO to funnel the monies out of the company."

"We could do that simply by investing poorly," Tammy said. "It would be a drain on the company but we can sell it as a long-term investment in other projects. Since we control the board, it should be doable."

"That's why you are in charge," Jack said, smiling.

"Yay, Mom!" Chrystal joined in. She was still Tammy's biggest fan and was hoping she would find someone as good as Jack in her life.

Tammy didn't say anything but reached for the langoustines and smiled demurely.

∞

The trio, with the help of the twelve funds, purchased three cement companies located in China, India, and the US. They then focussed on mining sand for fracking as well as construction. With the sand mines, they found they also ended up with gravel and other non-sexy investments, which were the meat and potatoes of the construction industry. The acquisition of public companies was only part of the strategy. They had the cash to augment the existing cash flows and purchase the mines that would make the companies even stronger. It would be three years before they purchased their first ocean-faring ship, but the strategy was mapped and all Tammy needed to do was follow it. Jack and Chrystal saw less and less of her as she remained firmly in the legitimate world of industry while Jack pulled Chrystal into his world of revenge.

"But I need to see you and feel you," Chrystal said. "If you disappear for three or six months at a time, I don't know if I'll be able to cope."

"You'll be fine," Jack said. "I need you to stay on the right side of the law. You are the safe pair of hands holding our investments. Your mom is running the business. You can't get involved in what I am about to do."

Chrystal didn't agree with this logic at all. She had also felt those dirty hands grope her, filling her with their slime, hitting her with their ignorance. She wanted revenge. "And you can't tell me to stop loving you."

Jack's eyes closed for a second too long as he exhaled. "But this is dangerous, and you'd be jeopardising everything we worked for up until now."

"I only did those things for you, Jack. I don't care about the money. I just want to be next to you. If you leave, I'm afraid I'll never see you again."

"You can't get rid of me that easily," Jack said as he pulled her next to him from the waist. He loved the way she felt next to him, her scent and perfume mixing in a heady concoction that stopped him thinking clearly. He kissed her and held on to her with one arm. "And I love you, too."

"My life isn't worth living without you."

"That's not true. You are spectacular and are more capable than any person I've ever met."

"Blah blah blah," Chrystal said. "This sounds like you buttering me up to make me let you go. I'm not having it. I'm coming with you." She glared at him.

Jack pursed his lips in defeat. "Then let's figure out what we're doing and how we're going to do it. Tammy will redirect cash from the operations. You'll need to receive it in a jurisdiction that doesn't ask too many questions and that's not part of the global sharing of bank account details."

"I suggest Panama. The government is pliable and we'd be among thousands of other companies that use it as a base," Chrystal said.

"Then let's start looking into it. If it checks out, let's get something set up over there and that will become our base of operations for what we need to do next."

Chrystal's body began to shudder with excitement. "So I'm doing this with you?"

"We're doing this together," Jack said. "Just don't complain about the heat or the stench or the people we're dealing with. I want to have these pimps and assholes killed. We aren't dealing with sensitive types."

Chrystal didn't care. "I'm in!" She jumped on top of Jack and wrapped her legs around his waist. They fell over and remained tangled as she kissed him passionately until all discussions ceased.

Chapter Fifteen

A Dish Best Served Cold

"Can I help you?" The woman's voice was directed through thick glass and helped by a small speaker.

"Yes, I'd like a ticket to Beijing, please."

The ticket woman looked at the blonde girl on the other side. *An American*, she thought. She was dressed in tight-fitting jean shorts with long tanned legs that ended in sandals. Her nails were painted pink on both her toes and fingers. There was a little anklet chain that hung loosely but not as low as her heel. She had a flannel shirt, which was unbuttoned low, and her knapsack was on the floor, leaning against her. She had striking blue eyes and a smile that was pure innocence, complete with those big white America teeth. *Braces*, thought the ticket woman.

"That's a long way to go. Are you travelling by yourself?"

"Uh, yes, but I'm sure I'll meet some people along the way. People have been so kind to me everywhere I go."

"Are you American?"

"Yes, why?"

"Just wondering. Look, I'm about to take a break. Do you feel like a coffee? No, don't be concerned. I'm looking at going that way as well and I also don't have anyone to go with."

"Uh, OK. Why not? The schedules say the next train isn't due to leave for a couple of hours. I'll grab us a seat there?" She pointed to a small café within sight of the ticket window. "What do you want?"

"Don't worry. Anything's fine. I'll be off in ten minutes."

"Great. See you there."

Chrystal picked up her knapsack and went to the café. She ordered two pastries and two coffees and waited facing the ticket window.

"Hi, my name's Valeria." She held out her hand.

"Hi, I'm Chrys."

"Nice to meet you." Valeria pulled up a chair and made herself comfortable. She dunked a piece of the pastry into the coffee before eating it. "Have you been travelling long?"

"Yeah, about three months, mostly on the trains around Europe."

"By yourself?"

"No, I was travelling with my boyfriend, who turned out to be a complete jerk. We broke up last week and I decided to go as far away as possible—hence, Beijing."

"Sounds crazy." Valeria was smiling and took another sip of coffee. "I don't have any stories like that. My life is extremely boring. I sell tickets to glamorous people like you and watch myself grow old in the mirror."

"That's nonsense," Chrystal said. "Besides, it takes a lot of guts to ask me for a coffee and leave your post like you are."

"I've been leaving for six months but I haven't been able to really do it. When I saw you, I knew today was the day."

"I told you I keep meeting the most interesting and nice people," Chrystal said. She was leaning forward and finished her coffee. "I noticed they make hot chocolate. I'm going to get myself one. Do you want one or possibly a sandwich?"

"No, thanks. I'm not as young as you. The sugar sticks to me like no one's business." She watched Chrystal walk away. Her care-free hips and nubile body grated on Valeria. *I could have been like that if I were born in America*, she thought.

Chrystal returned with a toasted ham and cheese sandwich. The smell nauseated Valeria to the point where she needed to find an excuse to leave. "How about I check on two tickets to Beijing? I won't be more than fifteen minutes."

"How much will it cost? My travel book said to expect something around 500 euros for a second-class sleeper."

"Don't worry, I get a special price. Give me 200 euros and I'll get us two tickets in a first-class sleeper." Valeria knew she had her and didn't want her to leave. She would have subsidised Chrystal's ticket if need be. She took the four 50 euro bills and pocketed them.

Chrystal watched Valeria walk away. *Scary stuff,* she thought. *If I was travelling, I would completely fall for this. A week in first class sounds like a something I could get used to.*

Valeria returned with two first-class tickets. It meant they had only two beds in their sleeper and had more privacy for their shared shower and toilet.

"You're a star, Val!" Chrystal looked at her ticket and ran her fingers along the paper. It all felt like a dream. "When do we leave?"

"At ten tonight. We have quite a while. I know it's not the next train but it's the only one I could get first-class tickets for. I hope you don't mind."

"Not at all. It gives me time to shop for some snacks and booze for the journey," Chrystal said with a wink.

"I think we're going to be great friends," Valeria said. "Shall I meet you here around nine tonight? That should give us plenty of time to get settled in our berth before the train leaves."

"Sounds like a plan."

∞

They met right on time. Valeria had changed into jeans and a T-shirt with a light sweater over it. She had a suitcase, not a knapsack, but was otherwise prepared to embark on their joint adventure. The sleeper was nicer than either had expected. The train was upgrading many of its tourist assets and this one had a private toilet and shower.

"This is great. There's no fridge but I'm sure we can pick up ice if we need it," Chrystal gushed. She sat on one bed and bounced up and down, then switched to the other bed and did the same. "I'll take this one if that's OK with you."

"No problem. They both look great." Valeria was also impressed. She had never seen the newly upgraded sleepers and couldn't believe she was able to purchase it at her discounted employee rate. It cost a thousand euros for the two of them but she knew Vlad and the family would be more than pleased with Chrys. She would be very popular and more than make up for her expense. Vlad constantly reminded her of the additional expense he needed to pay to her employers when she left at such short notice.

They eventually settled into a delayed first night's sleep after almost half a bottle of vodka. They swapped stories and made each other feel comfortable. The train's clicking and movement soon lulled them to sleep and the next thing they knew it was daylight.

"You know," Valeria said, "there is a big advantage in travelling first class. They allow you to get off and spend days at stations without penalising you when you get back on."

"That sounds fantastic," Chrystal said, teeth gleaming after their morning brush. *Bullshit*, she said to herself. *If we got off, we would need to book a place again. She's about to make her proposal.*

"I didn't think about it back in Moscow but we are actually going past my family's home. The station is only a few miles from the farm and they would love to see me. They haven't seen me since last year."

"I've never seen anywhere in Russia, so no problem for me. Are you sure we can jump off and get back on?"

"Sure. Happens all of the time. Are you sure you want to see my home? It's not much but my family is there and we'll treat you well. Good food at least. My brothers won't be able to stop staring at you, though. You're beautiful."

Chrystal blushed and turned her head away slightly. "You're too kind. Look, I'm in no hurry to get to Beijing. Let's do it."

"Great!" Valeria moved closer and hugged Chrystal. "You won't regret it."

"Are you going to call them or surprise them?"

"I'll text them. They'll come to pick us up at the station. Better than a taxi."

"Sound perfect. What time?"

"Tomorrow, just before noon. They'll be over the moon to know I'm coming." Chrystal was looking over Val's shoulder at something. She turned her head to see what was there and then became cold and couldn't move.

"Hi, Val. Miss me?"

Val froze, every cell in her body screaming danger. She managed to reply calmly. "Hi, Jack. What're you doing here?"

Jack grabbed her phone from her hand and pocketed it. "I just wanted to catch up with an old friend." He locked the door and sat down beside her.

"Quick, Chrys, get someone," Val cried.

Chrystal didn't move. Val began to realise the trouble she was in.

"You'll text them saying that Chrys will be arriving alone. You will send them a picture of her so they know who she is. You'll be grabbing the next train back to Moscow because there is someone else you need to bring them." Jack said this in a slow deadpan, devoid of all emotion. It was more effective than if he had screamed it in her face while whipping her. Chrystal noticed Val begin to shake.

"They'll know something is wrong," she said.

"You'll know what to do. And if there is any funny business, I'll be back to deal with you myself."

Val fiddled with the pen Jack gave her and wrote out the message. Jack then used his translation application on his phone to verify that she had texted what she had been told. There was a delay of fifteen minutes when a message came back. "OK, will pick up the package. Let us know when the next one is due to arrive. Vlad."

"What are you going to do with me?" The fear was real in Valeria's eyes. She knew what they did to Jack.

"I'll let you go. You did what you said you were going to do and the rest is up to me."

The relief was palpable. Her tension released and she crumpled in on herself on the bed. Her head was hung low, almost touching her knees, and Chrystal could see her shaking.

"How could you do that to Jack? To me?" Chrystal said. "I assume I was destined for the same fate?"

When she raised her eyes, they were red and puffy from rubbing. Her hair had fallen forward, dishevelled. There was silence as they waited for the reply. "Yes," she said quietly. "I am ashamed to say it."

Jack stood up, still keeping Val's phone.

"What are you going to do to me?" she said, head lowered again.

"You're going to get off at the next station. But now, I want you out of here. No, don't take anything. I'll walk you out." He grabbed her hand and led her out of the sleeper and down the narrow corridor. The scenery passed by through the windows but neither of them noticed. She didn't scream or make a sound.

Immediately before the first connection between the train carriages, there was a door that opened to the outside. Valeria started walking toward the next carriage but Jack stopped next to the door, deep in thought. She was too lost in her shame and misery to notice the pause. She just stood limply, silently awaiting her fate.

She heard something open and the wind fill her hair. It caused the hair to cover her face in a thin cowl. She lifted her head to see the distant trees and wheatfields passing without the hindrance of a window or door. It took a few moments before she registered that the sound was wind and that the door had been opened. She was like a rag doll when Jack's hand grabbed her shirt near the shoulders with both hands.

Valeria was broken. She didn't kick or scream. No knee to the groin or clever clawing at his eyes. She stood in his grasp as prey in a predator's mouth. He began to yell at her. Again, the adrenaline didn't kick in and she remained dazed and ashamed.

"You left me to die," Jack screamed in her ear. "I should have died there."

She was silent.

"They raped me and beat me and all I could think about was how badly they were treating you. It helped me carry on through the blood and shit and tears that I would someday help you. I feared the hell that you were being subjected to—daily rapes of hairy old men, alcohol on their breath, and dirt under the fingers as they probed you and pawed at you. Men who bathed maybe once a week demanding you to do things to them that would make a dog vomit. I almost didn't make it, but you kept me alive—until I learned that you are their sister. You're the bottom bitch who scours the country for fresh blood for their depravity."

Her eyes were vacant, as though something had snapped inside her. *I was only to find and bring people to Vlad and my family*, she wanted to scream. *I was never involved with the daily business. I just found people and returned to my spot in Moscow. I am innocent.* But she knew otherwise, deep in her heart. This realisation broke her. Perhaps if she had more time, she would have recovered. Perhaps she could do something to help make up for the pain and death that she had been part of. But her mouth didn't move, nor did her eyes.

"You have nothing to say for yourself?" Jack had white spittle at the corners of his mouth. The roof of his mouth felt waxy and he needed something to drink. He shook her hard, trying to get a response. He was met with a languid stare. "Maybe this will get you talking?" He held her so that her head and upper body was outside the train. He held onto her shirt and sweater with one hand, the other wrapped firmly on the interior bar.

Valeria did not tense up. Instead, her body went limp as she fainted. Jack was unable to hold up the dead weight and she slipped from his grasp. Her body fell backward and the bottom of her spine was broken instantly as it hit the creosote-filled railway ties. The velocity of her body's flight caused it to tumble upon impact. When her head hit the stones at sixty miles per hour, her neck snapped and her skull tore open. All Jack saw was a crumpled bundle of clothes, like litter thrown from a vehicle. His body went cold with the realisation of what he had done and it took all of his energy to push himself away from the open door, close it, and sit down.

No one came running. No door opened. In fact, he didn't see anyone for quite some time. He sat there long enough for his pulse to calm and the pain from the adrenaline to subside. He had never killed anyone before. Yes, he was complicit in the June Terror but it was always theoretical. *Pull yourself together, Jack*, he said to himself. *It's going to get a lot worse before it gets better.*

He pulled himself upright and began walking, one foot in front of the other, toward Chrystal. When he opened the door, she rushed to him.

"What's wrong? What happened? Are you OK?" Her hands were tracing his face and body, looking for injuries.

"I'm fine, Chrys. Just tired."

"You look grey, like you've seen a ghost," she said. She pulled out the vodka and poured him a large shot. "Here, drink this." He did.

"Thanks. I just need to sit for a while."

"Where's Valeria?"

Jack wanted to say something clever like *"I let her go,"* but remained silent for some moments. "She's gone," he said quietly.

"What do you mean gone? Did she escape?"

"No. Gone. I was talking to her with the door open and, the next thing I knew, she fell outside and hit the ground. I can only assume she's dead."

Chrystal was silent and poured herself a large shot and drank it. She moved next to Jack and put her hand in his. "You know she's as guilty as, if not more than, all the others," she said.

"I know but it's harder than I thought it would be."

"Come, lie next to me. We'll need our sleep before you confront Vlad." She pulled him down and they curled up on the narrow bunk. Jack fell asleep almost instantly while Chrystal's mind raced, everything becoming much more real than it had been when they were discussing it on a small yacht in the Caribbean.

The next day came faster than Chrystal wanted. She had moved to the other berth to give Jack more space. She was also increasingly nervous. If anything went wrong, she would become the sex slave of an exceptionally brutal Russian pimp in a whorehouse somewhere east of nowhere.

"Have a shower and try to eat something. Today's a big day."

"I know," said Jack. "I've been dreaming of and fearing this day since I left. How about you? You must be nervous."

"I am," she admitted. "Just don't hesitate. I know we are doing the wrong thing but it is for the right reason." She saw Jack pull a gun from his small rucksack. "Just don't miss."

"I won't. Just be calm and don't let them rush away. I need some time to make this happen."

"Hug me, Jack. I'm afraid." They embraced as the train slowed.

"I need to get to the third-class carriages," Jack said. "They can't see me coming out of first-class carriage with you."

"I love you." There were tears forming in her eyes.

"I love you, too, Chrys. Be strong." He closed the door behind him and disappeared.

When the train finally stopped, she was already at the exit door. She had packed everything into her knapsack and was wearing what she considered to be her sexy-backpacker outfit. She wanted Vlad and his crew to see her and not think about anything else. It was already suspicious that Valeria was not accompanying her to the pickup. She needed to be perky and unsuspicious in all other regards.

When she cleared the other people disembarking, she found herself in the courtyard of a small town's train station. It had only the bare essentials, one of which was a circular roundabout with a statue in the middle. The taxis were over ten years old. She wouldn't have been surprised to see a donkey and cart go past. Instead, she saw a newish blue van parked with its doors open. There were three people inside, the driver and two others. The driver came out and met her like a long-lost relative.

"Chrystal," he said in a thick accent. "Welcome. My name is Vlad. I am Valeria's brother."

"Nice to meet you," Chrystal said.

"I understand that you wanted to see some real Russian family life? Then you have come to the right place." His smile was real and he seemed to like her. His body language was full of deference and he couldn't have been more polite.

"I'm always up for an adventure," she said. This caused Vlad to smile even more broadly.

"I think we're going to be good friends," he said. "Let me get your things." He reached over and grabbed her knapsack. "I have two of my brothers in the van and the rest of the family is at home. We've cooked a special meal just for you."

"You really shouldn't have," Chrystal said sincerely. "I just want an authentic Russian experience."

"You will. You will," he said as he led her to the van. He put her things in the back of the van and made sure she was in the backseat before he closed the sliding door on her. He hopped in the driver's seat and started the engine.

Where's Jack? Chrystal thought. She felt a panic rising in her stomach and a tingling in her armpits and biceps. Vlad walked around and took up his position behind the steering wheel. He looked to be the most confident of the three men. The one next to her in the backseat looked placid, almost timid. The third man, in the passenger seat up front, hadn't said a word. His hair was a dirty blond, slicked back. He would have looked handsome except for the length of his hair, which hung in greasy-looking strands across his leather jacket. His face was covered in stubble and he had a strong jaw that looked like it could be hit with a crowbar and feel nothing.

Vlad started the van's engine and the vehicle began to move. Chrystal could feel her confidence drop as her brain knew that she was no longer the executive of a multimillion-dollar family office. If anything went wrong, she would become the punching bag and sexual toy of these men and countless others. *Where the hell is Jack?* She craned her neck to scan the horizon. *How could he leave me like this? Why?* The panic began to numb her legs and arms. She could feel her heart pounding in her chest.

"Woah! What do we have here?" Vlad said loudly, hitting the brakes. The van stopped suddenly and Chrystal was flung against the back of the front seat.

She wasn't wearing a seat belt. "Sorry, Chrystal, but I need to talk to this man. Don't be alarmed. Andre, keep an eye on her." Vlad opened the door and the passenger did the same. They had seen someone and wanted to greet them. When Chrystal cleared her hair from her face and sat back down, she was able to see who they were greeting.

"Hey, Jack. Remember us?" Vlad walked up and offered his hand.

When Jack proffered his, Vlad took it and pulled him toward him and punched him in the gut with his free hand. The passenger gave Jack a downwards punch into his head, just behind the ear, while Jack was doubled over.

"You remember Nicki as well, I assume?" The thick accent had a sinister jollity to it.

"Hi Jack. Didn't you forget something?" Nicki hit him again, this time in the side of the face.

Jack was staggered by the blows. He hadn't ex-pected the two meanest brothers to show up. He was winded from the sucker punch and seeing stars. "That's why I'm here," he managed to say. "I've got your money. I wanted to give it to your father in person."

Nicki didn't deliver the third blow, arm held in readiness. Vlad still was holding onto him so he couldn't escape. "Search him."

Nicki did a cursory patdown of Jack and nodded that he was clean. After a nod from Vlad in the direc-tion of Jack's knapsack, Nicki opened it and found a brick-sized object wrapped in plastic. He took out his knife and cut the plastic.

"It's cash," Nicki started laughing. "The dumb asshole actually brought us cash."

"You are probably the stupidest sonofabitch I have ever come across," Vlad said. He gave him one final punch straight in the nose. Chrystal thought she could hear something pop from inside the car and saw blood streaming from Jack's nose. "Put him in the van. We'll let Father decide what to do with him."

Jack didn't resist being directed into the back of the van. He didn't look at Chrystal when the door opened and she did everything she could to not scream when she saw him bloodied up close.

"Sorry about this, Chrystal," Vlad said. "Long story. I'll tell you all about it over dinner. Sit next to the window behind me. Andre, you sit between her and our old friend Jack."

When the three of them were securely in the back, they continued toward the farm. Nicki couldn't stop laughing and pulled out a bottle of vodka to relax. He handed it to Vlad, who took a small swig but otherwise concentrated on the road.

After half an hour, Jack noticed Nicki's head lean back heavily against the headrest and then lean against the window. There was grease on the window from his hair and occasionally his head would bounce when the van hit a bump. He slept soundly. Andre was also drowsy and Jack could see his head bobbing as he fought the sleep. Chrystal was stock still and didn't look left or right.

Jack could feel his left eye closing and he had one hell of a headache from the ear punch. *Who punches someone in the ear?* he thought. He scratched his thigh. Andre didn't seem to notice. Vlad couldn't see him in the rear-view mirror, but could probably see him in his peripheral vision if he turned his head slightly. Jack unbuttoned the top button of his jeans and slowly began unzipping his fly. Andre was either comatose or thinking about something else because he didn't move. Jack put his hand into his underwear and shifted his weight onto his left buttocks as he found what he was looking for. He looked at the back of Nicki's head, saw Andre dazed and uncaring, and chanced a glimpse at Vlad. No one was paying him any attention. He knew he had only one chance and began to play through the scenarios in his head. *Good thing they underestimated me. They were more interested in hitting me than searching me properly,* he thought. *I just wished I didn't have to allow myself to be sucker punched like that.*

When he pulled his hand from in his pants, he held a .38 calibre revolver. He put it behind Nicki's ear and pointed it slightly left and upwards so that it would go into the sleeping bastard's brain. He pulled the trigger and felt the kickback of the gun. It wasn't much but it caused the back of his hand to bang against the side of the car, almost dislodging the gun from his hand. When he brought his hand back toward him, it was clean. He had expected blood.

The next thing he felt was his face against the back of the passenger seat. Vlad had slammed on the brakes and Jack flew forwards, but so did Chrystal and Andre, causing a tangle of bodies. Jack had anticipated this and kept his target clear in his mind. He knew he had the element of surprise. He also knew that Andre was not a concern and could be dealt with last. Nicki and Vlad were the most dangerous pitbulls in the operation. This is why he allowed himself to be taken in the way he had. He couldn't have simply gone in with his guns blazing. He had to trick them. Their arrogance was the one thing he could count on. A shoddy pat down allowed him to hide his revolver high in his crotch. The punches just made it easier for him to pull the trigger. Until then, he had doubts about the morality of what he was about to do.

The second bullet missed Vlad but the third hit something. He was counting on the fact that speed required Vlad to pay attention to the road or die in a car crash. The van had slowed and Vlad was trying to pull his gun out. Jack regained his senses as his vision tunnelled to see only Vlad and feel the trigger of the gun. He felt his index finger move and saw the impact of the bullet as it hit Vlad's head. His body stopped struggling and he slumped over the wheel.

The van was still moving and, without a driver, careened into the ditch. The crash hurt but was more startling than dangerous. Andre had flown between the two front seats and was splayed pathetically between his dead brothers. Chrystal was shaken but OK. Jack relished his revenge.

"Are you okay, Chrys?"

"Yeah, you?"

"Yeah. This isn't over. Just wait." Jack got out and ran around to the driver's seat. The engine was still on and the wheels were trying to turn but ended up spinning. Vlad's foot was still on the accelerator. Jack turned off the ignition and found himself staring into the uncomprehending eyes of Andre.

"How could you do this to us?"

Jack was incredulous. "How? Are you insane? Do you not know what goes on in your family's home?"

Andre was quiet and tried to push himself into the backseat. Chrystal had already exited the van and was standing nearer Jack, who was running his hand along Vlad's torso to find a gun. It read "Grach" on the side; a 9mm Luger. Andre was just sitting in the backseat in stunned silence, so Jack went over to the other side and searched Nicki. "Chrys, check the back of the van for anything interesting while I look over this guy." Jack found a PP-200 machine gun tucked in the side of the van door next to Nicki and another handgun like Vlad's.

"I found a weird shotgun," Chrystal said. "It has a pistol grip instead of a normal stock."

"The stock will be a metal piece that folds out," Jack said.

"Ah, neat. Like a video game," Chrystal said. The whole thing had become surreal.

With his stash of weapons secured, Jack turned his attention to Andre. "What's wrong with you?"

"Nothing. I was told to come along for the ride, that's all."

Jack looked at the van. It was ruined. "How far to the farm from here?"

Andre looked around him. "About five miles, I think."

"Can you lead us there?"

"You're just going to kill me," he said.

"I won't kill you," Jack said.

Andre looked uncertain and then nodded silently. He let himself out of the van and started walking on the abandoned road. Not one car had passed.

"Does anyone come down this road?" Chrystal asked.

"Only to visit the farm," Andre said.

"Then we can't leave the van. If someone comes along, it'll alert the rest of them," Jack said.

"It looks like there is a farmhouse over there," Chrystal said. In the far distance, they could see some silos for grain storage.

"OK, let's head there first," Jack agreed.

They walked along the perimeter of the field and found the driveway. No one was home but they heard the dog barking furiously. "We'll have to brave it. Hopefully the dog is more bark than bite," Jack said, half smiling.

There was a truck but they couldn't get it started. In the shed, they found a tractor and keys and they all hopped on. It was slow, but faster than walking. Twenty minutes later, they were within sight of the farm brothel. When it came into view, Jack began to shake. He had faced his demons and even killed Vlad, but just seeing the innocent-looking white house amidst the swaying fields of wheat jolted him. He felt the cold crawl up his arms to his elbows and his stomach tighten.

"I wanted to come here at night," Jack said. "But if Vlad and Nicki don't show up soon, alarm bells will sound."

"I agree," Chrystal said. "We don't have a choice. The good news is that we have the element of surprise."

"Andre, how many guards are there and what type of firepower should we expect?" Jack had parked the tractor just out of sight of the house and the three of them were standing next to it.

"Vlad and Nicki dealt with security," Andre said. "Doron carries a gun, as does Father. Everyone else is either a client or a . . ." he didn't finish the sentence. Jack knew what he was about to say: "a whore."

Jack completed his sentence with a smash to the back of Andre's head. He fell to the ground, bleeding.

"But you said you wouldn't hurt me." He was crying. "You said everything would be OK."

Jack looked down at the pathetic figure. "I lied." He had taken a large spanner from the tractor's toolbox and brought it down with all his strength on Andre's head. It bounced off on the first hit, but he heard the crack. He brought it down in the same place again and again. The skull gave way to the soft grey matter inside. He kept smashing the same place until he felt a hand touching his shoulder.

"I think he's dead," Chrystal said softly.

Jack turned around, blood splayed up the front of this shirt and on his face. "I had to," he said quietly. "I just had to."

Chrystal lowered herself next to Jack and put her arms around him. "I know," she whispered. "I would do the same."

Jack dropped the spanner and began to cry, his body shaking with sobs. Chrystal held him as tightly as she could and kissed him softly on his neck and ear. "It'll be OK," she said. "Everything'll be OK."

Jack needed a few minutes to gather himself and prepare for the final assault. He tucked the 9mm pistol into his waistband and hoped he didn't blow his ass off in the process. He held the machine gun that Nicki had tucked into the side of the van's door. He gave Chrystal the other pistol, and she carried the shotgun. They both had two extra magazines of ammunition for their pistols. Jack also had two mags for his machine gun.

Chrystal only had the shells in the shotgun and couldn't find any more.

Jack had taken off his bloodied shirt and tried the best he could to get the blood off his face. All he had on was a white T-shirt and jeans with good hiking boots. His adrenaline was flowing and he could barely feel the weight of the guns. Chrystal was still in sandals and short shorts but ignored the stinging nettles and scrape of weeds as they walked to the back of the house.

"I'll go in first. You stay here and cover me. If you see anyone, shoot first and ask questions later." Jack was looking her straight in the eye and could see she was ready.

"Be careful." But he was gone, running at full tilt toward the house.

When he reached the front door, it was open. He pushed and it didn't even squeak. He walked in, his mind on full alert. *There's no one here*, he thought. He walked more easily into the lounge and then kitchen, just to be thorough. As he opened the door to the kitchen, a head turned around to look at him with dis-interest, mouth full of the sandwich he had just made. Doron.

Jack started shooting too early. His finger pressed against the trigger and held it. He felt the vibration of the machine gun and saw the flash from the muzzle as the magazine emptied. He raised the gun toward Doron but the bullets had all been shot before he got there.

Doron instinctively raised his right arm to cover his face defensively. When the explosion of sound ended, he realised he was still alive. He reached for his gun but it was too late. Jack had reloaded the next magazine and didn't make the same mistake twice. With the barrel aimed, he emptied the entire clip into him. Doron's body shook as the bullets riddled his flesh and he fell to the floor. The ceramic tiles on the wall were bloodied and smashed by the bullets and flesh. The kitchen cabinet splintered from the bullets. Without a word, Jack replaced the magazine and left the room.

He knew where the father would be and he marched to the study. He stood next to the door but not in front of it. He banged his fist on it before opening it. In response, he felt the thumping of the bullets against and through the door as the patriarch of the farmhouse brothel made his last stand. *He's got a machine gun as well*, Jack thought.

"I just want to talk," Jack said.

"Bullshit. You've come to kill us all."

"Then what do you have to lose?"

The father responded with a fury of bullets. When there was a pause, Jack went into the room and found the father struggling to change the magazine.

"It's over," Jack said. "Arms up. You know I'll shoot you dead where you stand so no funny business."

The father raised his hands in defeat and came out from behind his desk.

"Now, slowly take off your shirt," Jack said.

"What are you playing at?"

"Take off your shirt or die now." He took off his shirt.

"Take off your shoes, socks, and pants."

"If you're going to kill me, just fucking kill me. You don't need to do this as well."

"I just need to ensure that you aren't armed," Jack said. "Take it off now."

He did.

"Now, walk. Walk slowly. This way. OK. There. Out the front. Yes. Down the stairs. OK. Stop." Jack had marched him in front of the house. "Chrystal, can you please come here? Thanks. Can you get something to tie this piece of shit up with? Look for some duct tape or rope, anything." Chrystal ran into the house and returned with a roll of saran wrap.

"This is all I could find," she said sheepishly.

"OK, we'll work with it. Stand ten feet away. If he moves, shoot him. I'll use it to tie his hand behind his back." He instructed the father to put his hands behind his back. He was a fat bastard and it wasn't easy for him to stretch that far.

"This isn't working. Put your hands in front of you," Jack instructed. He began wrapping the arms from the elbow to the hands as tightly as possible until the plastic wrap was all used up.

"I don't think that'll hold him," Chrystal said doubtfully.

"I agree. I'm just going to get some people. If he even blinks at you, shoot him." Jack ran toward the garage he knew so well. He opened it to find twenty-three young people cowering in their bunks.

"It's OK," he said. "I'm a friend." They didn't understand him. He motioned for them to follow him. They were too afraid to move or to follow. Eventually, they came. As Jack walked through the garage, he noticed a framed photo of all the brothers covered in a white powder grinning at the camera. There were some girls and a little boy in the photo, as well. He looked at the garage and realised that this was where the photo was taken. He then remembered the first lesson he had received from Vlad on this very floor. It was covered with a white powder. He never thought about it then but he remembered getting it in his eyes and mouth as he was gang raped and beaten by those four masochists. That picture must have been taken either just before or just after he arrived. He grabbed the picture and some cabling wire next to the fridge.

When he returned to the father, he saw Chrystal holding the shotgun straight at him. They were talking and she was scowling. He feared she would shoot him before he got to her.

"Everything OK, Chrys?"

"Everything's fine. Good thing you returned. This motherfucker was about to have a religious experience."

Jack returned to the father's side and used the electrical cabling to tie up his legs at the ankles. He made sure it was as tight as possible and then he twisted the cables until the skin was white underneath and purple on either side. He did the same with the hands, tying the cable over the plastic wrap. The father remained defiant until he saw the children come out of the garage.

"Do you remember the people in this picture?" Jack said, putting the frame in front of his eyes.

There was a nod.

"I don't know who the girls and boy are, but the men are all dead. Andre, Vlad, Nicki, and Doron."

"Go to hell, you bastard!" the father squirmed, torn between grief and fear.

"Oh, don't worry, I won't kill you. I promised you that," Jack said. Then he turned to the children, all armed with forks, knives, and anything else they could find in their hellish barracks once they realised what was happening. "They will." It took a while before the children braved the space from where they were being housed. One young man was first and a hesitant second followed. After that, the rest poured out.

The father's eyes opened wider as the small mob descended on him. Jack and Chrystal walked back to the tractor. They would need to get out of there before too many questions were raised. As it was, a bad guy got what was coming to him. The police and other regular customers would need to find another brothel to frequent. Hopefully the victims were taken care of by whomever found them, but that wasn't why Jack returned to this place. He wanted revenge. As he heard the feral screams fade, he felt relief. *Payment given in full and final settlement*, he thought as he pulled Chrystal close to him.

Chapter Sixteen

CHRYSTAL SERVES NOTICE

"How do you feel?" Chrystal had just returned from a session at the spa and was still in her robe. After their Russian adventure, they returned to the train and continued on to Beijing. They were able to use their tickets, but they needed to wait until a space was available. It was a long wait to get to Beijing and there were times when Jack's nerves got the better of him. But it was also a time for them to spend together, decompressing the terrible events of the last week and to plan for Chrystal's revenge. When they reached Beijing, they checked into the Rosewood Hotel to relax.

"I shouldn't be feeling good. I should be feeling guilty or ashamed. It took six months as a sex slave, being submitted to things I can barely confess to my god, before I realised I was no different from them. They fuck body parts. For them, a man or woman is reduced to their constituent parts. The client chooses as per his preference. He buys porn, rents a girl or boy, or fantasises about an amalgam of sexual or violent images and calls it desire. They may be animals but they are just like me, merely unleashed."

"You are not like them. At least you called in the location of those children to the police," she said as she came next to him. She held his hand and stroked it, both of their hands smooth from the spa oils.

"Possibly, but I just killed six people and I feel no remorse. I used to anguish over the meaning of life, where we should be going as a society, and how to make the world a better place, and now I'm a confirmed murderer." He didn't tell her about his other guilt, about the June Terror. Somehow, that didn't bother him as much as it should have.

"Life should be about love," he continued. "These people destroy all innocence, enslaving those directly and indirectly involved. They have changed the way in which we view each other and how we think about love. Love, if it exists, is about the whole person. We are not beings of cravings to be satisfied by eating, drinking, or sex. We are human. We are more than our parts. Pornography and sex trafficking does more than stain the soul. It attacks the fabric of society. It attacks what it is to be human. It fools us into believing that a vagina or asshole or mouth is the pinnacle of desire. Then it morphs into violence when the user needs more to satisfy his desensitised cravings. But it comes down to a lowly evolved sense of existence. Sex is great. Love is better. Porn is neither."

Chrystal was nodding. "I agree with you, Jack, but at least you have done something. You still have the passion in you. You are a good person."

He pulled his hand away and got up. "I hope you're right, because right now I don't feel much different than the rest of them."

"But you are. Those weren't humans. I know it's not right to say something like that. We live in an age where we are all special souls but that is bullshit and you know it. Some people are angels and some are demons. The rest of us are somewhere in between. All you did was slay a demon. There's nothing wrong or evil about that." Chrystal had also stood up and was next to Jack. She allowed her gown to fall to the ground and to slide his off his shoulders. Their skin was smooth, tanned, and muscular. Jack had regained his weight in muscle, his torso tight as ropes where he turned, and his stomach boasted the chinks of a six-pack. Chrystal traced the curves of his muscles with her fingernail, no longer talking, just allowing her body to touch, caress, and heal Jack's wounded soul. She took his hand and guided it across her body, from her shoulder across her breasts, and along the curves of her thighs. She tilted her head up and kissed his chin, following his jaw with kisses and down his neck. Her hands found themselves in his hair as she pulled him toward her, kissing him deeply. She had never imagined such a man existed and would do anything for him.

∞

When they landed at LAX, they knew what they needed to do. They rented a truck, bought two pistols and two shotguns, and rented a hotel a block away from Lyle's headquarters. They called to ensure that he was in town and watched the building from the truck to see who was coming and going.

"I remember her," Chrystal said. "She was a quiet one." She pointed to a slim Asian girl in a small black dress and high heels on the arm of Dino, one of Lyle's minders.

"We need to hit Lyle first. He's the main man," Jack said. "Strike the shepherd and the flock will scatter."

"Yes, Sun Tzu," Chrystal giggled. They were on deadly serious business, but it felt electrifying to sit next to a man who was prepared to do this for her. He was like a father, big brother, and best friend all rolled into one. He was her protector and lover, her beginning and her end. She had fallen madly in love with him and hoped he felt even a fraction of the same for her.

"Quiet, grasshopper," Jack said.

"Different movie," Chrystal said.

"Sun Tzu wasn't a movie," Jack countered.

"You always ruin things with facts," she said playfully. She wanted Jack more than she had ever wanted anything. She slid closer to him and put her hand between his thighs. She liked his muscular legs and the way he carried himself, not realising how beautiful he was. She began to trace her fingernail along the seam of his jeans when she froze. She withdrew her hand and sat bolt upright, her body leaning away from the windshield.

"What's wrong, sweetheart?"

"That's him," she whispered hoarsely. "That's Lyle."

Jack turned to see the sandy-haired man breeze out of the building toward a car parked twenty feet away. He wore expensive-looking pants, not jeans, and a stylish shirt with stripes, with the top two or three buttons undone. "He doesn't look like much," he said.

"He's my demon," Chrystal replied. Her hands were together in her lap and her shoulders were rolled inward. She began to take on the posture of a whipped animal, cowering in front of its abusive master. Instead of continuing her downward spiral, something inside her clicked and she straightened, her eyes shining with determination.

"We'll deal with him together, Chrys," Jack said. "Let's get out of here for now. There's no hurry." He put the truck in gear and drove off. Lyle would be there later or tomorrow or the day after that.

When they had driven fifteen minutes, they began to see signs for the sea. "Do you want to go to the beach and regroup?"

"No, I think I'd prefer to deal with this bastard head on." She was becoming mad.

"How do you want to do it?"

"I want it bloody and brutal. Nothing elegant about what we're about to do. Let's just do it."

"In broad daylight? What about the cameras and our truck? CCTV will have captured us passing."

"Then we approach from a different angle. There aren't a lot of shops in the area. It's mostly businesses and not a lot of off-street traffic. The businesses located there are studios like Lyle's and industrial suppliers."

"It's dangerous and we will probably get caught or do something wrong," Jack looked at her increasing rage. "But this is what we are doing. Let's just do it the best we can."

Jack turned the truck around and found a place to park it within a five-minute walk of Lyle's studio. *This is crazy*, he thought, but he owed his life to Chrystal and Tammy. *Let's just hope the* CCTVs *aren't working.*

They checked their pistol magazines and loaded their shotguns. At the last minute, Jack decided to put the shotguns in a gym bag he had in the backseat. *At least we won't look so conspicuous getting there,* he thought.

"It's corny, but have your hat low and wear dark sunglasses. Hopefully no one will be able to identify us without a clear shot of our faces. We'll walk there, deal with Lyle, and leave."

"OK. Let me call to see if he has returned." She called and found out he was in a meeting on-site. "No, thanks, I'll try again later," Chrystal replied and hung up. "Let's go. He's there."

Jack got out of the truck as casually as he could and made his way down the street with her by his side. "Don't hold my hand or arm," he said. "I don't want them to have any clues as to who we are, or whether we are men or women."

Chrystal was silent, face set. She walked beside Jack and let her arms swing naturally. He had the bag slung on his shoulder, the zipper open for quick access. When they opened the door, the air conditioning hit them and sharpened their focus. The receptionist looked up as they entered and asked if she could help them. Chrystal walked past her without a word and Jack followed. She opened the door to the boardroom and faced Lyle, Dino, and Jeremy, as well as two other guys she didn't know. They all looked at her in surprise.

"Can I help you?" Lyle said. So far, nothing was out of the ordinary.

Chrystal took off her hat and glasses and stared at him. Lyle sat taller, as did Jeremy and Dino. The two new guys looked on, uninterested. When Jack entered the room, they all got up. Jack held two shotguns and passed one to Chrystal.

"Yes," Chrystal said. "I left your employment without giving due notice. I have just come back to say that

I quit." She pointed the shotgun at Lyle and pulled the trigger. She staggered in surprise at the recoil but then pointed it at Jeremy.

"What the hell, Chrystal? Why?"

Jack held his shotgun in readiness at the other men in the room. This was Chrystal's show and he didn't want to get involved if he didn't have to.

"Why?" she screamed. "What the fuck?! You rape, beat, and whore me out to others on the promise of me becoming famous. You promise me money but tell me I'm in debt after I've given you everything I had. You are evil motherfuckers and you all deserve to die!" She pulled the trigger at Jeremy, then at Dino.

Jack shot the two other guys when they started to run toward Chrystal.

"They're not all dead," Jack said. He saw the shot spread on Jeremy's face, blood coming through the torn skin. *He's probably dead.*

Chrystal walked to Lyle's squirming body and shot him in the head point black. "Now he's dead." She did the same with Dino. She took Jack's shotgun and did the same with the two new guys.

Jack could hear the receptionist screaming and assumed she would have called the police by now. He collected the shotguns and put them back in the gym bag. Chrystal had her pistol in her hand, pointed at the receptionist's head.

"Did you call the police?"

"Nnnnno," the receptionist said.

"Are you sure? Did you see what I just did to those fuckers?" Chrystal was raging mad and no one would doubt her sincerity.

"I'm sure."

"Is there anyone else here?"

"No, just me and the boys."

Chrystal looked at Jack with her jaw set and eyes blazing. She pulled the trigger and walked away. Jack found a rag in his gym bag and cleaned the surfaces where their hands had touched—luckily only the door to the boardroom and the entrance door.

"Chrys, wait!" Jack didn't want her to open the door just yet. "Calm down first. Give me the gun and I'll put it in the bag. Breathe. Now, we'll leave and walk slowly with our hats and glasses on. There, good, put them back on. We walk and look like we don't have a care in the world. People only notice people who are acting agitated or differently than they expect. Walk normally and you are invisible."

Chrystal was breathing heavily and had started shaking. He could see her eyes weren't focussing too well. He needed to get her out of there before shock really kicked in.

"Let's go," she said and reached for the door. Jack wiped it inside and out as he followed.

Chapter Seventeen

PORTAL OF PIMPS

"Pimps in the US make, on average, $5,000 per week in small to mid-sized cities. They make upward of $40,000-50,000 per week in the larger centres such as Atlanta and Vegas. That's from $260,000 to $2.5 million tax-free cash per year." Jack was talking to Tammy and Chrystal in their New York suite at the Lotte Palace. "We have taken care of our personal issues and now need to focus on the bigger plan."

"For my part," Tammy said, "the business acquisitions are going well. We have leveraged the available $6.5 billion capital into a company with combined assets of nearly $70 billion and gross cash flow of nearly $10 billion. Our profits should be around $3.5 billion."

"Wow, Mom, that's amazingly scary stuff. You sound all corporate."

"It's easy when you have the advisors and professionals running the place the way we do. Besides, business is a language and if I can't learn it, I can't be of much use to either of you or myself."

"But are you enjoying it?" Chrystal said.

Tammy paused before breaking into an enormous grin. "Are you kidding? A few years ago, I didn't have money for fuel, I became a prostitute, and was contemplating killing myself. Now I'm sitting on top of a Fortune 100 company enjoying the best things life has to offer. I'm loving it!"

Even Jack grinned. He could see the difference in Tammy already. It had been three years since the start of the acquisitions and she had become polished. She was now forty-two, but looked at least ten years younger. Her face glowed with the pampering of the best spas and her clothes were tailored haute couture. She still enjoyed high heels but opted for four inches instead of six. Her body was sculpted by personal trainers and admired by a number of romantic interests. She looked happy.

"What can we budget in our fight against these bastards?" Jack asked.

"The annual profit of $3.5 billion is after us siphoning off almost a billion this year alone. I think I have put the correct mechanisms in place to keep that amount invisible—and provide us with a similar annual budget capable of doing what we hope to achieve."

This time it was Jack who was speechless. "Wow, Tammy, that's unbelievable. I had a feeling you were the right person for the job. I don't think anyone in the world could have done better." Tammy positively glowed from the praise.

"Thanks, Jack. It is a collaborative effort, and the markets are favouring this type of commodity. If things change, I may not be able to make so much invisible and available to you."

"And the charities, Chrys? How are they going?"

"Isabella has been amazing. She has been in contact with Frank from the States, the pastor who picked you up in Tucson. He doesn't know anything other than that his causes are exceptionally well funded. She was given $700 million to invest and make work for her, no strings attached. She has tapped into the volunteer market and is making that capital sweat. She is determined to keep the bulk intact and only operate from the interest. She has told me she will add interest to the capital at the rate of inflation and only spend the real return— that is interest earned minus inflation. Jack, you never told me she had an MBA."

"She doesn't. She's just smart and she will do anything for her kids." When Jack saw Chrystal's eyebrows raise, he added, "Everyone is her kid. Did I tell you she wanted to dedicate her life to helping AIDS orphans in Africa?"

"She sounds like a saint," Chrystal said. "But she has the financial acumen of a Wall Street titan. She is investing in small projects where labour is the largest component of the business while still generating nearly ten-percent net return. She is replacing the labour with her kids, giving them training and an honest income. She wants them to understand that they can live within the system and that they can earn an honest dollar and live in a home to raise their families."

"In other words," Jack said, "we don't need to worry about her or what she gets up to."

"Not at all. She is getting a lot of free publicity and volunteers are lining up around the block to help her keep her profits for her kids. No one in the organisation takes more than the national average income and she refuses to take a salary. That has shamed all of the wealthy wives and helpers into not taking a penny. In fact, she has launched a fund-raising effort to increase the capital base of her fund. I wouldn't be surprised if she grows it into a Fortune 500 company in due course."

"That all sounds great, but I need her to use her contacts in the government and police to get us lists of our targets. I want to know who the main pimps are and then we can work down from there."

"Even if you have a list, how're you going to get at them?" Chrystal said. "Look how dangerous and violent—and time-consuming— it was just for ours."

"I've been thinking about that. I know that for every one we remove, another will take its place. But if we attack this on multiple fronts, at least it will be pushed back to where it should be—in the shadows to be frequented by people who will always seek it out. I just want to stop it being pushed onto mainstream consciousness."

"Sounds like a good start. How do we achieve that?"

"We get Isabella to take up the cause. It helps her kids and she has a lot of grassroots support. She can go on the talk-show circuit and raise awareness so that hopefully we can get some effective legislation passed."

"What do you call effective legislation?" Tammy asked.

"Something that protects the downward spiral of human abuse. I would push for punishing the people paying for sex. I would set a fixed fine of $5,000 or one month's salary, whichever is higher. Right now, some of the most frequent repeat visitors to prostitutes are police. I would move toward fines instead of imprisonment, except on repeat infractions. I would also look to publish all the names of the people caught—whether paying a fine or time in prison. Societal pressure is the most effective tool against these people, and it will keep the fringe users out of the market. We can't change human nature, but I want to see it kept in the shadows."

"But then the women and men caught in that cycle will have even less hope," Chrystal said. "They'll still be stuck with monsters who beat and rape and whore them out to the scum of society."

"Possibly, but they don't have hope now, either. All I'm trying to do is reduce the volume of abuse that goes on. Until this changes, we are, effectively, allowing for legislated rape of our wives and daughters."

"So you want to extinguish mass demand and, in so doing, reduce those victimised into this modern slavery. What about the pimps?" Tammy asked.

"We should be chasing the pimps back to where they belong. They can only make money by operating in areas willing to pay for their girls' services. Let them scour amongst the crack and meth addicts. Let them be devoured by the lifestyle they promote rather than feast on the unsuspecting carcass of modern society. But my solution for pimps is not for Isabella or the courts."

"What are you thinking?" Chrystal got up to get some water.

"I want to put a bounty on every pimp's head in the US. For every confirmed kill, we pay it into a non-US bank account or in Bitcoin. We need to be anonymous in payment and block chain currencies achieve that. Our budget is $1 billion per year. That's huge. We can't hire an army, so we get the animals to devour themselves. The question is, how big of a bounty do we need to get results?"

"How about a month's earnings', acknowledging that each pimp is different? If a pimp earns $50,000 a month, that's what the bounty should be," Tammy said. "You will need to guestimate initially, but if Isabella's people can provide us with a list, we can then establish the size of the bounty based on the size of the population involved."

"Good idea," Jack said. "That'll give us enough to have thousands eliminated each year. It may take some time, but eventually they'll get the message that they are an endangered species."

"Which also means we need to be even more careful going forward," Chrystal said. "We need to start using 1024 bit encryption for emails and communications. And no talking about this to anyone unless you are both naked and in a hurricane." She smiled at the image.

"What about the websites that sell the porn? Can't we target those, as well?"

"I don't know how to do that, Tam," Jack said. "But maybe Sylvia does. Let's get this in motion. I'll get in touch with her to get the web presence and bounties into cyber-space without a trail leading back to us. Chrys, you get the list from Isabella. Tam, keep up the amazing work."

"I think this calls for a celebration," Chrystal said. "Anyone for a champagne lunch followed by an afternoon of debauchery?" She had sidled next to Jack and slid her arm around him.

"I think two's company and three's a crowd," Tammy said. "I'll leave you to it and I'll call up someone I've been dying to spend some time with." She got up and kissed Chrystal on the cheek and touched Jack on the shoulder as she left.

∞

"My sister Alice was reaching breaking point. It all started when she needed a little extra to keep her child fed and the rent paid. Victor had been pestering her since she was fifteen to make a few extra bucks and she, at the time, smiled as though it was a compliment but never took him up on the offer. When she got pregnant during grade 12, she was proud to keep her baby and give him the best she could offer. After high school finished and she was flipping burgers, she soon realised it wasn't enough. During a moment of weakness, she accepted Victor's advances and agreed to sleep with him. He gave her $200. Further desperation caused her to seek his companionship and money until she quit her job and began working for him. He was good to her initially and she was able to provide for her little boy, who was now almost ready to go to kindergarten. Over the years, things got harder and Victor helped her take the edge off with pot, then heroine, and finally meth. It wasn't long before she was a skeleton with hollowed-out eyes doing anything for her next hit. Her child was taken by family services and she could no longer look at herself in the mirror. She was twenty-eight when she walked in front of the crosstown night bus. The police put it down as an accident, but I know better. I believe she took her own life as a statement. It was the only dignified way for her to check out of the hell she found herself in." Sandra's eyes were wet.

"That was two years ago and I feel at times like it was yesterday."

"Thank you, Sandra," a voice said amidst the group sitting in a circle facing each other. A person next to Sandra put her hand on her shoulder to comfort her. "I think now would be a good time for a tea and coffee break." The voice got up and walked to the table set up alongside the wall in the elementary school's gymnasium. "Sandra, can I have a word with you?"

Sandra had been coming to meetings like this since her sister died. Initially, she could barely speak and just attended to be around other grieving people. When she finally started talking, she felt the burden of her grief lifting but never leaving.

"I know it's hard and I have noticed a lot of improvement these last six months. Do you feel like anything's different?" asked Dr. Phillip Scowe, a sixty-two-year-old psychiatrist who had also lost his son to methamphetamine two decades earlier. He had joined a similar group and decided to head it up when it looked to disband.

"I feel like something's dead inside of me," she said. "I know that she was a different person to me but she was still my twin. I feel as though I'm still connected to her even through death."

The doctor put his hand sympathetically on her shoulder. "I have an idea of your pain. Mine still haunts me. It's hardest on his birthdays and Christmas, but I try not to think about the day of his actual death. We are still here and are still alive."

Sandra put her hand gently on his face and let it fall slowly. "I just wish there was something I could do. Something to avenge her death. It just feels so hopeless, so pointless."

Phil took her by the arm away from the rest of the group. "I have heard about something. It's not for me, but I told myself I would tell you when I saw you." He pulled a piece of paper from his pocket and handed it to her. "Look up this site. If it's for you, don't tell me or anyone else. Maybe it'll help toward your own healing."

Sandra looked at the paper and then back at Phil. "Really? A website?"

"Take a look and keep your thoughts to yourself."

"OK," she said, but the doubt was obvious. "I'll take a look. Thanks." She went back to the table and grabbed a chocolate chip cookie and coffee. She put the website out of her mind.

It was laundry day before she remembered it and that was only because she habitually emptied her pockets before throwing her jeans in the washing machine. As she felt the paper in her hand, she remembered Phil's words. She turned on the washing machine and headed to her computer.

"You are entering a restricted site," the website said. "All communications are private and must be secured by way of encryption. Do you want to sign up and join? Yes or No." She clicked "yes." "Click on the button below to download the encryption software," it said. She clicked on it. When it was finished, she installed and restarted her machine. She retyped the website address. "Welcome. In order to proceed, you need to create an identity for yourself. Using the encryption software, click on 'create identity' and then 'send'." Sandra did it. When she went back to the website, she entered her identity and password and then waited.

"Welcome to Alcalde, your portal for justice," it said. It had the normal home page, About Us, and other tabs, but it also had a tab called "Bounty Claim" and another called "Most Wanted." Sandra clicked on "Most Wanted: and realised it was a list of a thousand names along with what looked like police photos. When she started reading further, she realised that they were all pimps and the photos looked like they had been taken from police files. Across a number of them were the words "bounty claimed" in a red slash. She rolled her cursor over them but it was greyed out. She rolled her mouse over a picture without the red slash and clicked on it. Up came the photo, name, last known address, and list of crimes committed or suspected. There was also a number with a dollar sign next to it.

There was a search bar and she had an idea. She typed in the name Victor Ivanov and the city. It was only a second before his picture appeared. She sat back in her seat, mouth suddenly waxy and dry. She looked at the confident features. He was younger in that picture; it must have been an earlier arrest. Underneath, she saw the bounty of $150,000.

She went back to the site's homepage and explored matters further, reading about the organisation. "We will pay a bounty as indicated when two things are confirmed to us. First, we need to have proof that the pimp is dead. This can be by way of a video but is better if we have a death certificate or police report. Second, we pay out the bounty to the first person who submits the details of the killing. The details will need to be verified and such verification will be reserved to us in our absolute discretion. As you can appreciate, this is not a perfect system and it requires you to admit to either killing or knowing about a killing. Therefore, all communications will be done via the 1024 bit encryption software downloaded onto your computer. You will never receive a request for your personal details. We do not want to know. We will pay you in the block chain currency of your choice. It will be up to you to convert it to a conventional currency."

Sandra looked away. *Is this a snuff site? How could Phil give this to me? What does he expect me to do with it? This sounds like Star Chamber vigilante courts handing out death sentences with no due process.* She shut her laptop and went to the kitchen, her mind suddenly racing. She returned to her laundry and folded the dried clothes and double-checked the washing. Still working. She made herself a coffee and some toast and stared out the window at the passing school bus. It didn't help and she soon returned to the computer.

This time, she noticed a tab called "Upload Pimp Details." She clicked on it and saw the instructions on how to post pictures and details, and how to estimate the size of the pimp's business—everything from the population of the city, the estimated population that the pimp was servicing, the estimated number of workers he or she was employing, and the number of minders or security people they had around them. When everything was entered, you just pressed "Calculate Bounty"and a figure appeared. It was subject to verification but it provided the public a way to put bad guys onto a death hit list. Sandra found herself growing cold and warm with excitement at the same time.

Three weeks later, she was able to locate Victor. He was easy to spot and wasn't afraid of people he grew up with. Sandra looked just like Alice so, in some ways, Victor was almost nostalgic.

"How's it goin', Sandra? You're still looking fine," Victor said with a smile. He didn't have the gold teeth or chains, just a quality suit and no tattoos. His blonde hair was combed back and he walked with the confidence of a man who knew a secret. He paid the police their cut and was left alone. He kept his nose clean and didn't start fights in other pimps' territories. He was the closest thing the world of pimping had to a straight shooter.

"I'm fine, Victor, just missing Alice at times."

Victor's face clouded. "What a terrible tragedy what happened to your sis. I did everything I could to keep her straight. You know, it's not good for my business either." He moved closer to Sandra for a hug. She let him and she could feel the gun he carried in a shoulder holster against her breast and something else as he put himself next to her. She cringed at the thought.

"Thanks, Vic. I know what she meant to you. Anyway, it was good seeing you." Sandra untangled herself from the lingering hug and started walking toward the subway.

"Maybe we should get a drink some time," he said. "You may like it." He adjusted his suit and scratched his crotch.

Sandra stopped and turned around. "You know, that sounds like a good idea."

Victor was surprised. "Great. Tonight when you finish work?"

Sandra smiled. "Tonight at seven. Shall I come to your place?"

"Meet me at the club. I'll be in the back."

Sandra nodded and left. Victor smirked and turned to his boys. "Looks like I'm going to get some replay action. She is looking good, that girl. Uh-huh."

Victor's club was the main way for him to launder money earned from pimping the girls. He also used it to recruit. They start by dancing and stripping and soon they were earning him some real money. Victor was surprised when the club actually earned a good profit on its own merit. What he didn't touch was drugs. He considered it too dangerous and left the profits for someone else. *When it's just girls, it's harmless*, he explained to his boys. *The police leave me alone and I give them a taste every once in a while. But if I start moving blow and meth, my life isn't my own anymore. I'm just a simple businessman. As you can see, everything we do is legit.*

When Sandra arrived, she was ushered past the red curtains and black tables to his office in the back. It was all in black with spotlights and a large leather sofa and some overstuffed leather chairs. There was a desk in the corner with a computer and a massive TV on the wall. The music and noise from the club was muffled but was still audible. Victor was sitting behind his desk and got up when Sandra arrived.

"Champagne?" He was already pouring two glasses of Cristal.

"Love some," she said. "Shall we sit here?" She sat on the sofa. She wished she had taken the chair because he chose to sit next to her, just a little too close.

"How'd you like my place?"

"Amazing. You must be doing really well."

"I try. It's a lot of hard work and red tape. I'm looking to open a new club next month, a little more upmarket. Trying to target lovely women like yourself." He smiled the best he could but it made Sandra's skin crawl.

"Well, here's to your ongoing success." She finished her glass and he refilled it.

"So, what made you agree to see me tonight after all this time?"

"I don't know," she said, twisting her hair with her finger. "I guess I've been blaming you all these years when really all you are is a successful businessman. I guess I've been unfair to you and wanted to clear the air."

Victor was taken aback. "Wow, that really means a lot coming from you. Alice always spoke lovingly about you. We haven't spent any time together and I would love to be your friend."

"Here's to friendship." Sandra lifted her glass and finished it.

"Friendship." Victor did the same.

"Did you make reservations? Is it a nice restaurant?"

"I thought we were just meeting for drinks?"

"A woman agrees to meet you for drinks at seven and you think you're not going to take her for dinner?" Sandra was looking at him in her most suggestive look.

"Uh, of course. I booked us at La Grenouille. I hope it will be OK."

"Wonderful." She batted her eyelashes. "I've never been there but have heard great things." She got up and gathered her handbag. Victor took the hint reluctantly and stood up. He opened the door and they walked through the club to the early night air.

"Shall we walk?" Victor was trying to act the gentlemen the best he knew how. He offered his arm. Sandra took it and they began walking.

"I think there's a shortcut," Sandra said after a few minutes. "The restaurant is on Fifth. If we cut through this alley, we'll shave at least ten minutes off our walk. No sense walking around the block for no reason."

Victor looked unconcerned. "I like walking with you. I don't know many women who would even know how to walk like this. And alleys are dangerous. You shouldn't be walking through them at night."

"But I'm with you," Sandra said. "I'm not afraid."

That did the trick. Victor adjusted his trajectory toward the alley and they walked in silence. *She really is a classy broad*, he thought.

As they passed the large metal garbage bins, Sandra twisted her ankle and grabbed Victor's arm. "Are you OK?" he said with alarm. "Here, lean against this for a second and let me take a look at that." He helped her to a parked car and let her lean on it as he removed her shoe. "Heel's broken," he said.

"It's OK. I just need to let the pain pass," she said, holding her ankle. She opened her bag, "I have some aspirin here. That should help."

"I knew these alleys are bad news," he said. "I shouldn't have let you convince me otherwise. Now look at you." He had been cursing himself and pacing back and forth while Sandra found her aspirin. When he looked back at her, he was looking down the barrel of a gun. "What are you doing? Is this some type of joke?"

Sandra pulled the trigger and the bullet went right where she was aiming—through the nose. As his body fell backward, she walked nearer, making sure that he was dead. She took a picture of his face with her phone's camera and then a few more from different angles. She didn't need to shoot him again.

"That's for Alice, you sonofabitch." She had played out this scenario in her head a thousand times and knew she couldn't engage him in conversation. She had to just shoot him and be done with it. She had sawed into her heel before coming and knew that a drain cover or crevice would provide sufficient leverage to snap it off. It was perfect and now all she had to do was get out of there before anyone saw her.

The next morning, she was amazed that there was no report of the murder in the newspaper or on television. She had uploaded the pictures and details of the killing to the website using the encrypted software. The site sent a message that they would investigate it and let her know when the death was verified. Three days later, verification was approved and she received $150,000 worth of bitcoin. No police contacted her and none of Victor's boys thought of connecting her with the death. Just another inevitable outcome in the world of crime.

When Sandra shot Victor, it was as though two years of pain were released in an instant. She knew intellectually that she was killing a person and that it was wrong, but she was also exorcising herself of what she considered the source of her pain.

"You are looking particularly happy today," Phil said, greeting her and taking one last look to ensure that the chairs were set up and refreshments all in place. Sandra had arrived early and they were the only ones there.

"I am happy. I feel like I slayed my demon. Thank you." She gave Phil a kiss on the cheek that made him go red.

"I'm sure I don't have any idea of what you are talking about," he said, restraining a small smile.

"Whatever the case, I just wanted to say thank you and that you have helped me more than I could have imagined."

"These groups help. It just takes time," he said. He paused. "I also slayed my demon. It felt good."

Sandra didn't say anything but came closer and put her arm in his. Thoughts of professional impropriety flitted through Phillip's mind but were quickly dismissed.

∞

Detective Ernest Kay sat at his usual place when Sergeant Pat O'Leary clasped him on his back. "How's it hanging, Ernie?"

"Low and to the left, last time your wife checked," he said without missing a beat. "What's your poison?"

"Whatever you're having's fine."

Ernie kept his elbows on the bar and ran his index finger around the top of his glass. "Greg, we'll have another two rounds here," Pat said when he finally was able to grab his attention. Greg took Ernie's empty, wiped the surface, and put the two new drinks in front of his patrons. "That guy's pretty good," Pat said. "He's like Tom Cruise in that movie."

Ernie was not in the laughing mood but that was too much. "He's as much like Tom Cruise as I am," he said. Ernie was six foot four inches and had the looks of someone who had been hit once too often with a blunt instrument. The result was great for intimidation but hardly got the ladies swooning.

"Got you laughing, you sorry sonofabitch," Pat said, grinning. "It's all in the delivery." Ernie's face returned to its sullenness and his partner eventually calmed down. "What's eating you, Ernie?"

"Life, I guess. Every once in a while, you have to wonder what it's all about."

"You need to stop thinking about Diana."

"It's not Diana. She's a whole other saga. I'm more or less over her. It's Ronny."

"Laughing Ronny? What's that piece of shit done now?"

"Anything he wants, as you know. We should have been able to bust him by now. We've been watching him for, what, nine months? We know he's guilty as sin but we can't get anyone to testify and when we do, they suddenly change their minds."

"You know how it is." Pat's voice showed concern. "It's the status quo. We chase and keep them from getting too out of control and they push us back. We find ourselves in a bizarre balance between chaos and a police state."

"Yeah, but wouldn't you want to get those bastards?"

"Sure, who wouldn't? Look what they did to that little girl. Some fat fuck broke the child's hip. How in Christ's name is that even possible? I'd like to shoot the fat bastard as well as Ronny for supplying him the little girl."

"We know it was him and we have a dead twelve-year-old. Yet we do nothing."

"You know, you're a real buzzkill." Pat shifted his weight on his seat. "Greg, another four drinks please."

"Four?"

"Neither of us feel the first few so may as well move things along." Pat smiled. "Now, get those shitty thoughts out of that fat head of yours and enjoy yourself. We're alive, single, and not a person would give us a second look." He raised his glass and waited for his partner.

Ernie raised his and they downed the remains of their drink just as Greg brought each of them two more.

He took his elbows off the bar and turned slightly toward Pat.

"Atta boy, Ernie," Pat said. "Now let's settle into a proper session and put that nonsense behind us."

The days passed and Ernie couldn't put it behind him. He had heard during one of the daily briefings of a new encrypted site offering bounties on pimps' heads. He decided to check it out. When he saw Laughing Ronny's picture with a bounty of $425,000, he knew what he needed to do.

Laughing Ronny got his name on account of the scars he carried on his face. When he was fourteen, an older boy in his school pulled a knife on him and cut him from the corners of his mouth to his ears. It was, in part, an experiment to see if the jaw fell off, and partly just out of shear meanness. The older boy was expelled and spent some time in juvenile detention. Ronny spent months in and out of state hospitals but no one was able to reconstruct the skin to erase the event. Each morning he stared at himself in the mirror and was reminded of that day. Every reminder made him feel weak and he vowed to never feel weak again.

Ronny had every sympathy from teachers to parents to politicians, but girls left him alone and he began to feel like a circus freak. He dropped out of school at sixteen and worked with his uncle, who was a petty criminal dabbling in pimping. Ronny realised that dealing in flesh suited him. He flourished and, by the time he was twenty, was making two grand per week. That was twenty-three years ago and he was now a major operator, known to every police department and criminal for five hundred miles.

Today, he listened to a girl pour out her heart to him. He had realised early on that in order to control his girls, he needed to understand them, care for them, and make them totally dependent on him. *It's an art*, he thought. *I'm not some brute who knocks his women around. They love me and depend on me. They know if they hurt me or are disloyal to me, their fates are sealed. But what child wants to be disciplined? They just need to see the whip, not feel it.* In front of him was Caroline, a seventeen-year-old from Eritrea. She was a perfect specimen. If she wasn't so damaged emotionally, he'd call her beautiful.

"Then they came for me, I was twelve. I hid behind my parents. The sound of the pounding on the door was terrible. It felt like my world was ending. Neither my father nor mother said a word. When the door gave way, my mother screamed and put me firmly behind her. My father stepped forward to face the inevitable.

"On that day, my god died. My father was shot, stabbed, and kicked. My mother watched in stunned horror as she was torn between grieving for my father and protecting me. In the end, it didn't matter. My father dead, the hyenas focussed their attention on my mother. There were eight of them. They filled the room with their aggression and male-ness. They grabbed at her, ripping the front of her dress. She was ashamed as only a thin cotton separated her from the attackers. Even that was ripped, exposing one of her breasts.

"My mother pushed me into the corner, only for me to watch as they pulled at her until she was bare to her waist. She was punched in the face for no reason. Her body prone, they ensured she was on her back. Her dress was lifted and their leader pushed his way into her until he was satisfied. When done, he flung her legs aside, smiled at the boys, and nodded to the next. Each invader took their turn. My mother made no sound, except the occasional gasp of an unforeseen cruelty.

"All eight pushed themselves into her. When finished, they turned their attention to me. I was young, barely twelve. The leader came forward and held my face. He turned it to see whether I was something to be savoured or devoured.

"He grabbed my hair and dragged me to a clear area of the room. My father lay dead within my sight. My mother lay in shock; I would have hoped she was unconscious so she didn't need to see what they did to me.

"The leader hit me for no reason other than to establish his dominance. His hands began tracing my body, finding the points of my textile defence. Exasperated, he took his fingers and pushed them down my chest until they reached between my forming breasts. I was an early bloomer and my mother said I needed to get something, I forget what. He pulled heavily and violently toward him, exposing me to his lecherous eyes.

If I could, I would have killed him at that moment. Instead, I was silent. My father was dead, my mother defiled. Who was I to fight?

"What happened next was a repeat of what happened to my mother. All eight entered me, came, and withdrew. All by men, all warriors for their cause. All I could do was stop myself from crying and screaming. My entire being shut down and I just wanted them to finish.

Caroline was crying by now and Ronny brought her next to him, hugging her gently. "That's OK, I understand. You've had to live through a nightmare, but you're safe now. I'll take care of you."

Her tears lessened and she looked up at him. She only reached his shoulder and she could clearly see the white shadows of the scars on his face. She didn't care; he would be her saviour. *Yes*, she thought, *I will need to lie with men for money, but he will make sure I'm not beaten or harmed like that again. Besides, who would want me after what I've been through? I'm damaged goods. I could never be a wife, for what type of man would want a dirty woman like me raise his children? No, this is the best option I have.*

"Tom, take Caroline and put her with Candice and the other girls. They'll take care of her and show her the ropes. Caroline, if there is anything I can do to help, all you need to do is ask."

"Thank you, sir," she said. "You won't regret this. I'll be good."

"I know you will," he said. "Now run along. I have some important things to attend to." He turned around and let Tom remove her from his office. Ron didn't like these types of meetings. He didn't need to hear all of their past. But they needed it and he needed them to work, so he listened and pretended to care. *Besides, if they don't perform, I'll put them to work servicing the illegals.*

∞

"Pat, do you remember when we did the drop on Jerry the Jew?"

"The Chinese guy?"

"That's the one. Anyway, we kind of got out of hand and may have crossed some lines at the time."

Pat didn't respond immediately. He was concentrating on the road, watching the monitor and filtering the voices coming across the dispatch radio. "Yeah, and?"

"And I think I am ready to cross some more lines, but I need you on board."

Pat turned his head and then decided to pull into a 7-11 and see if he could find a decent coffee. He knew he'd be disappointed, but this was a conversation that needed some privacy—even if that just meant turning off the car.

"What are you talking shit for, Ernie?"

"I have a plan and I need you to help."

"I already don't like it but I'm probably in. What is it?"

"Remember that pimp snuff site we were told about at our briefing a few weeks back? I went on it and noticed that our friend Ronny has a bounty of $425,000."

"Holy shit. He must have pissed off someone."

"Look, I don't know if they'll even pay out. Word is that they do, via bitcoin or some other block chain currency. Totally anonymous and untraceable."

"I'm not sure I like where this is going, but OK."

"I want to take him out."

"To dinner?"

"No, you asshole. I want him dead and I want us to claim the bounty. We'll be killing two birds with one stone. Ron doesn't deserve to breathe and we just can't seem to get him on anything."

"Yeah, he's too clever that one. But this is serious shit, Ernie. I don't fancy seeing myself gang raped in the shower by the perps we put away."

"Me either, and that's why I need your help. I'll do what needs to be done but I need a backup in case things turn south."

Pat pursed his lips. "I don't like this one bit, I just want to say in advance. But I'm in. Just don't go getting our balls shot off in the process." He opened the car door and walked toward the shop. He needed a drink but a coffee and donut would have to do.

It took another three weeks of planning before they actually decided to act. They didn't want to chance a frontal assault, so they would try to get him when he was sleeping or make it look like a turf struggle.

"The good news is that he's king of the heap at present," Ernie said. "As a result, he's overconfident."

"And he's not expecting an ambush. His security team is bare bones," Pat said.

They were dressed in jeans and leather jackets, their badges clipped firmly to their waistbands. They carried two semi-auto pistols each, one in a shoulder holster and the other on the ankle.

"Remind me why we want to do this?" Pat whispered.

"Because it needs to be done," replied Ernie. "You stay here by the back entrance and make sure you take care of any runners. I'm going through the front."

"Ernie?"

"Yeah?"

"Be careful, you sonofabitch. There's no turning back once you go through that door."

Ernie nodded and stood erect as he walked from the alley to the front entrance of the club. It closed officially at 4 am, or at least that was when they couldn't serve any more alcohol. Ernie knew that Ronny was serving up other goodies and that the booze was just icing on the cake. Tuesday mornings were quiet and he didn't see any patrons coming or going. He nodded to the bouncer at the front door, pulled back his jacket to show his badge, and walked in.

The entrance was dark and relatively narrow with a counter on the right. There was no one behind the counter so Jack kept on walking. It wasn't a strip joint and there were people of both sexes talking and occasionally dancing. It was a place to hook up with a stranger—whether paid for or not. Ronny just made sure that unaccompanied men soon found a willing partner.

All of this was a front for his real business of pimping girls. He had other legitimate outlets to move the cash—restaurants and bars—and that element was constantly growing. *Why does he stay in this world when he has more than enough to go totally legit?* Ernie thought. *I guess none of us knows when to get out while the getting's good.*

The music was subdued but not quiet. He noticed a handful of bodies in the shadows but he walked straight to the back room where he knew Ronny and his gang would be.

"You can't be back here," said a voice before Ernie was able to focus on the figure.

"Police. I just need a word with Ronny. Is he back there?"

"Stay here. Let me check." It was less than two minutes before he was back. "OK, you can go through."

I wasn't searched, wasn't told to show my ID; *all I did was say I was police. They don't know me from Adam. Very sloppy,* he thought as he walked through a set of double doors into Ronny's inner sanctum

"My policeman," Ronny said joyfully and a bit loud. "How can we help you today?"

"Ronny, I just wanted to see if you were prepared to turn yourself in."

That was met with a loud round of laughter from Ronny and his three minders. They had been watching a movie with some girls. Each goon had a girl and Ronny had two. They each had their own sofa.

"Caroline, take yourself and the other girls back to the residence. We'll be around shortly. I just need to talk to this policeman." He was looking directly at Ernie as the girls removed themselves. The minders all stood up. Ronny remained seated.

"You come into my place of business and embarrass me in front of my friends?" He waived his hand towards his security detail, obviously enjoying the drama he was currently directing.

"It looks like your friends are missing their companions," Ernie said.

"I'm sure, but that is also your fault. It was your rudeness that made them leave."

Ernie pulled out his gun and, in one fluid motion, shot the three minders in their heads. It happened so fast none of them reacted. Even Ronny watched with detachment.

"Did you save a bullet for me?"

Ronny was looking straight down Ernie's barrel when the doors opened behind him. It was the man from outside, a mass of muscle and teeth. He wasn't drunk and moved like a man half his size.

"Police," Ernie shouted. "Put your weapon down." He was backing away so he could see both the mountain and Ronny, moving his gun from one to the other.

"It's okay, Edgar, nothing's going to happen," Ronny said. "You can put the gun down."

Ernie was astonished at Ronny's calm.

"Okay, Mr. Policeman. You have my attention. What do you want from me? A job?"

"No. Your bounty." Ernie pulled the trigger and watched Ronny's head snap back. He swirled toward the mountain and emptied the rest of the clip into his head and torso. He reached to grab his phone and called Pat. "Call it in, major incident at Ronny's. We'll need some ambulances. Five confirmed dead. Bring in backup." He pressed the red button to end the call. His fingers were shaking. He depressed the button holding the clip and watched the empty magazine fall to the ground. He put in a fresh clip and walked toward the three minders. Feeling inside their jackets, he found their guns. With a tissue, he pulled out their guns and fired two shots in the direction of where he was standing. He did this with each of them as well as with the mountain man. He didn't find a gun on Ronny and swore to himself.

"Holy shit," Pat said when he finally arrived on the scene. He looked at the holes in the walls, the people, and the blood. "You'll get a medal for this." He put his arm around Ernie and walked him past the gathering crowd of police detectives and sirens breaking the silence of the growing dawn.

Chapter Eighteen

IN SEARCH OF NORMALITY

"These hot springs are sensational," Jack said. "But the green water is tough to get used to."

"Don't listen to him, Mom," Chrystal said. "It was a great idea. Look at the stone with the beautiful moss on it. It's as though we are the only people on the planet, tucked away in this little miniature gorge."

"Vale is beautiful. Most of the hot springs are pretty basic, but this little section of rock is unbelievable. Hector was right; this would be something special to share with both of you."

"This Hector sounds like he is making quite an impression on you."

"More than an impression." Tammy's voice was soft. "I really like him."

"Congratulations, Tam. You deserve to be happy. I'm really excited for you."

"Yeah, me too, Mom."

"Thanks. It's been a while since I felt safe enough to feel something toward anyone." She was silent for a moment and the three of them sank neck deep in the hot water. The weather had turned cooler and it was below freezing with snow dusted on the horizon to make the picture even more complete.

"Do you think we could get sick like this?" Jack said. "The cold air and hot water are great, but what happens when we get out of the water?"

"We run like hell!" Tammy said with a toothy grin.

"Hmmm. I think I'll stay in until I become all wrinkly and someone comes to throw me out," Chrystal said. Her eyes were closed, enjoying the unending warmth, steam, and company.

"I'm with Chrys for at least another ten minutes," Jack said. "But I'm going to need to start planning my escape. Where to next?"

"We'll wrap up in the fleece robes and casually walk to the car," Tammy said, half smiling. "Then we'll go to the lodge and enjoy the rest of the day." She paused and then added hesitantly. "Do you want to meet Hector? He'll be there but I didn't commit to introducing you two to him."

Chrystal opened her eyes, suddenly interested. "Hell, yeah. I've been dying to meet him for three months." She started getting out of the water. "I'm ready to meet him now."

Tammy laughed. "We'll see him soon enough. We can have lunch together when we are all settled in." She couldn't have been happier. A new man who cared for her, a daughter who loved her, and a friend who changed her world for the better.

The transition from heat to freezing air didn't go down well with Jack and Chrystal at first, nor did the fifteen-minute drive to the lodge, but they were laughing and joking too much to care.

"The hot springs in winter really get the blood flowing," Tammy said.

"Sure Mom, almost as much as Hector." She had her hand lightly on Jack's leg as he drove. Tammy just smiled in the backseat and towelled her wet hair.

"Not everyone is as lucky as the two of you, Chrys," Tammy said. "I'm just happy at my age to have found someone."

"Are you kidding? You're hot and smart and rich. I would have thought you'd be beating them off with a stick."

"Not the ones you want, unfortunately," Tammy said with a sigh. "But Heck is one of the good guys. He's educated and, to me, gorgeous. He's got a strong jaw and looks you straight in the eye. Tall, but not freakishly so; strong with muscles, but not so much that he's in love with himself. And most of all, he seems to genuinely like me. He listens and talks about interesting things—from opera to philosophy—and likes to watch the romantic movies I like instead of only the violence most guys are into."

"So you've fallen for him hook, line, and sinker."

Tammy sighed. "Yes, I think so."

They reached the lodge and went to their respective suites. It was rustic luxury with lots of wood and glass and expansive views of trees and snow. There were real fireplaces in each of their suites with cosy armchairs beside them.

"Romantic stuff," Jack said. "You'd think we needed buttering up. I'd be happy with a tent and a single sleeping bag for the two of us." He reached for Chrystal and pulled her toward him.

"It works for me," she said.

∞

Lunch was at 1:30 with drinks before at the bar. Jack and Chrystal arrived a little late and noticed Tammy sitting in an overstuffed Queen Anne chair, leaning forward. The winged edges prevented them from seeing who she was talking to. They walked in an arc to reach her and saw a refined gentleman in a tailored suit. He had a cravat instead of a tie and stood when they arrived.

"You must be Chrystal and Jack. I'm Hector. I've heard a lot about you." He accepted Chrystal's handshake but then leaned in and kissed her lightly on each cheek. He gave Jack a firm handshake.

"Mostly good, I hope," Jack said, finding a seat in one of the winged chairs.

"All good. Almost too good to be true, if I didn't trust the source so much." Hector looked at Tammy and smiled. She melted. Chrystal watched them with a genuine smile, eyes wide and full of happiness.

"Shall we order some drinks?" Tammy asked. "We decided to wait for you."

"Unless anyone has an objection, let's have champagne," Jack said. When everyone nodded, he got up to go to the bar.

"No, Jack, please. Sit. I'll order it and get some bits and pieces to go with it." Hector was trying hard to impress. So far, it was working. When he was gone, Tammy leaned in.

"Well?" She was nervous and her eyes darted between Jack and Chrystal.

"I think he's like a modern-day Prince Charming, Mom."

"He's got a good handshake and he's not shy," Jack said. "So far, so good."

"He makes me so happy," Tammy said. "I feel like a teenager."

"I'm so happy for you. Sorry, I'm going to cry," said Chrystal. Jack handed her a napkin from the coffee table.

"Don't or you'll start me off as well." Tammy reached for another napkin and dabbed her eyes.

When Hector returned, the eyes were dried, but a little puffy if someone looked closely.

"I ordered some specialities of the house. Hopefully they're not too fattening or tasty. I was looking forward to lunch. They have one of the best clam chowders on the west coast and the rest of the menu is locally sourced and prepared purely with what is fresh."

"You'd think every restaurant would be forced to serve fresh food," Jack said, but regretted it as soon as it left his mouth. He didn't want to sound like he was ridiculing Hector.

"I agree," Hector said. "It's a sad indictment of our eating habits that the vast majority of what we eat is either reheated or frozen, even in restaurants."

"Especially in restaurants," Tammy said. Jack could see she was going to agree with anything Hector said.

Soon the oysters and caviar arrived with their bottle of champagne.

"The caviar is local, so try not to be snobbish about it," Hector said with a smile. "I'm told it's as good as Beluga but I've yet to be convinced." He put some on a little cracker and put it in Tammy's mouth. She closed her eyes and nodded. "Not bad?"

"It's excellent," she said. "I'm no expert but I can get used to whatever that was."

Jack and Chrystal reached for the oysters as their glasses were filled. They had to hold the oyster uneaten in one hand while toasting and clinking their glasses in the other. When the first toast was made and drunk, they were able to finish the oyster.

"I really like this place," Chrystal said. "Good recommendation, Hector."

"Thank you. I wanted to make a good impression and for you all to be comfortable."

"Scored on both counts," Jack said.

They continued their light banter for the duration of the champagne and snacks before moving to the dining room. Another bottle was ordered and they all started with the chowder. Another bottle, this time a vintage white Burgundy, was had with the catch of the day. Another bottle, a sweet Moscato, was enjoyed with their dessert, which ended up being a selection of house sweets ranging from a gooey chocolate brownie to a sophisticated work of art that towered on each dish.

"That was an excellent meal, as was the company," Hector said. "Thank you for making this a truly memorable day."

"The pleasure has been all ours," Chrystal said. "You have been the mystery man and now you are real. I've been dying to meet you."

Jack sat, full, extending his torso and eying the triple espresso in front of him. Tammy was flush with both alcohol and happiness as Hector fit so well with the two most important people in her life.

Hector hesitated and then said, "There's a cigar room here if any of you smoke." He looked cautiously at Tammy and Chrystal and then Jack.

Jack salivated at the words. He told himself he didn't smoke, despite the odd cigarette, but cigars were one of the few pleasures he allowed himself. He had only two provisos: that the cigars would be the best quality and that the person he smokes with enjoy them just as much. It was a guilty pleasure that harmed his body but made his soul sing. "I'd be very interested."

"If Jack's in, I'm in," Chrystal said.

"Then it looks like we're going to the cigar room," Tammy said. She didn't smoke but would join the others and have a puff or two.

"This day just gets better and better," Hector said. He was grinning like a schoolboy about to play hooky.

They decamped to the cigar room and expanded themselves into the leather chesterfield sofas and admired the oak panelling and flooring. In the shelves were leather-bound first editions and bottles of the finest brandies and scotches. An extensive list of alcohol on offer was bound up in a leather book, which sat on the edge of each table.

"Cuban or Honduran?" Hector looked at Jack.

"I'm easy going. I like Cuban; I don't know Honduran. I have tried Nicaraguan and liked those. But, to be safe, it'll be Cuban."

"Any preference?"

"Cohiba Siglio VI, if they have it." Jack was embarrassed to know this, but Hector wouldn't find it snobbish if he was a connoisseur.

"I'll have one of those, as well," he said.

"Me, too," said Chrystal.

"I'll just kill myself indirectly then," Tammy said, smiling. She was standing next to Hector with her arm gently on his back as he opened the humidor. She watched as he cut the ends and passed the cigars to her daughter and Jack. She found it hypnotising.

They lit their cigars and sat back down onto the chesterfields. The smokers puffed and played with their cigars, rolling them in their fingers and admiring the glowing ember. Tammy took a tentative puff and coughed, causing laughter as they settled into more conversation.

"So tell me, Jack, where are you from?"

"Nowhere, really. Middle of nowhere, USA. You?"

"Just outside New York City in a small town called Shirley. You probably have never heard of it."

"Can't say I have. Is that north of New York?"

"East."

"East?" Jack put his eyebrows together. "Isn't that Long Beach?"

Hector smiled. "Busted. Shirley is just west of the Hamptons."

"A real hardship. Tough childhood? Bullying and missed meals growing up?"

"Yeah, back in the 'hood." Hector smiled. "Life was good but that was as much about being young as being rich."

"Being rich doesn't hurt," Chrystal said. She was puffing away like an expert, the white ash forming in the wake of the glowing ember.

"And how did you meet Tammy and Chrystal?"

Jack gulped, not really wanting to go there in his mind or conversation. Tammy and Chrystal held their breath imperceptibly. "You know how things go. I bumped into them and one thing led to another, and here we are." The woman resumed their breathing.

"Well then. To good fortune." Hector raised his glass of brandy.

"To good fortune," Jack clinked his glass. They drank, changed the subject, and smoked for another two hours before retiring to bed.

∞

"What do you think of Mom's new man?"

"He's a hell of a nice guy," Jack said. "There were moments where I needed to remind myself to be careful. We need to impress this on your Mom as well. There are some secrets that need to remain unspoken."

"She knows that. She's just happy, that's all."

"I'm sure. Things are going well. We've had over 612 confirmed bounty collections so far. Some were expensive because of the extent of the person's operations. We'll see as time unfolds how much more we can do." Jack had showered and brushed his teeth. The cigar was great to smoke but it lingered if you didn't clean up.

"Looks like your plan is going well."

"It is. I'd like to implement phase two soon—targeting the purveyors of porn and prostitution. There is no reason for any five-year-old to be subjected to this when they turn on their computer. Parental locks can be overcome by any kid with half a brain. We need to find a way to prolong innocence in our children. We will all fall at some point, but let's give them until they are older before they start facing the world."

"If we had kids, I wouldn't want them to face what I did—ever," Chrystal said. She looked at Jack and saw the father of her future children. She couldn't imagine a better man to be with or to raise their children.

"If we had kids," Jack said, "I wouldn't let them out of the house until they were twenty-one." He rolled onto his back and looked at the wooden beams with their artistic knots. He wondered at the beauty of nature to create so much life and at humankind's tendency to use and destroy what was around it.

"Don't fool yourself, Jack. You'd be a good father."

He rolled back on his side and looked at Chrystal. She had let her hair grow and it was now a mane. She loved him despite his murderous actions and urges. He thought himself a peaceful man but found himself killing or causing people to be killed. The solutions he came up with to problems involved killing. He had begun to think of himself as an intolerant man, unprepared to listen to centuries-old wisdom about the sanctity of life. He had begun to think that this unwillingness to kill was the weakness in society's assumptions and prevented it from removing the cancer from society's body. He also knew that many innocent people would die, but he lacked a better solution. And that was not a sufficient reason to do nothing.

He rolled off the bed and stood up. He went to his luggage and pulled something out and put it in his pocket. When he turned to Chrystal, she had sat up and was on the edge of the bed, a quizzical look on her face. "Is everything OK?"

Jack stood in front of her. Looking at her, he began to lower himself until he was kneeling. He reached into his robe's pocket and pulled out a small box. He opened it without a word and put it in her hand. "Chrystal Alberts, will you marry me?"

Her mouth opened slightly and tears began to flow freely down her cheeks. The silence lasted a moment before her head started to move, imperceptibly at first, and then more definitely. She was nodding, then smiling. "Yes. Yes, of course I'll marry you."

Chapter Nineteen

SHADOWS CAST LONG

"So where are you planning to get married and when's the big day?" Tammy was beyond excited. Her life had seen the lowest of lows and now the highest of highs. She was in a job she loved, meeting powerful people who impacted the world in significant ways. She was, dare she whisper the words, in love with Hector. Her daughter was overseeing a multibillion-dollar investment fund and was marrying its owner and patron. It was a real-life fairy tale come true, complete with a princess and prince.

"We haven't set a date yet and we're not sure where," Chrystal said. It had been three weeks since the proposal and they were back in New York City. Tammy was able to carve out an afternoon tea at the Ritz-Carlton with Chrystal and go through the details.

"What do you mean?"

"Jack wants to get married in a church, synagogue, mosque, and Buddhist temple. Just don't tell him any other places or it'll be impossible." Chrystal smiled. "He said he wanted to make sure that whatever we did was recognised—just in case we got married in front of the wrong god."

"Buddhism doesn't have a god," Tammy said dryly.

"You know what I mean. I think it's sweet."

"Okay, it's romantic but nonsensical. You can't have four weddings."

"It gets worse. He wants to get married in the Vatican, Jerusalem, Mecca, and Nepal."

"He's crazy. You can't even go to Mecca unless you are a confirmed Muslim, and I don't think the Pope is going to let dear old Jack pop around for a quick confirmation just to get married in the Holy See."

"Don't be such a party pooper. Have a scone."

"I just want it to be perfect for you."

"Anything we do will be perfect. At least the honeymoon will be spectacular. We'll stay at the Taj in Mumbai for as long as we feel like before heading to Capetown for two weeks. Our final destination will be Paris, wandering the Champs Elysees, aimlessly crossing the bridges and soaking up the romance."

Tammy looked at her daughter, glowing in anticipation. "I bet you'd be happy with a marriage at the registry office and a trip to a campsite for your honeymoon."

"You bet. I can't think or breathe when he's around lately. I'm so excited, my mind is upside down."

"And your biological clock is hammering you so hard, nothing else matters," Tammy said. "I'm so happy for you, I can't put it in words."

"Speaking of which, he wants enough children to form our own soccer team." Chrystal tried not to burst laughing when she said it. "Ever since his proposal, he's like a different man. He is talking about the future with hope and I haven't heard anything about, you know, the other stuff at all."

"Whatever you plan, let me know and I'll be there. I am starting to like the idea of the Vatican, Jerusalem, Mecca, and Nepal." Tammy took a bite from her crust-cut sandwich and poured some more tea. "Enjoy the excitement. Before you know it, the big day will be upon you."

"I'm taking one day at a time. Are you bringing Hector?"

"Try to stop me. We're having a charity function tomorrow night at the Rockefeller Center. Perhaps you and Jack would like to come? I think it would be fun."

"That sounds good. I'll run it past him just in case there is a conflict, but I think you can count us in." She raised her glass of pink champagne and they toasted their good fortune.

The next day was a Friday and the sun made it glorious. The early spring sun in New York transformed

the otherwise stoic city faces into smiling hopeful vis-
ages. The indifferent Rockefeller Center stood sentry
over the shoppers, tourists, and business people. At 9
pm, Jack and Chrystal joined Tammy and Hector after
the initial charity auctions were done and the food was
eaten. The fun was in the mingling with famous faces.
Past presidents rubbed shoulders with Hollywood A-
listers, future presidents rubbed shoulders with titans
of industry, and everyone else did what they could to
be noticed or recognised.

"Quite the crowd," Jack said to Hector. "Do you
come to these events often?"

"Not really my scene," he replied. "You?"

"Never. First time."

"Jack, do you want to get us some shots? Everyone's drinking champagne and it's getting boring."

"I like your contrariness, Chrys. Coming right up."
Jack got up to go the bar. It was three deep in people
before he could reach the glass and marble top.

"What'll you have?" The bartender looked like a
guy but Jack wasn't sure. Ever since transgender had
gone mainstream, he'd become conscious to adjust his
first impressions.

"Some shots if you have 'em. Four flaming B52s
and a couple beers."

"Coming right up." Jack saw him, or her, swivel
and grab the shot glasses and pour the booze in layers.
S/he grabbed two bottles of beer, not asking a brand
preference, and placed them all in front of Jack. "I'll

give you a tray or you'll never handle the flames. Just bring it back later." The shots were lit and Jack turned to go.

"Can I get four G29s?" Hector said it to the bartender in a way that was intended for Jack to hear.

"No such thing, buddy."

"OK, not a problem." He turned and followed Jack.

Jack walked in silence, not acknowledging Hector's remark. *It couldn't be a coincidence,* he thought. *G29? No one knows what that is. How could Hector, of all people?*

He didn't need to walk long before Hector put himself in front of Jack before they got to the table. "We need to talk," he said.

"Not here, not now," Jack said. *Shit, shit, shit.*

"Then soon." He spun around just in time to hand out the flaming B52s to Tammy and Chrystal.

"To Jack and Chrystal." He raised his shot to the others and drank it back.

"To the future," Chrystal said.

"To love," Tammy said.

Oh shit, Jack thought.

∞

"You were looking a little off tonight," Chrystal said. "Is everything alright?"

"Yeah, it must have been something I ate. You know, there are so many people with their hands touching everything, sneezing on things, I may have picked up a bug. I'm not feeling great."

They hailed a cab and Jack opened the door for Chrystal to get in. As he began to bend into the vehicle, he felt a hand on the door and a presence next to him. He turned to see Hector. He must have jogged to close the gap between them on the way out. He didn't look out of breath, but he did have a serious look on his face.

"Jack, I just wanted to catch up before you disappeared. Remember that thing we were talking about? Do you want to meet up tomorrow to continue our discussion? I think you may find it interesting."

"Actually, Heck, I'm catching an early flight to Miami. Perhaps when I'm back and you're here, we go through things in detail."

Hector's hand was still on the door, leaning in toward Jack and Chrystal. His body language said he didn't believe Jack but to act otherwise would have been even more suspicious. "Have a safe flight and I'll see you on your return." He closed the door and tapped the taxi's roof.

"What was that about, Jack?"

"I'm not sure."

"I didn't know you were heading to Miami tomorrow."

"I'm not, but I think I'll pop over to Winnipeg and see Isabella. I have a bad feeling about Hector."

"I think he's adorable." Chrystal came close to him. "He is so nice to Mom and he is rich, to boot. No gold digging from his side. No agendas. Just a nice romantic story of boy meets girl."

"Like us, you mean."

"Like us," she said before she kissed him. Her body was soft and gentle against him. Her perfume was like an entire world to his senses as she shared her space with him. He never tired of her and repeatedly found himself being surprised by her. He knew he could trust her. She was a strength in his world of uncertainty; the only good thing he truly knew. He put his arm around her and they cuddled contentedly while the taxi made its way back to their suite.

In the end, Jack didn't go to Miami or Winnipeg. He woke up feeling strangely calm, resigned to what would happen. He had a long, hot shower and went for a shave and a haircut at the hotel's barbershop. He enjoyed the resurgence of men's hairstyling places—old-style barbers where you could get a shave and a haircut while talking politics or sports while a real gentleman cut your hair. No gimmicks or skinny models with weird haircuts in black-and-white posters in the window or walls. No salon products being flogged on every surface. If you wanted, you could get your shoes polished at the same time. For the regulars, there was a stack of dirty magazines in the back they would pull out, or the *Financial Times* on the front table next to the *New York Times* and *Washington Post*. Jack opted for *The Economist* as he didn't feel like talking.

When he was done, he grabbed a second cup of coffee and called Hector. *May as well get this over with,* he thought.

"Hi Hector, it's Jack."

"Yes, the meeting was cancelled so I thought I'd give you a call and see what your movements were."

"That sounds good. Should we say eleven this morning?"

"Perfect. See you then." He put his phone back in his shirt pocket and began walking.

The joggers and cyclists were never ending and it began to unnerve Jack. *I guess it's better than a tread-mill, but it's still running in circles,* he thought. Central Park was an oasis of controlled green in a jungle of concrete. He sought out water and found himself at the pond. Coffee long gone, he found a food cart and got another, along with a pastry. *I need my blood sugar at the right level. Now I'm talking to myself again. Calm down, Jack, calm down.*

Hector showed up at 10:30 and sat on the bench next to him. They nodded and shook hands but neither said anything for a short while.

"I know this must come as a shock to you, Jack."

"I'm not sure what you are talking about."

"You're not in trouble. I'm just reaching out. I've been given orders to take over and wanted to give you the courtesy of being part of the team again."

"What team?"

"You know what team. The same team that Joe and your parents were on. The same team I'm on. The same team you should be on."

Jack nodded in realisation more than agreement. "Then you are real."

"Real as a heart attack. We've been monitoring you since the untimely death of your parents and Joe. We let you run because there was no benefit in bringing you in."

Jack looked at him. "You knew where I was all this time and you did nothing?"

"You must understand. We deal with every nationality and personality on the planet, from dictators to little old ladies. As far as we were concerned, you are a patriot."

Then they don't know about the June Terror, Jack thought. *Good. He's fishing.* "What do you want from me?"

"We were impressed when you finally began to be proactive with the tools Joe gave you. We actually didn't know he had access to all of that money. It was one of the reasons we let you believe you were free. We didn't want to reel you in until it was worthwhile."

"And now it is?"

"Exactly. You have created an admirable entity that's invisible but in plain view. Even our group can't do what you did anymore. Those swashbuckling days are over. Everything requires oversight, committees, permission, and politics at every level. It's amazing we are able to do our job at all."

"So what are you saying?" Jack wasn't going to volunteer anything and wanted to hear it directly from the horse's mouth.

"I think it's time you returned what's rightfully ours."

"And?" It couldn't be that easy. Jack couldn't see himself getting off that lightly.

"And we want you to join us and be responsible to us. We can't have players within the US borders operating internationally and being above the law. We know about your little bounty scheme. Clever. Effective. But it is going to end now."

"Then why did you allow it in the first place?"

"We wanted to see if it worked. If it was a disaster, we would arrest you and be heroes. If it worked, we would simply take it over and redirect the siphoned funds to projects more deserving than a few whores and runaways."

Jack bit his lip. "And Tammy? Was that all part of the trap?"

Hector shrugged. "Sometimes we get pleasure with business. We have engineered one of our companies to be taken over by your group and I am now on the board of directors, as you know. Tammy is the chair and CEO, and she has the votes from the shareholders."

"And Chrystal represents the shareholders," Jack said.

"Yes, but you are the shareholder." Hector said this and waited. It had the desired effect. "Your silence speaks volumes, Jack. We were impressed with your cover story and the lengths by which you tried to cover things up. This is one of the reasons we value this asset. It is the perfect front for what we need."

Jack found his voice. "The CIA needs to take over private companies to do its wet work? I find your whole premise insane. We spend hundreds of billions on wars and defence annually. I'm sure G29 could find some spare change without harassing me."

"But Jack, the money you used is ours. We are prepared not to charge you or drag you through the mud. This is as much a complement to your efforts as us exercising our right to utilise assets that rightfully belong to us."

"If I refuse?"

"Then we will apply pressure," Hector said, leaning back on the bench. "You remember the effect Detective Clog had on you all those years ago?"

Jack would never forget. To a large extent, it was because of Clog's behaviour that he was sitting here now. He was underhanded and untrustworthy; typical CIA. "What are you going to do? Kill me? Kill Tammy and Chrystal? And then what? Congratulate yourselves on your ability to pull a trigger?"

"You are upset, Jack. Think about this and let's get together soon. I'll be in touch." Hector put his hand on Jack's shoulder and left.

Jack watched the ducks swim in formation and the children squealing to feed them. Mothers pushed their strollers and the old timers read their magazines or simply stared into the distance. *What difference does it make?* he thought. *It was never about power or money, just getting things done. It has been twenty years since that night when Joe shot my parents and then himself. Twenty years of being on the run. Twenty years of thinking I was free from those animals.*

∞

When Jack returned to their suite, Chrystal was in full bridal mode. She was meeting with her mother to try on dresses later that day and was determined to nail down what the actual wedding ceremony would look like.

"You want to have a multi-faith ceremony? Why not have a priest, rabbi, and imam preside in one place and get it over with in one shot?"

Jack laughed at the idea. "You may as well ask why we can't have peace in the Middle East. Yes, we could get representatives from each religion but they would be so liberal we may as well not use them."

"Come on, Jack. I'm trying. I know you want to have a grand statement of how you love everyone and everything, but this is about us."

"Then why don't we have a simple ceremony at City Hall and get it over with?" Jack didn't need the ceremony at all. "The idea of getting married four times was just me getting carried away with the romantic gesture of being recognised as having chosen you before all others."

"Aww, Jack. You are the most romantic person I know." She put down the bridal magazines and kissed him deeply.

"Careful or I'll make you late for your dress fittings," Jack said as he grabbed her.

Chrystal pushed away playfully and resumed looking at the magazines.

"Chrystal, I met with Hector this morning."

"How's he doing?"

"He's OK, but he said something that may affect us deeply."

She put down her things in her lap. "Like what?"

"I don't know how to say this, so I'll just blurt it out. He's from a highly secretive group with the CIA. It's called Group 29. G29 has been tracking me for the last twenty years and are fully aware of our company's real ownership structure and purpose."

Chrystal's hands let go of the magazines and they slid onto the floor. Neither of them reached to pick them up. When she spoke, it was with a quiver in her voice. "What does that mean? Are we all going to jail? Or worse?"

"To tell you the truth, I don't know."

"Then what does he want you to do?"

"He wants me to join the group and he wants G29 to take over the company."

Chrystal was relieved. "That's all? Then do it. Join his stupid little party and give him the company. We don't need it."

"I don't think you understand what this means. You don't leave this group. It doesn't even exist if you try to find it. You leave when you die, and you do what they say or die. It's not the Boy Scouts."

"We haven't exactly been acting like the Boy Scouts, either."

"But it was for a purpose we both believed in. I have only scratched the surface. Killing scumbag pimps was the tip of the iceberg. I haven't managed to stop internet porn. Someone needs to do something. The government has only one solution: regulate and oversee. The problem is that further regulations and laws are only followed by the law abiding public. Their solution is to further enslave the citizenry. It's not the way. All it takes is a bad leader and, along with these bad laws, we will become actual slaves instead of the figurative slaves we currently are."

"Jack, I don't want to lose our life we built together. It's been almost ten years since we met on that road to Las Vegas. I still have nightmares of being caught and the things they made us do. I can't return to that."

"I don't want to return to that either, Chrys, but at least we were free, or felt free, in our decisions. We did what we wanted to do. If I join this group, my life is over. If Hector takes over the company, then Tammy becomes irrelevant, as do you and I."

"He wouldn't do that to Mom," she said.

"They aren't normal and they don't have any choice. They are merely agents working for invisible people behind the scenes who call the shots. We don't know what their objectives are, but our happiness doesn't factor into it."

Chrystal was silent. "Then we don't need them. We'll give them the company and tell them to leave us alone."

"I wish it was so simple. I tried that once, many years ago. Do you want to know what they did to me?"

"What?"

"They stabbed me in the stomach, almost killing me. Then they broke up my relationship with a girl I was with by showing her faked pictures and phone records." *Then they put a girl with me who spied on me constantly but who I thought was the love of my life. She didn't care about me at all.* He had thought occasionally about Carey and what became of her. He still couldn't determine whether she was spying on him from the start or whether she actually liked him and only turned against him later. He pushed those thoughts out of his head and concentrated on the present.

"I'm not some stupid girl and we'll figure this thing out together." Chrystal sat next to Jack and put her hands in his. She put on a brave face but was worried. She didn't know if she really had what it took to stand up to the CIA.

"Do you think we should talk to your mom?"

"I don't think we have a choice." Chrystal got up and went to the bathroom. She needed a shower. All of a sudden she felt dirty.

∞

"Yes, Chrys, he told me all about it a few days ago. I suggested he talk to Jack and work things out. That's why he raised the subject last night at the Rockefeller Center."

Chrystal was thunderstruck. "You knew about this and didn't say anything?"

"Only a few days."

"What did he tell you?" She became suspicious.

"That he worked for a secretive government agency and that he needed Jack's help."

"Did he tell you that he worked for the CIA?"

"No, but I figured it must have been one of them." Tammy seemed more preoccupied with the dresses in front of her than the subject at hand.

"Did he tell you that his agency ordered the death of Jack's parents?"

Tammy stopped fussing. "No." Her face became ashen.

"Or that they aren't allowed to retire? They work for the agency until they die or are killed."

"I can't imagine Hector being part of that. He's a businessman who was recruited himself. I only got to know him as a result of our merger with his company.

His family is established. He's not a government spy and definitely not a killer."

"Maybe you can talk further with him. Maybe Jack's mistaken," Chrystal said, becoming uncertain in the face of her mother's absolute confidence.

Tammy visibly shook herself as a bird might after a winter's snow. "Let's focus on you and your big day. I think this pattern is divine." Watching the strain on her mother's face as she pushed the news aside and willed everything to be OK, Chrystal laughed and forced herself to forget about Jack's news. Neither one fully believed things to be as bad as Jack said.

Chapter Twenty

ROCK AND HARD PLACE

"You care about your women and that is admirable," Hector said. He took another draw from his cigar and sip from his brandy. "This really is a great place, isn't it?"

Jack was also having a cigar and a large scotch whiskey, neat. The room had a high ceiling and was enclosed to keep the humidity at the perfect level. "Spectacular," Jack said. "Shame about the company."

"You don't need to get nasty. I'm just doing my job."

"I've been thinking about your offer, Hector, if that is really your name. I need to know that both Tammy and Chrystal are safe. You can have your money and company, but I won't join your club. I'm out. I'm done with all of that."

Hector finished his drink and stood to pour himself another. Jack shook his head when he lifted the bottle.

"Let me tell you how this is going to happen. If we don't get you, then the rest falls by the wayside. The entire bullshit history that you created is predicated on your existence. Tammy and Chrystal are irrelevant. They're expendable, as are you or I. But you are less expendable than them."

Jack didn't like where this was heading. "So what are you going to do if I simply refuse? You can't make me do this."

"We'll see. Is that what you are telling me?"

"That is what I'm telling you." Jack finished his scotch and put his cigar in the ashtray, barely half smoked. "Thanks for the cigar and drink. This really is a nice place."

Hector watched him leave and poured himself another brandy.

∞

"Hector!" Tammy waived her hand as she saw him on the sidewalk. She had hoped to have had a chat with him yesterday after seeing Chrys and trying on the dresses, but their schedules didn't allow it. She hadn't been able to contact him on the phone all day and it was just by chance that she saw him.

"Tammy, what a pleasure. Sorry about the phone. I've been chalk a block all day so far." He kissed her on both cheeks and held her hands. "What are your plans for lunch?"

"I am pretty tied up with meetings. Can you do dinner?"

"I prefer dinner," smiled Hector. "By the way, I just saw Jack and he's a bit upset. I don't think he understands the facts of the situation."

"He's usually a model of pragmatism," Tammy said. "Can I do anything to help?"

"Yes," Hector said, still smiling. "You can tell him that if he doesn't co-operate, I'll be forced to disclose some unfortunate information that has come my way about you and your daughter. Nothing too drastic, just videos. I have no intention of disclosing the murders Chrystal committed or you condoned."

Tammy went cold and her tongue felt a piece of leather. The sirens of a passing ambulance cut through her head and the horns of the taxis sounded like heavy artillery, their percussive force pounding her body. She shook her head as the love of her life said these words. The words and actions were incongruous to the man she knew. And dinner? What was that about? How could he talk about dinner with a smile while blackmailing her about her most embarrassing and demoralised time in her life?

"You don't need to say anything now," he continued pleasantly. "We can talk later. Shall I pick you up at seven?"

She nodded numbly and he kissed her on the cheek again, then walked away. Even his gait looked hardened as she could feel his footsteps on the pavement as he disappeared into the crowds. Suddenly, she had trouble standing and her legs gave way. All she remembered was shouting and arms helping her back to her feet and into the hotel lobby. Chrystal arrived within the hour and they went to her suite.

"You know, I don't even have a home to go to when this is all over?" Tammy said through tears.

"Don't worry, Mom. We'll figure something out. Jack made sure we each had some money stashed away in a rainy-day fund."

"Well, it's raining today."

"What came over Hector to talk like that? Has he ever said something like that to you before?"

"Never. He's been the most gentle and understanding man I've ever met—except for Jack. I didn't think they actually made men like that anymore. A proper gentleman." Tammy blew her nose and looked at Chrystal. "Is there any chance you can convince Jack to join? How bad can it be? It's the US government, for Christ's sake. They're on our side. They're the good guys."

"I know. I don't understand why he doesn't want to join." Her head reminded her of the real reasons, but she couldn't accept that the CIA would do that. "When I heard that's all they wanted, I was relieved. I didn't realise Jack would walk away from everything instead of joining."

"There's something we don't know about Jack. Maybe he is as bad as Hector, Chrys. Maybe he's just like all the other men who have hurt us." She started crying again, as much from her breaking heart as from the words. "All we have is each other."

Chrystal put her arm around her and held her tight. "I'm with you, Mom, whatever happens. We're a team. Don't cry. I love you. Please don't cry." She became the little girl, comforting her mother when her father left them all those years ago. Chrystal started crying as well, unable to do anything else.

∞

"I won't do it. I won't join them. I did it once and it almost killed me. It killed my parents and my biological father. If I join now, they'll end up killing you both. I don't know how or when, but it'll happen. I don't trust them. Don't ask me to do this, Chrys. They are not normal. They have no emotion or logic. They follow orders." Jack was pacing, already mad as hell after meeting with Hector that morning. When he found out what Hector said to Tammy, he became incandescent with rage. He grabbed a lamp and flung it across the room. It was lying in a pathetic pile on the edge of the room's fake Persian rug.

"Things are different this time," Chrystal said. "They need you. They need us."

"They don't need anyone or anything. All they do is use us and dispose of us when they are finished. They just need me because of the way we set up the structure.

Once they have their hands on the money and the company, they'll get rid of all of us."

"You don't know that, Jack. They work for the US government. They can be trusted."

"I don't know who they work for anymore," Jack snapped. He didn't feel like rehashing his suspicions about a shadowy group called the Order of Prime who had a hand in most of the major decisions made by world leaders.

"You're just being paranoid. Think about Tammy. Think about me, and us. How are we going to live if he does this?"

"I thought you said you could live with me in a tent?"

"And I can, but why would you want to when you could be living in a penthouse overlooking Central Park?"

"I need some air." Jack grabbed a sports jacket and left the room. Tammy was sitting quietly in the corner, unable to speak. When Chrystal looked at her, all she saw was a steady stream of tears as her mother stared straight ahead, body rocking gently.

"Mom." Chrystal shook her shoulders. "Snap out of it. We're stronger than this. Just you and me. We'll figure something out. You're meeting Hector tonight for dinner, right? Then we have a few hours to think of something."

Tammy's body began to nod before her head. Eventually she found her voice. "Yes, Chrys. Let me have a shower and then we'll have some coffee and a nice lunch. Then we'll figure this out. I'm not going to work. I'll call my PA and tell her to clear this week." She got up and dragged her feet as she willed herself into the bathroom.

"That's it, Mom. Never say die. We'll get through this."

∞

Jack was walking briskly, crashing into the shoulders of other pedestrians, some swearing at him, most ignoring him. He got to the park and started to walk the pathways. He just needed to walk and think. *What am I going to do? I never thought I'd see Chrystal flip like that. One day we're a team, next she's back with Tam. I guess she's her mom but, when the chips are down, is she going to choose me? Probably not. Blood is thicker than water.*

He walked the entire perimeter of the park, watching the demographics of its visitors change as he went north toward the end that was closer to Columbia University and Harlem and then back to the end that was closer to Carnegie Hall and the luxury hotels and residences of the really rich and famous people who ran the country. Somewhere in his thought processes of society's incongruous juxtapositions of people, he thought of Sylvia and decided to give her a call.

"You're in the city? Great. Can we meet now? Where? How about Tavern on the Green in Central Park? Yes? Great. I'll see you there."

When she arrived, Sylvia looked like she was in her element. She carried an air of sophistication and detachment many in New York strive for but few pull off. Her walk pointed her toes and extended her legs to make her look like a silhouette that had come to life. Everything about her was like an extrusion of what most people were like. She was like everyone else, just better, taller, and more beautiful—and she knew it, despite her age.

"Hello, Sylvia." Jack rose and gave her a kiss on each cheek. She snuck in a third on his lips. He didn't make a fuss.

"Hello, Jack. Nice to see you. Success suits you."

"And you are looking magnificent. Success definitely suits you."

They took their chairs and ordered water as they waded through the menu. When they made their choices, they leaned with their elbows on the table. Seeing this, Sylvia motioned Jack to move and sit next to her so they weren't talking across the table. She put her hand on his leg. "Hey," he said.

"Relax. It would look more suspicious if we were having a business meeting. Lovers are boring. Get over yourself." She said it in a blasé manner that left Jack wondering whether she ever did anything spontaneously. But the way her hand rested left no doubt as to her inclinations toward him. He ignored the signals and focussed on the business at hand.

"I was visited by an old friend," Jack said.

"Hmmm. Is this a good thing or a bad thing? I am assuming the latter or I wouldn't be here." She leaned in and whispered this in Jack's ear, playing the part too well. Her hand was so far up his leg, her pinkie touched his belt.

"Remember Joe's club? One of its members decided to pay me a visit. They are aware of our history lessons and were admiring the artwork in creating the masterpiece currently enjoyed by all." Jack tried to talk as circuitously as possible in the event anyone was listening.

This got Sylvia's attention and she sat back in her chair, hands returning to her own lap. "And did they approve of the exhibition?"

"So much so they want to buy the artwork. Or perhaps I should rephrase that. They want the artwork and intend to take it."

Sylvia was silent. "Let's eat and see what our thoughts are after lunch."

"I was thinking of something. Perhaps you may ruminate on this as you eat." Jack leaned in again. Sylvia did likewise, putting her hand where he didn't want it and leaning in to kiss his earlobe. *What's wrong with this woman*, he thought. But, her putting her lips on his ear put his mouth next to hers. He whispered his idea and felt her hand against him and her teeth bite into his poor ear. It caused a strange sensation of pain and then pleasure as she moved back into her seat. Anyone who would have been looking at them would have turned away either to give them privacy or in disgust. Either way, her tactics worked.

"Interesting," she said. "I am feeling like some red wine with our meal. Will you join me?"

"Of course. I look forward to the inspiration it gives you."

"Me, too," she started to smile. "If you pull this off, you'll need to really disappear, Jack." He could tell that she genuinely liked him. In a strange way, he was starting to like her, too. She was quirky verging on weird but, so far, he trusted her.

"To madness." Jack raised his water, not wanting to wait for the wine.

"To madness."

∞

When Jack returned to his suite, Chrystal was waiting for him. She was distinctly cooler than normal. *She never could hide her emotions*, he thought. *It is one of the things I love about her.* "What's wrong?"

"Did you have a nice lunch?"

"Huh? Yes. Thanks. I just needed to spend some time by myself."

"By yourself?"

"Yes," Jack lied. *No need to tell her about my plan just yet.*

"I just received an envelope with some interesting pictures. Recent pictures. Lunch pictures of you and an elegant woman who seems to be very friendly." She put the pictures on the table in front of Jack. It was of him and Sylvia in Central Park, her hands in sharp focus as well as her kisses. "Are you going to deny it or tell me this is also some conspiracy cooked up by the CIA?"

"It's not as bad as it looks."

"It looks pretty bad. And we're about to get married!" She couldn't keep it in any longer. "How could you?"

"Don't you think it's suspicious that pictures all of a sudden show up like this and so quickly after the event? Don't you think if there was anything going on between me and this person you'd have much more damaging photos?"

"Those are damaging enough, thank you very much," she said. "It looks like she's giving you a hand-job in public. I don't want to imagine what she does for you in private."

"It's not like that at all. You must believe me, Chrys. I need her j. . ."

She cut him off before he could finish. "Need her?" She got up angrily. "Then go to her. You men are all the same dogs in the end. Can't be trusted off a leash. I should never have been so stupid!" She used her arm to sweep all of the papers and pictures off the table.

"Don't follow me!" She grabbed her bag and phone and left the suite.

This is feeling eerily similar to what happened with Sarah, Jack thought. At the time, he didn't follow Sarah and regretted it. This time, he wouldn't make the same mistake. He caught the door and opened it. He saw Chrystal stomping down the hallway. "Chrys!" She stopped but didn't turn around. He ran to her. "Chrys, don't leave me. We need to stick together more than ever. These are the tactics these people use. The woman I saw was the same woman who did the papers for us, the one I met in Montreal with you and your mom. She's just nuts that way."

"With her hand there and kissing you? That's more than nuts, Jack."

"I agree. But she is talented and connected."

"Then be with her. I'm not as talented. I'm just some whore you picked up when you were down and out." She started to cry again.

"You're not. I love you, Chrys."

"I can't look at you right now. I need to be alone, or with my mother. Just leave me alone." She didn't look at him the entire time. She started to walk again and he let her go.

Chapter Twenty-One

IVANHOE TRUST

Mary-Anne Coleman pushed her shopping cart down the supermarket's aisles, looking at the stuff she could never buy. She carefully counted the costs as she put a tin of beans, a package of bacon and some cereal from the shelves into her cart. She had to buy bread and butter, and today she would also buy peanut butter for a treat. She looked longingly at the strawberry jam and the steaks sitting tantalisingly behind the glass where the butcher's station was. Maybe one day. She picked up some sliced bologna sausage and kept walking.

When she reached the check-out counter, the other shopping carts were overflowing with Cokes, chips, and junk food, but her eyes were on the fruit and salad veggies handled carelessly by the woman in front of her. Mary-Anne didn't have a fridge large enough to keep salad stuff. Her whole kitchen amounted to a dirty oven, hot plate, and tiny sink. Her trailer wasn't ancient but also wasn't one of those new luxury types—those were usually bought by wealthy retirees and not by divorced single moms.

"You OK, hon?" The cashier was a middle-aged woman with big hair and stretchy pants. She hadn't seen a zipper or buttons for years.

"Yeah, thanks. You know, same old same old." Mary-Anne unloaded her cart onto the conveyer belt. She noticed the disapproving looks of the well-dressed woman behind her.

"Weather's pretty nice out, don't you think?" The cashier was all sunshine and smiles and it was hard for Mary-Anne to stay miserable.

"Sure is."

"Nice day for a BBQ or party," the cashier continued.

"Uh huh." Her world became small again and the smile disappeared. There would be no BBQ. There would never be a BBQ or party for her. She needed to feed two children without a job or any prospects for one. No man was interested in her, not except for what they always wanted, and she couldn't afford to even meet any good men. She couldn't remember when she looked forward to waking up in the morning.

"That'll be $43.55. Will that be cash or card today?"

Mary-Anne wished the cashier wasn't so loud in announcing the price. She didn't reply but pulled out some food stamps, ashamed to show the woman behind her that she was a leach on society. She handed the papers to the cashier quietly.

"That'll be $1.45 in change. You have a good day now." The cashier was interminably happy.

Mary-Anne took her bags and began walking home. There was no car and the children were in school, thank God. It was only a fifteen-minute walk to the trailer park on the edge of town. *Could be worse*, she thought. But she wasn't sure how.

The trailer park had been established over fifty years earlier when the area was still relatively prosperous. Coal was still being mined. The best bourbon and tobaccos were still being created in Kentucky's fertile soils and Reagan was still in office. Now, those same facilities were old and tired, just like the town. Water and sewer mains were connected to the homes and the roads were paved, except where holes appeared and no money was available to patch them. Management tried to upgrade the old trailers by setting regulations on their appearance. As the people in trailers didn't own the land underneath them, they were subject to the rules of the park. The only problem was that there simply was no money to comply with the regulations or to enforce them. The result was the Green Acres Mobile Home Community that Mary-Anne found herself walking home to.

"Hi, Mary." A young shirtless man sat next to his brother. At first glance, she thought they were wearing T-shirts because of how white their skin looked and how red-brown their faces, necks, and arms were. It would have been funny if she had a sense of humour.

"Hi, Stewart, Dan. How's it going?"

"Just fine. Enjoying us some suds. You want to join us?"

"Maybe later. I just want to get the shopping dropped off and do a few things." She kept walking, not breaking stride to talk to them. They were always just having some suds and she had no intention of becoming their next talking point.

Her home was on the third row in, fifth back. The park held almost five hundred homes and it felt a bit like a maze at times. The steps to her unit were tired and needed replacing. The post box hung at an angle and its little red flag was up, indicating that the mailman had been around. She pulled the post out and put the key in the door. It took a while to put her shopping away.

The post had its bills and normal letters from government agencies requiring her to confirm that her income was below $10,000 per year and that she still needed assistance for her rent and food. She would fill those in later. What interested her was an official-looking letter with the words "Important Document Inside. Do Not Throw Away." She opened and read it. There was a covering letter along with a fancy-looking certificate. She re-read the covering letter.

Dear Ms. Mary-Anne Coleman,

You have been specially selected to be the recipient of a capital sum of money in the form of a share certificate. This is not a scam and you do not need to send any money to us. Please keep reading. We are a charity called the Ivanhoe Charitable Trust and we would like to help you by giving you $100,000 worth of stock in TNT *Holdings Limited, a global investment company worth over $100 billion. Your certificate and ownership will entitle you to an annual dividend of approximately $7,000. This won't change your life but hopefully will help take some of the stresses away that you are feeling. You are free to sell this certificate. To do so, please contact the website at the bottom of the page. Someone will be in touch with you. We would hope that you are able to keep the certificate and continue to benefit from the annual income it provides. We hope it will not adversely affect any benefits you receive but that is something you will need to take up with your case officer. We understand that they may take away the food stamps if you have assets of more than $2,500 in total. Hopefully the roughly $7,000 per year will be able to replace those food stamps and allow you to eat better and live a better life.*

What you need to do next: nothing. If you move or change address, please let us know via the website. The Ivanhoe Charitable Trust will continue to manage and vote on your behalf so you needn't do anything. Please also find enclosed your first cheque for $7,000. This is *not a dividend but a further gift to you from Ivanhoe Trust.*

Yours   *faithfully,*

The Ivanhoe Charitable Trust

Mary-Anne was doubtful. She constantly received letters saying that she was the recipient of a million dollars and all she needed to do was sign or post something. Not knowing what to do, she took the letter and its contents to the town's local bank.

"No, I don't have a bank account," she said when asked. "Yes, I'd like to open one, please."

"How much would you like to deposit?" The young woman on the other side of the desk tried not to look at Mary-Anne's clothes or shoes.

Mary-Anne handed over the cheque. "I got this in the post today. I don't know if it is real or not. If it is, I'd like to deposit it here."

The young woman's eyes opened slightly wider. "OK, Mary. I'll check and get back to you. I just need to have a word with my manager."

"Can you also show him this?" She pulled the letter out. "I don't know if it is real or not."

Mary saw the young woman walk away with a puzzled look on her face. When she returned, the manager was with her.

"This is some extraordinarily good fortune, Ms. Coleman," the manager said. "We'll set you up with an account and a debit card so you'll be able to access your money easily."

Mary-Anne was surprised at the deference he showed her. Usually, people either tolerated or just ignored her. "Thank you, sir."

"And Ms. Coleman, if it is safer for you, we have the facility in the bank to safeguard documents like the one you brought in. It is an important document and you wouldn't want to lose it."

Mary-Anne thought about it. Her trailer was not the best place for documents. She barely had space for her food or clothes. She didn't have a book in the whole place. She nodded. "Yes, thank you, sir." Then she remembered that nothing is for free and added, "What is the cost for that?"

The manager knew who she was. He had gone to school with her parents and understood the delicate nature of her predicament. He decided that the Christian thing to do would be to make arrangements to help her, even if it cost him something personally. "We would be prepared to store your share certificate for free. We would put it in one of our fire-proof safes. It's not foolproof, but it is as safe as we can offer."

"And what happens if it gets stolen or lost?" Mary-Anne said.

"The certificate is issued to you from the company. You would just need to ask them to provide you with a copy."

"And you'll do that without charging me?"

"Yes, Ms. Coleman."

She sat thinking for a moment. Good things didn't just happen to her, but it was a bank and she knew Mr. Janka was an honest man. A lot of people said that, despite his being a banker. "Thank you, Mr. Janka. That is very kind of you."

"With pleasure. I will leave you with my capable assistant. She can discuss setting up a college fund with you if you'd like. With that amount of money, you need to be careful that it doesn't get eaten up and is applied carefully to what you want most."

Mary-Anne nodded and smiled.

∞

In other developments, CNR news has learned that thousands of people across the country have been receiving gifts out of the blue from a group known only as The Ivanhoe Charitable Trust. Having obtained copies of the documents, our reporters went to the Securities Exchange Commission to find out if they are real. The SEC confirms that, to the best of their knowledge, these are genuine. Naturally, there are many scams around and we continue to advise our listeners to be wary.

Jack turned off the radio of his pickup truck. He had been monitoring the impact of his move and believed it to be the best thing he could have done. The downside is that Hector and his crowd would no longer have any use for him. His life was over if he didn't drop off the radar for some time.

"Are you sure you want to do this, Jack?" Sylvia had said. "It's suicide. Noble, awe-inspiring, just, and right, but suicide." She was in her private studio and wasn't displaying any of her other antics.

"But can you do it?" Jack asked.

"Of course I can," she said. "But you can't go back from this. They've let you live like a guinea pig, watching from a distance as you built up this beautiful corporate money-making machine. Now they want it. It was their money that started it and they want it back. What you are proposing to do is to ensure that they lose twice—by giving away your ownership portion of the company and by ensuring they will not be able take over the remains of the company."

"That's down to your magic," Jack said. "And I want the recipients to be families who need it. Try to find single mothers; hopefully, they will be able to use it wisely. From my calculations, we can give away 100,000 share certificates worth $100,000 each and still have change left in the bank."

"That's a lot of money and we don't have much time to do all of this. Papers need to be filed. There are procedures," she said.

"We are not asking anyone for money. We are giving away what we already own. All you need to do is to create this Ivanhoe Charitable Trust and ensure that it still has the proxy vote for all of the shares we are giving away. Chrystal must be specifically named as the only person capable of exercising the proxy. If we don't protect her, Hector and his people will eat her alive."

"You love her, don't you?" she said with a tinge of sadness and admiration.

"I do. But she's in too much danger. With me out of the picture, she becomes collateral damage. Hell, she was with me around, too."

"I hope you're right, Jack. These bastards may just retire her for no other reason than that they are pissed off at you."

"I know. Which comes to my second point. We have a lot of money in our discretionary bounty program. I need to get as many names as possible from the G29. I want to put Hector and his goons on the site with a bounty of $2 million each."

Sylvia straightened. "This is treason, murder, and just downright wrong. If they catch me, I'll never see the light of day again."

Jack grinned. "And?"

"You know, if I was twenty years younger, I would give Chrystal a run for her money. I'll do it, but only because I know you're dead without me."

"Sylvia, you're a star."

"I know."

The conversation had gone better than he expected. Jack snapped back into the present and veered out of the way of a box on the road. It probably fell off some pickup truck when it wasn't tied down properly. *The cops will stop and pick it up. Too dangerous to stop on a highway*, he thought.

Telling Chrystal about his plan was more difficult, and hadn't gone as well.

"Whatever you are about to say, Jack, I don't want to hear it." She was still fuming about the pictures of him and Sylvia.

"Stop messing around. I need to talk to you," he said.

"There's nothing to say. You want me to turn my back on a successful life to live in a cave with you? You, a back-stabbing, two-timing piece of shit who doesn't know how to tell the truth? We've been together almost ten years. You were the one person I could swear on a stack of bibles was good. I trusted you. I believed in you. I loved you."

"Loved, past tense?" Jack said.

"Don't play word games with me. You want to tell Hector to go to hell because he wants you to do your patriotic duty and serve your country. Oh, and by the way, if you don't serve, your fiancée and her mother will be either killed or fired—which is more or less the same in my books." Her anger blinded her to the possibility that he was telling the truth.

"But I love you, Chrys."

"I don't want to hear about it. I want to know about the other women you've been seeing behind my back, the ones I don't have pictures of. All those sluts and whores who you needed to boost your ego. I thought you were better than that, Jack. I really wanted to believe there were good people in the world. But I was living in a fantasy land. This whole thing was a fantasy and I'm a big girl. I don't believe in the tooth fairy, Santa Claus, or you."

His throat tightened and it became hard to swallow. He couldn't hear the word "slut" or "whore" without being physically affected. He was someone's slut and whore back in Russia, as was Chrystal in LA. All his efforts since then had been to attack those who abused their power and shaped people into thinking they were "sluts and whores" or people who used them. He wanted to say something clever or philosophical. He tried to close the gap and kiss her but received two hands against his chest, pushing him away. She wasn't prepared to listen to him yet. He'd give her time. He'd give her a message through Isabella in due course. For now, all he said was, "I love you, Chrys." He hoped she would remember that in the coming months. He didn't tell her his plan and wasn't sure whether she could be trusted in her current mindset. He turned and left quietly, the door closing between them.

That was a month ago and he hadn't seen or talked to her since.

When the news broke that Hector had been killed in a car bomb in Syria on a "peace mission," he was described as an American aid worker by the international press. Hezbollah claimed the bounty. Fourteen more members of the G29 were assassinated by the Triads, mainly in China and its territories. The CIA never acknowledged the deaths or the existence of its ultra-secret organisation. Instead, it redoubled its security and began its own offensive against leaders of the Triads and Hezbollah. The Triads claimed the bounties without any organisation ever discovering the connection.

"Sylvia," Jack had said at their last meeting, "I have one more favour to ask of you."

"In addition to saving your life, setting illegal bounties against members of the CIA, and generally rebuilding your life from bottom to top?"

"Yes," Jack said, his grin returning.

"Of course. What else am I here for?"

"I need Hector's file on me deleted, and anything else the G29 has."

Sylvia inhaled deeply. "You don't ask for the easy things, do you? I can't promise anything but I'll work on it. If you wake up one day to find yourself dead, I've failed. Otherwise, you should be OK."

"You're a real piece of work," he said.

"I know. Just stay alive and give me a call the next time you're in New York. We'll have that dessert I've been looking forward to at the Tavern."

Jack shook his head incredulously. He regarded her and smiled again. "Sure thing. It's a date."

Now he was alone again. His eyes began to get heavy as the sun set. He would be at the border shortly and reached for his clean passport. Sylvia had assured him he wouldn't get picked up easily, at the border or with a traffic ticket. He hoped she was right. He still needed to make his way through the Canadian provinces and up to Alaska. There, he would lay low for at least six months. *No cell phone, no email, no computers, no electronic devices of any kind.* He could still hear her words of warning. *Stay off the grid. When you re-join the world, check out our encrypted site. I'll have instructions for you and let you know if things are safe.* The US-Canada border was an easy formality and Jack decided to see Isabella before he took the deep breath and went underground.

"I'm going to disappear for some time, Izzie," Jack said. "And I need you to get a message to Chrystal and Tammy for me. We haven't spoken for just over a month. She's mad now but she'll be worried later."

"What have you done now?" she asked. She didn't ask too many questions, not after receiving the money that had since grown to almost $2 billion for her charity.

"The money I used to build my empire may have been less than clean," Jack started. "And the original owners want their money back."

"I'll give you all of it," she said immediately.

"No," he said, "That's for the kids. They will never even know about that. Besides, these are bad people who will do bad things with it."

Isabella was silent. She guessed what Jack had been up to but was also hoping he would be allowed to continue. *The world was a better place without those predators on the streets*, she thought.

"Whatever the situation," Jack continued, "I need to disappear."

"What do you want me to do?"

"When the time is right, tell Chrystal I love her and always will. Hopefully by then she'll understand. Tell her it was the only way for her and her mother to stay safe."

"Will she know what I'm talking about?"

"She'll know."

They talked for another hour before he decided to continue on his way.

"Take care of yourself, Jack." She kissed him on the neck and hugged him.

"I will. You take care of your kids."

"I will. Just remember, my door is always open to you, day or night, rain or shine."

Jack nodded his thanks and closed the door behind him. Next stop, Alaska.

∞

Actually, the next stop was Minnedosa, and then every four hours as he allowed himself to refuel and relax, never allowing the tank to get too empty. He took highway 16 to Edmonton and then followed the signs to Juneau. In Edmonton, he stopped in a sporting store and bought more clothing to help him survive—fleeces and waterproof clothes but also the foam mattress to keep him from ruining his lungs when sleeping on the ground. He wasn't much of a fisherman but he bought enough gear to make mistakes and still hopefully get something edible. He bought bottled gas as well as the flint lighters and survival gear in the event things really went bad. He hoped to buy a gun when in Juneau; it wasn't easy to buy one in Canada, especially when just passing through.

When he finally reached Alaska, it was breathtaking in its rugged beauty. He had put his finger on a map randomly when deciding where to go. He wanted to be out of the way and Alaska was certainly that. What he didn't realise was that he couldn't drive to Juneau at all. *Who makes the capital of the state inaccessible by road?* He decided he didn't need to go there after all, and just made his way into the woods near the end of the road at Haines.

Jack backed his pickup truck off the road and pointed it toward the untamed salted water, which was serene at the moment. He opened the all-weather cap that sat bolted to the flatbed part of his truck. His foam mattress was set out like a bed in readiness, complete with pillow and sleeping bag. *Better than a tent*, he thought. He cleared an area and began to form a campsite for himself. He found some stones and dry wood. He put a grate over the new fire pit that could be removed if needed. He had bought a rifle in Haines and made sure it was always within reach. *No sense surviving the* CIA *just to be eaten by a bear.*

The air was so clean it smelled sweet. There were no sounds except the water, wind, and the animals. *I wish I brought an encyclopaedia or something to read. The novelty is wearing off already.*

Jack caught fish on his second day. He shot his first deer on his fifth and realised he couldn't keep the meat without it going bad. He cooked as much as possible but realised he couldn't morally shoot game until the weather turned cold. It was July and the flies were unbearable at times. He spent his time walking, exploring the crevices and pathways. He tried to gather wood at least twice a week to stockpile for the coming months. He knew he would need to keep a fire going almost continuously except for when he slept in the flatbed of his truck.

His first visitor came when he lit his first fire, on the second day, to cook his fish. It was the park ranger.

"Hello," a big man in boots came out of nowhere, startling Jack.

"Uh, hi. Is everything OK?"

"Yeah." The ranger looked at the truck, gear, and campsite. "Do you have a licence to be in this park?"

"Yes, of course." Jack went to the truck and fished it off the dashboard.

"And the wood you've been collecting—you're not allowed to cut down trees. Keep it to the dead ones."

"Yes, sir." Jack didn't know if the guy was serious or kidding. There was no one around for miles.

"I also notice you have a gun. You plan on using it?"

"I was hoping to, but I thought it was good to have something just in case."

"That should be fine. I'm Ranger Martin Thompson and I patrol these areas. Are you planning on sticking around for some time?"

"I was hoping to stay as long as my determination holds," Jack said.

"Are you used to camping? You have a lot of gear in there," he motioned to the truck with his head.

"Not really. Just wanted to clear my head. If it gets too much for me, I can get in the truck and head home."

"Where's home?"

"Not sure. Fiancée was in New York the last time we talked and that was three months ago." Jack noticed the Ranger's eyes drift back to him. "A bit of a soap opera."

"We get 'em all up here. Just make sure you don't get yourself killed trying to be all Mr. Nature. Any problems, call me."

"I don't have a phone."

"There's no cell service here, anyway. I meant call on me at the ranger's station near the entrance to the park."

"Will do, sir."

"Enjoy your stay and remember to gather your litter and burn it or bin it. As there's no bin, use your truck or burn it. The bears like fatty leftovers." He smiled and carried on walking, disappearing into the endless expanse of trees.

What the hell was that? Surreal. I wish I had a dog. I wish Chrystal was here. What the hell am I doing here? I hope the fish tastes OK. His thoughts pinged from one subject to another. At night, he began to fear the image of Vlad even though he knew he was dead. After three months at the campsite, he was beginning to develop an agitation he never knew he had. The night temperatures dropped below freezing and the daytime wasn't much better. At least he was able to eat meat again. He gralloched the deer, throwing its guts and inedible bits as far into the woods as possible. He cut the remaining meat into steaks by taking off the silver tendons and separating the muscles of the haunch and other body parts. It wasn't pretty but it gave him something to do and he was able to wrap each piece of meat in a plastic bag to be eaten later. It all went into his cooler. Unfortunately, he still found that half of the meat went off. *Third time's a charm. I'll get a nice young doe and have enough meat to last me until I leave.*

By the fourth month, even his internal voices became quiet. He fished in silence, his mind as quiet as its surroundings. He even began to enjoy fishing. He didn't have a boat and was forced to throw his line in from the shore. Ranger Thompson had come down a few times to visit and give him tips.

"You're doing well for someone who never camped before," Thompson said.

"Thanks. The first few days were the worst. It's the isolation that was the hardest to overcome."

"But when you do, it's the thing you seek out the most," smiled Thompson.

"Until recently, I would never have agreed with you. It took until the fourth month and the snow had already begun to fall. The fish weren't biting and I had just shot my third deer—the other two rotted as I didn't have a cool place to store the meat—and there was nothing in the world other than that deer, my knife, and ensuring I harvested all the protein from the carcass. The snow muffled all the usual agitated bird sounds and even the wind was still. Before then, I would have just heard a ringing in my ears. But at that moment, even my ears relaxed. All was silent."

"Sounds like you had a religious experience, Jack. And the ringing in the ears is something I'm still struggling with. I think I shot too many times without ear protection. Doctors say there's nothing they can do about it."

"Don't ruin it, Martin," Jack laughed. "I really thought it was something."

The ranger knew that shooting three deer was not allowed but he also knew Jack wasn't just a hunter or camper. He had seen his share of nutters come and go, but this one represented a tormented soul determined to be calm. He could tell there were many unspoken things that Jack preferred not to discuss, but it was no different than nature remaining silent on things it preferred undisturbed. "Look, Jack, I've got some firewater up at the cabin if you ever care to leave your hermitage."

"Thanks, Martin. I'll take you up on that. I haven't had a drop since I got here."

"Are you punishing yourself from something?"

"No." Jack laughed again. "Just trying to live off the land and get my mind to stop racing."

"Sounds good to me. How much longer are you planning to stay?"

"I think I am coming to the end of my time. I'm not looking to survive an Alaskan winter on my own. We're already into October. Probably by the end of the month I'll pack my things and be on my way. I need to drive back and see if I still have a fiancée!"

"Sounds like something to drink to."

"For better or worse," added Jack with a grin. His mind was at peace and he was ready to face whatever fate had in store for him.

Chapter Twenty-Two

THE ROAD NOT TAKEN

"Isabella! I'm so glad you came." Chrystal could barely contain herself. Her eyes were puffy, hair dishevelled, and her clothes looked slept in.

"Hi, Chrystal. I needed to come in person."

"Is he alive? What's happened? Why couldn't you talk on the phone?"

"Jack's alive. He saw me yesterday, which is why I'm here now."

"How is he? Where's he been? When can I see him?"

"He's fine. He looks a bit like he walked out of the wilderness, and he only stopped by long enough to use my shower and grab a change of clothes." She stopped as she heard a sob emitted from Chrystal. "Are you OK?"

"No. I feel like an acid has been eating away at my insides. I feel empty, alone, and worthless. I was angry at him. It was a fight. Normal people don't just drop off the edge of the world for six months. And now I've lost him."

"You haven't lost him. He wanted me to give you a message. He wants you to know that he loves you and, if you'll have him, he wants to see you."

"Why couldn't he just call me himself?"

"He's paranoid due to his recent actions. He believes he will be killed if he uses the phone or contacts you in any way. Everything he's done was to keep you and your mother safe."

Chrystal wiped some tears from her cheeks with a tissue. She simply couldn't stop crying. Even during her conversation with Isabella, the tears continued as if from a tap. "I realised that too late. We've been through so much together. I don't know why I doubted him so much. I don't know where it came from. It was just hatred and jealousy against ghosts. I felt betrayed when really I was the one who betrayed him."

Isabella moved closer and gave her a long, gentle hug. There was nothing to say. It was between Jack and Chrystal. All she was doing was helping an old friend.

"I still don't understand why Jack couldn't give you a burner cell phone so I could hear his voice."

"I said the same thing to him, Chrys, but he has been away for so long, he only wants to see you in the flesh." She felt like some messenger from a bygone age. "He loves you. He's waiting for my call for instructions from you."

Chrystal's tears abated. "From me?"

"He said you will know what I'm talking about. You will know if it is safe for him and where you could meet."

Chrystal wiped her nose with the back of her hand and sleeve before using a tissue to blow her nose. She drank some water and closed her eyes. "Tell him Hector is dead and there is no indication our friends are after him. I've been told by our other mutual friend that their dossier on him has been either lost or deleted. She wasn't able to elaborate. Also tell him that Operation Ivanhoe was a smashing success and is still receiving media attention. You can tell him that I am scheduled to fly to Churchill to inspect our shipping operations later this week. It may be a good first meeting place." Chrystal was spent, all emotion drained. "And Isabella? Please tell him I love him, too."

Isabella didn't know the whole story behind this blonde woman in front of her. She could see the trappings of luxury, the effects of the spa on her skin and hair, and the view from her penthouse suite, but it was the way she pulled herself together emotionally when given the hope of love that impressed her the most. "You two will be happy together. I'll tell him you'll be in Churchill waiting for him later this week. That should give him some spring in his step." She smiled and Chrystal smiled with her. They hugged and began laughing together.

∞

Jack was sitting on the grass next to where the two rivers met when his phone rang. "Hello, Izzie? How'd it go? She is? She does? I can't wait. What about the other matters? He is? It did? Good. I'm relieved. Does this mean I'm a free man again? Let's hope. I'm on my way now. Oh, Izzie? Thanks." He ended the call and felt the adrenaline crawling into his joints and muscles. He could feel the hair on his skin and suddenly smell the meat from the restaurant's BBQ. The air felt cool with an urgency to move. He looked over his shoulder to the table where he met Chrystal and Tammy when they first arrived in Winnipeg. He felt a longing and suddenly foolish at not speaking to Chrystal on the phone.

Enough about the past. It's going to start snowing soon, he thought as he looked at the grey white clouds. He leaned forward and levered himself upward on the slanted grass. It felt good to have a destination. *Life may be about the journey,* he thought, *but you can't have a journey without a destination. Otherwise, it's just called being a bum.*

His truck was parked nearby and the seat felt cold and brittle when he slid behind the wheel. It started in one turn and roared to life. *Next stop, Churchill.* He backed out and turned the wheel as far as he could. There was a high squeaking sound as he did so. *Must be colder than I thought. Couple of minutes should sort that out as it warms up.* As he tried to turn onto Main Street, the cars became actors in his final scene. They crowded him, pushed him, and refused to allow him to change lanes. *Stay calm, let this batch pass. A light will change and you'll get into the stream of traffic.* He slotted himself into his lane as he drove past the train station that could have taken him straight to Churchill. *I'd rather drive there than take the train. I'll get there faster.* He pushed down on the accelerator and moved into the fast lane. He just needed to clear this downtown traffic and get out onto the open road. When he cleared the perimeter highway, he stopped at a station to refuel. The weather was closing in and he didn't want to run out of fuel as he went north. He had seen how few and far between the towns became when he went to Alaska. Northern Manitoba would likely be the same.

"I'll take this map and these chocolate bars," Jack said to the cashier.

"Any fuel?"

"Number 3. And I'll have a large black coffee please."

"Help yourself. It's over there." He pointed to the wall next to the WD40 and antifreeze.

Jack paid the bill and went back to his truck. Looking at the map, he couldn't quite understand what was wrong. He returned to the kiosk where the cashier was sitting watching something on a small TV.

"Sorry to bother you," Jack said.

"Yeah?"

"I wanted to drive to Churchill but this map doesn't show the road. Do you have another map?"

"No. That map is correct. There isn't a road that makes it all the way to Churchill."

Jack wasn't sure he heard correctly. "What? But I thought it was a major shipping point to the rest of the world."

"All I know is the only way to get there is by plane or train."

"Do I need to go back to Winnipeg?"

"Probably your best bet. But you can drive to the end of the road, I think it's Thompson, and catch a train from there."

Jack was still trying to understand how, in the year 2036, there still wasn't a road that allowed you to drive to Churchill. "OK, thanks." As he left the kiosk, the wind was picking up and he turned on his radio to catch the weather report.

He drove in a numb state of disbelief, weighing his options. *Keep driving or turn back?* He answered himself with obstinacy. *Keep moving forward. Walk if you have to.*

The road opened in front of him and the vista became bleak as the miles began to tick past. Jack didn't measure distance, just time. One hour. Two hours. The truck was warm, the radio said snow was on its way and Jack could only think about Chrystal. It was shortly after the radio sang about a cowboy's lost dog, lost girl, and lost rodeo when the trouble began. A light appeared on the truck's dashboard. Jack ignored it. *Nothing much I can do about it now. Just make it to Thompson, put it in a garage, and let them deal with it while I take the train to see Chrys.*

The next symptom was a loss of power. Jack never used cruise control and he noticed that he needed to press the accelerator pedal further and further down. Usually it barely needed to be touched to maintain cruising speed. Within minutes, his foot was down to the floor and the truck was slowing down. It was clear things were not good. He pulled over so another driver didn't accidently smash into him.

Shit.

Shit shit shit.

Shit shit shit shit shit. What else is going to happen to me?

Jack sat for a few minutes behind the wheel, weighing his options. *I should wait here until someone comes by.* Then his stubborn side replied, *Just walk to the next town. Someone will pick you up before then. If not, you can get help there.*

He knew it was probably the wrong thing to do but he did it anyway. He undressed and put on his long thermal underwear and his jeans. He put on two sets of warm socks and some good walking boots. On top, he put on a thin sweater over the thermals and a heavy flannel jacket on top of that. On top of everything, he put a heavy overcoat. He needed layers to allow the body to breathe. He put the chocolate bars in his left pocket and a bottle of water in his right. He took one final look at the truck and started walking north.

Just my luck. Must be some holiday or something. Not one bloody vehicle in either direction for an hour. Jack put one foot in front of the other. The truck's engine wouldn't keep him warm so it was just as well he was walking. *Someone will stop. Someone has to come by.*

But they didn't. One hour of walking and nothing. The temperature began to drop. It was well below freezing and Jack was overheating. He began to sweat so he opened the layers but kept walking. *There's daylight and I've committed myself to my course. Where the hell is the next town?*

After four hours, he stopped. *I'm not going to get to a town. I need to conserve my energy and flag down a driver—if they ever pass this way.* He had seen some houses from the highway and walked down one of the quarter mile driveways to knock on the door. There were no cars and no sign of life. In the distance, he saw a car pass on the highway. *Just my luck.* He became resolved to stay on the road and wait for the next car. *It's impossible to not have any traffic. And people are decent; they'll stop for me in this weather.*

They didn't. The first car was a van with a family, full of children. The man driving looked at the woman before shrugging his shoulders at Jack. Another woman, alone, drove past with a fearful look. It was another hour and dusk was approaching. The sun was low and Jack realised he would have to walk in an even more dangerous situation. *I'll go back to one of the houses and break in if need be*, he thought. *I'm not walking on a highway at night.*

Jack could see the frozen moisture on his jacket's collar and had lost feeling in his face a long time before when a luxury sedan with a Texas licence plate pulled up next to him.

"Where you heading?" The stranger asked.

"North," Jack said.

"Hop in."

Jack put his travel bag in the backseat and joined the stranger in the front.

"Is that all you got?" he said, looking at the bag.

"Yep."

"Waiting long?"

"Yeah. Not too many people pick up hitchhikers these days. Thanks." Jack shrugged and tried to smile but the cold made even that difficult.

"I'll let you warm up before I start talking at you too much," the guy said. Jack didn't respond immediately. "I've got a thermos of coffee in the back if you want something to drink. There's probably a sandwich and some chocolate if you'd like."

"You sure?" Jack said.

"I wouldn't offer if I wasn't. Help yourself."

Jack did. He poured a coffee for the driver, black, and one for himself. It had the right effect on him and he took off his heavy outer jacket and unbuttoned the flannel one. He rubbed his hands on the thin sweater underneath, partly to warm them and partly to see if he was sweating and not realising it.

"Do you smoke?" the man asked.

"When I have the chance. What do you have?"

"Just tobacco," he said, suddenly a little awkward.

"Works for me. I only smoke tobacco," said Jack.

"Sorry, I didn't mean anything by it. I was just trying to be friendly."

"I've got cigars on me if you like but you may not be too keen on smelling up your new car."

"It's a rental," said the stranger.

That got Jack's attention. "Where you heading?"

"North sounds good to me. I've been driving since Dallas. Need a change of scenery. I looked on a map and saw Churchill and thought northern Canada was as good a destination as any. You know, polar bears and all that."

Jack smiled. There was much more unspoken with this guy. "Running or rough patch?"

"One hell of a rough patch. I just need to clear my head."

Jack paused. "You know you can't drive to Churchill?"

"Uh, yeah. I figured that out when I passed Winnipeg and picked up a map. Who would've thought?"

Jack was silent, not sure whether to share his plans with this stranger. "I'm heading to Churchill, too. My plan was to grab the train from Thompson. If you still want to go, that's really your only option unless you want to fly. But you don't seem like you're in any great hurry."

That made the driver smile. "Sounds like a plan."

"You driving through the night?"

"Was planning to but I think Thompson's only around seven more hours. That should get us in just before midnight."

"Assuming the weather co-operates," Jack added.

It didn't. The wind picked up and the snow on the fields started blowing across the road. At first it was a pleasant scene, something out of a National Geographic landscape. The grand expanse of white with a setting sun created an orange hue as they followed the black tarmac. There was no snow falling but the stuff on the ground was driven onto the road, clawing back at civilisation. Snow fingers thudded against the tires as they drove. Jack looked over and saw the terror on the Texan's face.

"Don't white knuckle it," Jack said.

"Huh?"

"Relax your hands on the wheel. Slow down and let the car drive. We'll be OK."

"Easy for you to say. I've never seen snow like this, let alone driven in it."

"Do you want me to drive?" Jack said.

The driver hesitated but then nodded.

"OK," Jack said. "Take your foot off the gas, but don't hit the brake. The last thing we want is to start spinning at this speed."

That seemed to cause the Texan even more anxiety but he managed it. "You OK?" Jack asked.

"Yeah. Thanks. I owe you one."

"No, I owe you for picking me up. Sit back, have some of your chocolate, and I'll get you to the next town. I think its Grand Rapids. It's not glamorous but I'm pretty sure they'll have some sort of hotel."

The Texan fell into a deep sleep, waking only when Jack they arrived at the motel. "They only had one room but it has two beds," Jack said, coming back from the office. "I told them OK. I don't think we have too many options. The restaurant is still open for another hour or so. That should give us enough time to unpack and grab a bite before everything shuts down."

"Thanks," the man from Dallas said. "What do I owe you?"

"Nothing. My treat."

The man looked oddly at Jack but grabbed his things. The room was basic but warm and the two fell asleep quickly.

The next morning, Jack awoke to find that the driver had already gone. Jack had a shower, dressed, and went to find the breakfast room. He found the Texan looking dejected.

"Heard the news?" Jack said. He had been listening on the clock radio. They were stuck in the middle of the season's first big storm, with up to fourteen inches predicted. It meant that they were stranded for a few days. Jack felt relieved to be off the road.

"Yup. Not too great."

"Oh well, can't complain. We're in a decent place with hot food and all the amenities. Could be a lot worse." Jack was upbeat. Nothing could put him in a bad mood. He would be seeing Chrystal as soon as the storm cleared.

"Not much," the Texan grumbled.

"Believe me, this is heaven. From what I can surmise from you and your situation, this may be just what you needed." Jack was feeling expansive. He usually didn't give advice or interfere, but he wanted to help this man for some reason.

The man from Dallas tried to smile. "I'm not sure you're qualified to say that."

"You'd be surprised," Jack said. "Let's grab some grub and I'll tell you a story that'll make you happy to be alive."

ABOUT THE AUTHOR

Baron was born in Canada.
He currently lives in South East England,
somewhere near the Surry/Sussex borders.
Sightings vary.

If you'd like to follow Baron and receive free samples
of his future writing before it is published, please visit
www.baronalexanderbooks.com